### "You said I was handsome."

"You are." And Jessica meant it. Yes, Topher was scarred, but the beautiful boy was still there, tempered by something that was deep and masculine. Something that appealed to her female sensibilities.

He shook his head. "No. But you're beautiful," he whispered. "That's the truth."

Topher smelled like the trade winds on a summer day, spicy and salty and so delicious that she leaned in to him. For a crazy moment, Jessica thought he might kiss her, and she wasn't even frightened by the prospect.

Instead he took a step back. "It's late," he said, even though it wasn't.

A wave of disappointment crashed over her with the roar of the surf behind. She wouldn't have stopped him. Good grief, she *wanted* him to kiss her.

But he turned and let himself out into the storm.

# Praise for Hope Ramsay

## *The Moonlight Bay series*

"*An Officer and a Gentleman* meets Nicholas Sparks' *Dear John* in the second captivating installment of the Moonlight Bay series."
**—Woman's World on Summer on Moonlight Bay**

"Ramsay mixes a tasty cocktail of sweet and sexy in this heartfelt launch of the Moonlight Bay series. Ramsay's expert characterization (particularly with the multilayered hero and heroine), entertaining cast of secondary characters, and well-tuned plot will make readers long for a return trip to Magnolia Harbor."
**—Publishers Weekly on The Cottage on Rose Lane**

## *The Chapel of Love series*

"[A] laugh-out-loud, play-on-words dramathon...It won't take long for fans to be sucked in while Ramsay weaves her latest tale of falling in love."
**—RTBookReviews.com on The Bride Next Door**

"Getting hitched was never funnier."
**—FreshFiction.com on Here Comes the Bride**

"Ramsay charms in her second Chapel of Love contemporary...[and] wins readers' hearts with likable characters, an engaging plot (and a hilarious subplot), and a well-deserved happy ending."
**—Publishers Weekly on A Small-Town Bride**

# RETURN TO MAGNOLIA HARBOR

# RETURN TO MAGNOLIA HARBOR

*A Moonlight Bay novel*

# HOPE RAMSAY

## FOREVER

NEW YORK   BOSTON

Copyright © 2020 by Robin Lanier
Excerpt from *The Cottage on Rose Lane* © 2018 by Robin Lanier

Cover design by Elizabeth Turner Stokes. Cover copyright © 2020 by Hachette Book Group, Inc.

Forever
Hachette Book Group
1290 Avenue of the Americas, New York, NY 10104
read-forever.com
twitter.com/readforeverpub

First Edition: June 2020

Forever is an imprint of Grand Central Publishing. The Forever name and logo are trademarks of Hachette Book Group, Inc.

The publisher is not responsible for websites (or their content) that are not owned by the publisher.

The Hachette Speakers Bureau provides a wide range of authors for speaking events. To find out more, go to www.hachettespeakersbureau.com or call (866) 376-6591.

ISBNs: 978-1-5387-0174-4 (mass market); 978-1-5387-0172-0 (ebook)

Printed in the United States of America

OPM

10  9  8  7  6  5  4  3  2  1

*To the friend I made in 1965*

# Acknowledgments

I was warned, before I started work on this story, that writing a *Beauty and the Beast* trope might be harder than I thought. I ignored this sage advice and ended up mired in a mess of my own making. And so I must acknowledge all of those who pulled me out of the quicksand, starting with the anonymous blogger at *You Call Yourself a Film Critic* (youcallyourselfafilmcritic.wordpress.com) whose wonderful blog about *Beauty and the Beast* finally helped me realize that my main character was a great deal more like Fiona from *Shrek* than Belle from the Disney version of *Beauty and the Beast*.

Also, many thanks to my longtime editor, Alex Logan, who had to read the first draft of this story, an experience that was probably quite painful for her, and stuck with me until we had fixed the problems. She once again helped me figure it all out as only she can do. Her advice is nothing short of brilliant.

I'd also like to thank my good friends and critique partners J. Keely Thrall and Carol Hayes for their thoughts about the hero as this project was first coming together and my writing pal Jamie Beck for listening to the whole plot line during a three-hour drive from New York to Vermont and for helping me brainstorm the ending.

Finally, my heartfelt thanks go to Elizabeth Turner Stokes for capturing my vision of a lighthouse and giving *Return to Magnolia Harbor* the best cover ever.

# Chapter One

Jessica Blackwood patted down her hair, hoping the humidity hadn't frizzed it too much. Granny would probably comment on it anyway, even if she'd managed to smooth it into the most perfect pageboy in the universe.

She stood on the sidewalk outside Granny's house in the historic district of Magnolia Harbor. Built in the mid-1800s in the Georgian style, the house was a study in geometry and symmetry. The plants in the garden were set out in careful rows too. Granny would have it no other way.

Jessica hurried up the brick walk, fixing a proper Southern-lady mask on her face. She rang the doorbell and waited.

It was funny, she'd once called this house home, but now it felt more like the scene of a crime, where her parents had abandoned her and disbelieved her and then sent her away.

So she didn't love the house because she'd never been loved here. And yet, like a good girl, she came back every

Saturday out of obligation. Granny lived alone now that Momma and Daddy had died.

When Granny finally opened the door, Jessica drew some comfort from the fact that, like her own hair, Granny's looked like a frizzy nimbus around her thin face. But that didn't stop Granny from frowning. The fold in the middle of her forehead could intimidate anyone, and frequently did. Granny had spent a lifetime frowning and had worn that groove deep.

"Darling," Granny said in a slow drawl, "you're late." And then the old woman inspected Jess. "Why do you insist on wearing that dress? The color isn't good on you."

The dress in question had been purchased at Daffy Down Dilly, the boutique that occupied the retail space below Jessica's brand-new office. It had a border of roses along the hemline in shades ranging from pastel to hot pink. Jessica loved the dress, but Granny had a thing about pink. Jessica should have remembered and worn something else.

Jessica said nothing because Granny didn't expect explanations or apologies. Instead the old woman turned away, and Jessica dutifully followed into the front parlor, which was furnished with Victorian antiques that had never been comfortable.

As if to punctuate the point, Granny's sister, Donna Cuthbert, who was about a hundred pounds heavier than Granny, perched precariously on the edge of the balloon-backed sofa. Aunt Donna looked as if she might slide right off that thing at any moment, and her purple jungle-print blouse clashed horribly with the sofa's red damask upholstery.

Granny gave her older sister one of her disapproving looks, with the eyebrow lowered just so. "Donna dropped in unannounced," she said. "I had to put another cup on the tray."

As if putting another cup on the tray was a major trial. Granny could complain about anything, even an unexpected visit from a member of her much-diminished family.

"Hey, darlin'," Donna said, hopping up from her unsteady seat and giving Jessica a big, warm hug.

"What brings you to tea?" Jessica asked, sitting down in one of the side chairs.

Granny took a seat beside Donna. There was a faint family resemblance between the two sisters, despite the fact that one was rail thin and the other quite large.

"Gossip, my dear," Aunt Donna said in a conspiratorial tone.

Jessica didn't rise to the bait because she avoided gossip at all cost. She'd been scarred by the stories people had told about her over the years.

She turned her attention to the tea tray, filled with Granny's pride and joy: her Lenox china in the Cinderella pattern. Jessica picked up the teapot and started pouring. From the time she'd been ten years old, she'd been expected to manage a teapot without spilling, as if this ability was an indication of her worth as a human being.

"What gossip?" Granny finally asked, unable to resist the lure Donna had set.

"About Christopher Martin," Aunt Donna said.

The teapot jumped in Jessica's hand, and she sloshed tea into Granny's saucer. Christopher, who was widely known by the nickname Topher, had been a hometown hero ever since he'd led the Rutledge Raiders to the state football championship sixteen years ago.

"Oh, for pity's sake," Granny said, reaching for a cloth napkin to mop up the spill.

"Sorry," Jessica said in a tiny voice and carefully put down the pot. "What about Topher Martin?" she asked, picking up her cup and saucer, hoping that neither woman noticed the slight tremor in her hands.

"The poor man has shut himself up in Ashley's cottage," Donna said.

"Oh, the poor dear," Granny said.

Jessica looked up from her tea. *The poor dear? Really?* "What do you mean, he's shut himself away?" Jessica asked aloud.

"Oh, didn't you hear?" Donna asked.

"I don't gossip," Jessica said in a tight voice, although technically she was gossiping right this minute.

"Well, it's not exactly gossip. I mean, it's practically common knowledge," Donna countered.

"Maybe only to the members of the Piece Makers, sister," Granny said. The Piece Makers were the local quilting club. The ladies had been meeting for decades to make charity quilts while they discussed everything and everyone in Magnolia Harbor.

She didn't ask what the heck Granny and Aunt Donna were talking about. She refused to give them any encouragement. She simply sat and sipped her tea and tried, without success, to think about something that would change the course of the conversation.

"Christopher was horribly disfigured in a car accident about nine months ago," Granny whispered in the same tone she often used when talking about someone diagnosed with cancer or having a heart attack.

"I hear it's a challenge to look him in the face now," Donna said.

"So have I. Such a pity. He's still unmarried, and a Martin. A *rich* one, evidently, since he was the CEO or something for one of those hedge funds. They say he made *billions*," Granny said.

"It's such a shame, and after the way he led the Rutledge Raiders to the championship that time." Aunt Donna let go of a long sigh.

Jessica kept her expression impassive while her emotions churned in her gut. Just yesterday, Topher Martin had called her office and asked her to design a house for him out on a remote island in the bay. She'd refused at first, but he'd been very persuasive, offering her a fee that was twice her going rate.

He hadn't really explained why he wanted to build a house so far off the grid. But now maybe she had her answer. Maybe he wanted to hide. Maybe he'd become a monster.

Although in Jessica's book he'd always been one of the villains—a member of the football team that had started the vicious rumors about her sixteen years ago. Now maybe everyone would get over their hero worship and see him for who he truly was.

If her architectural firm wasn't desperate for new business, she would never have considered his commission. But she was trying to move on in her life. And a girl had to eat.

"Have you seen him since he was disfigured?" Donna asked, pulling Jessica from her thoughts.

Granny shook her head. "No. But he was such a beautiful boy once."

"Well, it's water over the dam now," Donna said. Her aunt placed her empty cup down on the tray. "The juicy bit is that I understand he's so disfigured that he wants to build some kind of hideaway on Lookout Island." Donna paused here for impact before turning her gaze on Jessica.

"And I understand from the word on the street that he's hired you."

Jessica's face heated as the two old women stared at her. Granny glowered as if Jessica had been caught in a lie just because she hadn't rushed in to tell her that she had a new client. Aunt Donna leaned in ready for the next juicy morsel.

"I'm meeting with him on Monday to discuss the house he wants to build."

"So you've seen him?" Donna asked.

Jessica shook her head. "No. We had a phone conversation. And it would be an exaggeration to say that I'm his architect. I have no idea, really, what he wants to build. He hasn't signed any paperwork, either. We're meeting for a site visit. That's it for now. And since he might be paying me a lot of money to design a house for him, I'm not going to gossip about him." Although, way back in her mind, it struck her that maybe there was justice in the world. Let the old biddies of Magnolia Harbor gossip about him all day long. She hoped all that talk would make him miserable, and then he'd realize what he'd done.

Jessica leaned over and picked up the teapot. "Seconds, anyone?" she asked, hoping to change the subject.

"You know," Donna said, holding out her cup, "I've heard Ashley, Sandra, and Karen talking about Topher. His cousins definitely don't want him to build this house."

"No?" Jessica asked.

Donna shook her head. "I gather he's been deeply injured too. Has a problem with his leg."

"The poor dear. He has no business moving out to that remote island," Granny said, turning toward Jess. "You should tell him no."

"What?"

"You shouldn't help him, my dear," Granny repeated.

"Why not?"

"Because it wouldn't be right."

Jessica bit her tongue and just barely stopped herself from asking Granny the age-old question: Who elected her to be the arbiter of right and wrong, anyway? Because she was a really bad judge.

"It might not be," Donna said.

Jessica stared down at the stupid Cinderella teacup. Here was the exit door. She could walk through it if she wanted. She could tell everyone that she refused his commission because he had no business building a house in a remote location.

So maybe doing the wrong thing was exactly what she needed to do. She didn't care. Let him go live a miserable life in a drafty old lighthouse. It would serve him right.

The thought warmed her in some weird and unacceptable way. She looked up from the teacup and right into her grandmother's judgmental stare.

"I really don't care whether it's right or wrong, Granny," she said. "I need a client; he has money. And that's the end of this discussion."

\* \* \*

The only berth available for Topher Martin's newly purchased, forty-foot Caliber sailing yacht, *Bachelor's Delight*, was way at the end of the Magnolia Harbor pier. When he'd first returned to Magnolia Harbor three weeks ago, he'd planned to live on the boat. But the long walk from the berth to the nearest convenience store had proved impossible for him.

So he'd thrown himself on his older cousin's mercy.

Ashley Scott, the owner of Howland House, the five-star bed-and-breakfast in town, had allowed him to rent Rose Cottage for the next six months, through March.

The long walk from the parking lot reminded Topher that his earlier plans had been half-baked. He was annoyingly winded, and his bad leg ached by the time he reached the berth.

Isaac Solomon, at the marina office, had fueled up the boat and stocked the small refrigerator in the galley with drinks and box lunches. Topher hobbled down the ship's ladder and snagged himself a bottled water and gulped four ibuprofens.

Maybe that would take the edge off the pain.

But even if it didn't, he would endure it. He'd done that before when he'd torn up his knee between his freshman and sophomore years at Alabama. That injury had ended his NFL dreams and taken months and months of recovery time.

But that old injury was nothing in comparison to the pain that lanced through his leg with every step. He loved and hated the pain. It was a reminder of the alternative he'd narrowly escaped when he'd wrapped his Ferrari around a barrier when he'd swerved to avoid a deer on a blind man's curve. At the same time, he often wondered why his life had been spared and reduced to this living nightmare.

He dragged himself back above deck and sat down in the cockpit behind the ship's wheel. He checked his watch. He'd left himself plenty of time because he didn't want Jessica Blackwood to see him winded and limping down the pier. Hell, if he could have dealt with her entirely by telephone or text, he would have.

But how on earth would she ever design him a house if he refused to go with her to the island? If he left her to

back would hurt. And, of course, it would display his weakness.

She put her hands on her hips and cocked her head. "I'm not your crew, you know."

Great. She didn't know what a mooring line was. "Fine. I'll do it—"

"No. All you have to do is ask nicely," she said with another big, phony smile.

"Please," he muttered, semi-embarrassed. What the hell? He didn't want to scare this architect away. She was the only one who hadn't laughed at him when he'd said the words "Lookout Island."

She dropped her big tote into the cockpit and scampered down the dock to the big cleat where the mooring line was tied. She moved like a sprite, light on her feet. She was fun to watch.

Clearly she knew something about sailboats because she handled the mooring lines like a pro and even hopped from the pier to the gunwales without looking intimidated or out of her element.

"So you know your way around a sailboat," he said as he fired up the diesel engines.

"My grandfather was once a member of the yacht club. He had a J-22 we used to sail when I was a kid," she said as she stepped down into the cockpit and then perched on the portside bench.

He studied her as she looked up at the mast where the wind vane indicated a good breeze blowing from the southwest. Topher judged it at maybe eight knots or so.

"So we're not sailing?" she asked as he guided the boat into the channel.

"No," he growled, annoyed by her question.

He'd been sailing all his life, and the yacht had all

the technology money could buy. It might be forty feet long, but it was rigged to be single-handed. Topher could manage it even without his good health.

But he didn't want to embarrass himself in front of this woman. He didn't want to display his disabilities; otherwise she might join the chorus of people in his life who thought he was crazy to want to live alone on a deserted island.

* * *

Topher turned his head so that only the unmarred side of his face was visible. It was as handsome as ever. But Jessica was hard-pressed to recognize the man sitting behind the ship's wheel.

He wasn't the same clean-cut, letter-jacket all-American she remembered. He'd lost the roundness of youth and now had a tough, sinewy look to him. He was dressed like a beach bum, in a garish purple Hawaiian shirt featuring palm trees and bright-orange sunsets, faded jeans with holes in the knees, and a pair of dirty Vans.

The late-August sun highlighted strands of blond and gray in his shoulder-length hair. A bushy beard hid a tracery of scars on his left side, which he tried to keep hidden from her view. The way he turned his head might have broken her heart if she'd had any pity for him.

But it was the eye patch over his left eye that gave him the appearance of an anti-hero from an action movie. Looking into the endless blue of his right eye was more unnerving than the lack of symmetry in his face or his incredibly rude manner.

She settled back into the cushion and waited. Last Friday, when he'd set up this meeting, he'd been so insistent about her dropping everything, including her bid for the new City

Hall project, in order to do this site visit. She expected him to have a lot to say as they sailed out to the island.

Clients usually had more ideas than could ever be incorporated into a single design. It was her job to winnow out the important things at initial meetings like this.

But minutes rolled by and he remained silent. Evidently, he expected her to get the ball rolling. "So, about this house," she said, "are you planning to restore the lighthouse, or did you want to build additional structures?"

Instead of answering the question, he turned that blue eye on her and asked, "Do you think I'm crazy?"

"What?"

"It's a simple question. Do you think I'm crazy to build on a remote island?"

Oh boy. Obviously the man knew what the gossips were saying about him. She could stop this right now. But she suddenly didn't want to. If the man wanted to hang himself, she was happy to supply the rope.

But she wasn't rude, either. She simply sidestepped his query. "Building on an island will be difficult," she said.

"That didn't answer my question."

He was no fool, was he? "Well," she said, leaning back on the bench and looking away from his too-intense gaze, "you have to be a little crazy to want to build off the grid."

He barked a laugh. "So you think I'm crazy."

"Yes," she said as irritation mounted. The man obviously didn't know one thing about polite conversation.

"Maybe we should turn around," he said through his teeth. His gaze pinned her.

"Maybe we should. We're only here because you insisted." She forced herself to stare right at him, daring him to come about.

His mouth twitched, and he looked to the left, hiding his scars. He didn't turn the boat around, but he didn't say anything, either. The silence stretched out, punctuated by the wind whipping against the ties on the furled mainsail. She pressed her lips together, determined not to smooth over what had just been said, and watched the seabirds above them.

Ten minutes later, he spoke again. "My grandfather talked about building a big house on the island. I think he wanted to oust the Martin family get-togethers from Aunt Mary's. It galled him to have the Martin family reunion at Howland House. There was once a time when the Martins were as important as the Howlands."

So this was about family ego? Really? She wanted to hurl over the sides, but she continued her silence. She had nothing nice to say about his vision.

"What's going on in that head of yours?" He barked the question into the wind.

That did it. If he wanted the truth, she'd give it to him. "So basically you want to build a monument to your family's name, then."

He laughed without any mirth. "Yes." And then a moment later. "I loved my grandfather."

The longing in his voice yanked her back and reminded her that she was here for the purpose of moving on. Maybe she should quit being so angry and try accepting that he was a human capable of loving someone.

And she could understand loving a grandfather. She'd adored PopPop.

"I understand," she said, fighting to maintain emotional distance from the man who had ruined her life.

# Chapter Two——————————

$D$id she understand?

No way. She was whole, and beautiful, and... He didn't know what the hell word to use to describe her. She wasn't intimidated by his anger, and the way she pointed her face at him suggested that she wasn't giving him *the stare*.

He wanted her to understand about Granddad. But what the hell. It didn't matter if she understood. What he wanted was impossible. The dream of a family compound had died with his grandfather. His cousins were scattered around the country these days, and besides, who would want to bring their kids to visit a man whose face made babies cry?

No, he was alone, and likely to be that way for the rest of his life. So what he needed was a place to hide. But saying it out loud wasn't easy.

He tore his gaze away from Jessica and focused on the compass heading. Not that he needed the direction. He could see Lookout Island off the port bow, the old lighthouse rising up, seemingly from out of the bay itself.

"Maybe I should just restore the lighthouse," he muttered, feeling the need to say something.

"Well, that's an option. But are you ready for tiny-house living? A lighthouse usually doesn't have much square footage."

"Are you trying to talk me out of everything I want?" he asked in a disgruntled tone. He turned back toward her, irritated that she seemed so carelessly calm, with one leg tucked up under the other.

She shook her head. "No. I'm just doing my job. You haven't given me much to work with."

"No. I told you what I wanted and—"

"Not really. You told me what your grandfather wanted, and then you told me what you were willing to settle for. What is it you want, Topher?"

*I want my old life back.* That was what he wanted, but she was powerless to give him that. So instead, he asked, "What would be involved in turning the lighthouse into a residence?"

She leaned forward, pulling her cap down on her head against the breeze. "Well, I've never done a lighthouse restoration, so I'll need to do some research. But from what I've seen in photographs, it will be vertical living. You know, a room on each level. So lots of stairs to get from one place to another."

She pushed her sunglasses up her nose and looked in his direction. Damnation. He wanted to see her eyes when she said stuff like that. Did she have enough courage to look him in the eye and point out his obvious disability?

"I think maybe I want a little more room," he said.

"Is there a lightkeeper's cottage on the island?"

"There was once, but I don't remember it. Hurricane Hugo blew it down in 1989."

"Too bad. We could have restored it."

"I guess. I don't think it was very big."

"So you want something big, then?"

He shrugged.

"Are you planning to live there year-round?"

"Of course."

"Oh. Okay, that's important to know. We have to worry about winter storms in addition to the occasional tropical disturbance. I don't think we'll be able to build a sea wall, but we can—"

"I like the idea of walls," he said because he didn't know what else to say. "You know, to keep the storms at bay." *And to keep people out.* Then he added, "The lighthouse is made of brick, so maybe we should think about some stone to complement it." God, he sounded like an idiot. He knew nothing about architecture.

"Hmmm," she said on a long breath. "So basically you're telling me you want a castle with a tower."

"What? I didn't say—"

"Okay, I know that's not what you said, but a stone building with a wall and a lighthouse tower says castle to me."

A flash of anger hit him like a rogue wave. "Are you laughing at me?" he snarled.

"Not at all. I'm trying to understand what you want."

"Well, clearly I want something substantial, maybe built of stone, with a wall to protect it. And it needs to withstand the most ferocious storm, with a big enough freezer to lay in food for months at a time. I don't plan to make a lot of trips back and forth to the grocery store."

\* \* \*

Finally. She had something to work with, and it wasn't far from what Aunt Donna had talked about last Saturday. He wanted a hideaway.

It made sense, seeing the way he would turn away from her, exposing only his unscarred side. It almost irked her that she could feel empathy for him. It was probably hard for him. People probably stared at him.

So she got the picture. He wanted a place to haunt like some brooding, injured hero in a Gothic novel. She'd never designed anything like that, and she'd hate living in a place like that. But it wasn't her vision or her house.

That was the point. And she took pride in the fact that · she was good at her job because she could translate her clients' visions into reality.

So she gave him a businesslike smile. "I can design something like that," she said, standing up to make herself taller and maybe a bit more serious-looking. But the swaying motion of the boat almost knocked her sideways. She had to grab the back of the bench to keep from falling over. How humiliating.

She found him watching her out of his cobalt-blue eye, studying her as if he could see right through to her insecurities. She needed a moment to regroup.

"If you don't mind, I'd like to use the head."

"Sure. It's down the ship's ladder and to the left."

She headed forward and took the ladder down into the yacht's main salon, which had been decorated in a style that fit the boat's name.

And really, who names their boat *Bachelor's Delight*? But then, she already knew that Topher Martin had an ego the size of Alaska. Clearly, the whole #MeToo thing had completely escaped his attention.

As she snooped around his yacht, she got a real good

sense of his design style, which could be summed up as early–American Playboy Mansion. She wanted to barf all over the gold trim in the yacht's head. The whole thing was beyond tacky.

When she returned above deck, desperately in need of fresh air, *Delight* was nearing the iconic lighthouse. It stood on its lonely island at the mouth of the inlet, its red and white stripes faded to brown and gray. A cast-iron gallery and catwalk topped the tower and had left rust streaks down the faded paint of the brickwork.

The tower was solid and utterly isolated. A perfect place for an off-the-grid hideaway for a brooding bachelor.

Topher guided the yacht alongside a floating aluminum dock that appeared to be brand-new. She hopped out and secured the mooring lines as Topher cut the engines.

She had expected him to take care of the aft lines, but when he stood up from the captain's chair, she realized the truth. Aunt Donna had said something about his injured leg, and now she realized that it was, by far, the most significant of his challenges.

A few misgivings settled uncomfortably into her mind. Maybe it was cruel to do this—to make it possible for him to retire from the world.

She stomped on the thought. Who was she to tell him what he should and shouldn't do? The man was willing to pay her well. So she wasn't going to get all softhearted or worried. The man had money, he wanted a house, and she was an architect.

She headed down the dock and caught the mooring line when he tossed it to her. When she'd secured it to the cleat, she stood and turned, gazing up at the lighthouse.

"Tell me about the light?" she asked.

"It was built in 1870," he said as they made their way

up a flagstone walk. Topher had produced one of those folding aluminum canes with a rubber tip, which he leaned heavily on as they climbed the hill where the light stood looking over the inlet.

"It was decommissioned in the late 1960s," Topher continued, "and my grandfather bought the island back in 1973, years before I was born."

When they reached the steel door set into the masonry, he pulled out an old-fashioned key and slipped it into the lock. The mechanism squealed as he turned it. So did the hinges as he pulled the door open.

They stepped into the tower, a dim light filtering down from above. The porthole windows circling the building revealed a slightly rusty cast-iron stairway spiraling up around the building's interior perimeter. Jessica took off her sunglasses and hung them from the neckline of her T-shirt as she gazed upward. The helix of the stairway was a thing of beauty.

"There are one hundred and sixty-seven steps to the watch room. A ladder leads up from there to the lantern room," Topher said.

She turned, finally, meeting and holding his gaze. His cobalt eye gleamed in the dim light with a spark that welded her to the floor. She couldn't look away, as the memory of the boy in the letter jacket was cauterized forever from her memory, leaving this much more intimidating version.

He looked away first, and she yanked her gaze up toward the spiraling stairs and spoke the first words that entered her brain. "You can't make it up to the top, can you?"

The words were cruel in a way, but they were also true. And necessary. She'd need to incorporate an elevator into her design.

"No, I can't," he growled.

# Chapter Three————————

It was after four o'clock by the time *Bachelor's Delight* returned to its berth at the Magnolia Harbor Marina. During the afternoon, Jessica had taken hundreds of photos and measurements, filling a notebook with ideas, facts, figures, and even a few drawings.

She also had a signed agreement in hand to produce a house design. Topher Martin was willing to pay her twice her going rate.

Which was great, except that her new client seemed to know that she was overcharging him because the last thing he said, right before she left him at the pier, was that he wanted to see design concepts in a week.

A week!

Yikes. She was going to have to burn some serious midnight oil to make that happen because she needed to finish her submission to the review committee for the new City Hall project before she could even start work on his house.

Submissions were due on Friday, and she still had a lot

of details to work out. She was hoping that her hometown connection would give her a leg up on the other teams submitting designs. Of course, the review committee, most of whom had known her and her family for years, were also well aware that she was a one-woman shop with offices above a boutique.

But a girl needed to start somewhere. When she'd returned to Magnolia Harbor two years ago, she'd taken a leave of absence from the firm in Charleston where she'd been working to look after Momma in her final few months.

She'd reconnected with Colton St. Pierre, and his cheerleading and business connections as Magnolia Harbor's up-and-coming building contractor had helped her decide to start her own business. Colton had been the one to introduce her to Mr. Akiyama, who'd been looking for an architect willing to take on a big challenge. His house had won awards and brought her more business. A month ago, she'd moved her business into commercial office space on Harbor Drive. So what if her office was above a boutique?

If she'd allowed herself to listen to Granny's negativity, Jessica would never have been in this position—to accept a contract from a rich man for a challenging design on a remote island.

Call her crazy, but if she could carry it out, she might win a few more awards.

Her life might be almost perfect were it not for the fact that the gossips of Magnolia Harbor seemed to believe that her business relationship with Colton would eventually rekindle their teenage romance.

Like most gossip, this was wrong. They were friends and business associates, not lovers, and there had never been a teenage romance, even though her name and his had been forever linked sixteen years ago.

Nevertheless, it was still a bit disconcerting when she returned to her office and found Colton lounging in her swivel chair with his feet up on her desk. He looked mighty comfortable, as if he'd been there for a while.

Colton was a truly nice guy who'd straightened out his life, but sometimes he had boundary issues.

"Kerri let me in," he said before Jessica could even ask the question.

Kerri was the owner of the building and the boutique downstairs. And of course she'd let Colton in even though Jessica had never left any express instructions about who should and should not be let into her locked office.

Kerri had just assumed, because Jessica and Colton had a long, twisted history in this town.

After a long day with a difficult man, her landlady's assumptions irritated Jessica. But she wasn't about to tell Colton that because she owed him so much.

"So how'd it go?" Colton asked, dropping his feet to the floor. "You guys were gone all day. I was starting to get worried."

"Topher wants a castle," she said with a little eye roll. "Or maybe a bachelor's pad. I'm not sure which."

"What?" Colton leaned forward with a deep frown.

"Have you seen his yacht?" Jessica asked.

"No, why?"

"It's named *Bachelor's Delight*. Honestly, who names a boat—"

Colton started to laugh.

"What's so funny?" she asked, putting her hands on her hips.

"That's the name of a famous pirate ship," he said.

"What?"

He whipped out his iPhone and peered into the screen. "Siri," he asked, "who sailed *Bachelor's Delight*?"

Siri dutifully responded, "I found this on the web."

Colton made a few keystrokes. "Edward Davis," he said. "He lived in the 1600s and was some kind of English privateer. His boat, which had thirty-six guns, according to this Wikipedia entry, was named *Bachelor's Delight*."

"You and your pirates," she said with an eye roll.

He smirked. "If you had ever studied up on your local pirates, maybe the name of Topher's boat wouldn't have ticked you off. The original *Bachelor's Delight* is one of the most famous pirate ships around, along with Captain Teal's *Bonnie Rose* and Blackbeard's *Queen Anne's Revenge*."

"Okay. So I'm uninformed about historic pirate ships. But it doesn't change the way Topher Martin's boat is fitted out. Hugh Hefner would feel right at home." She stalked forward to stand in front of Colton. "Out of my chair. I need to think."

"And you can't think on your feet?" he asked with a smirk.

"Out."

"Yes, ma'am." He hopped up onto the edge of the desk, and she flopped back into her chair. "I spent the whole day thinking he was an egotistical maniac because of the boat's name. Although really, there were other things that convinced me of that. His grandfather wanted to build some kind of big house out there just to prove that the Martins are as important as the Howlands. And the bed in the captain's quarters is round, with satin sheets." She shook her head.

"Really?" Colton's tone changed to avid interest, or maybe concern. "How'd you get to see the captain's quarters?"

She cocked her head. "I went to the head, and I snooped."

"Oh."

"I don't know, Colton. He really wants a castle so he can retire from the world and brood. Did you hear about his accident?"

Colton nodded. "So, is it bad?"

She shrugged. "Not his face so much. But he's got challenges. Physical ones."

"Does this mean you've forgiven him?"

"No. It means my empathy has kicked in, and I wish it hadn't. I heard that his family is dead set against him moving out there, and I kind of see why."

"So you're going to shoot yourself in the foot and walk away from this job?"

"Heck no." She pulled the signed agreement out of her tote bag. "I'm charging him double my going rate."

"Well, if you can't forgive him, taking his money is an alternative," Colton said with a grin.

"Yeah. I guess." But in the back of her mind, something— probably her conscience—niggled. Did taking his money make her craven? Or ugly? Or . . .

She stopped the negative thoughts before they overwhelmed her. Even now, years later, she could hear Daddy calling her names that made her feel ugly and unwanted. And then he'd sent her away.

"What are you thinking?" Colton asked. "You've got that faraway look in your eyes."

She shook her head and forced a smile. "Nothing. Just tired."

"Well, I've got a solution for that. Let's go have dinner

at Aunt Annie's place." He stood, snagging her by the arm and pulling her from her chair.

She came to her feet but resisted his pull. "Um. No. I'm really tired," she said.

"C'mon, I'll feed you. And I'll assuage your conscience for having charged Topher Martin twice your rate."

She shook her head. "No." The truth was she didn't want to be seen at Annie's place with Colton again. They'd had dinner there three times last week. The food was bad for her waistline, but the gossip about them was worse for her headspace.

"Come on. Don't be a—"

"No." She pulled her arm out of his grasp. "I just don't want to go down there again. With you. I mean—" She bit off her words, suddenly mortified that she'd spoken her mind out loud.

It was the second time that day. Earlier she'd spoken the truth about Topher's injuries, and now. Well, now the words had hit their mark.

He blinked, his eyes going wide. "What does that mean?"

"It means that I've gotten five phone calls from my grandmother's friends who saw us at Annie's on Saturday and last Wednesday. And then there's the way you've been fixing my leaking plumbing. And the fact that you and your crew moved me into this office space a month ago. People are talking about us..." She ended the phrase with a gesture that wasn't terribly eloquent. Then she huffed out a breath and studied the exposed beams in the ceiling.

"And is that so bad?" he asked.

"What? You know what they're saying."

He nodded. "Maybe we should, you know, give them something to talk about."

She locked gazes with him as the earth shifted beneath her feet. What the...?

"Uh. Um. Colton. No. We don't...I mean, I don't...Oh, good grief." She turned away from him.

She didn't love Colton. Not that way anyway. Heck, she wasn't sure she could love anyone. Or that anyone could love the real her—the woman inside who sometimes believed the nasty things Daddy had said about her coming up.

No. She didn't want a man in her life. She didn't trust men. And besides, she didn't want to end up like Momma, domineered into submission.

Behind her, Colton's silence was like a physical thing looming over her.

"You better go," she said.

"Yeah, I guess maybe I should."

* * *

Kerri Eaton was having a less than spectacular day at Daffy Down Dilly until Colton St. Pierre came waltzing into the store around 3:30 p.m., looking for Jess. As if Kerri was Jess's keeper and not her landlady.

But hey, a beggar couldn't be a chooser, and the view out her front windows had definitely improved in the month since Jess had leased the office space upstairs. Colton came and went at will.

And why not? Jess was obviously the love of his life. And hell, if you listened to the gossip that had been raging for years, Jessica and Colton had been the Romeo and Juliet of Magnolia Harbor. Teen lovers who had been thwarted by the powers that be and forced into exile.

Everyone wanted to rewrite that story and give it a happy ending.

Kerri blew out a long sigh. It was kind of annoying that the most eligible bachelor of color, not counting Colton's older brother, Micah, had a jones for a white woman. But who was she to stand in the way of true love, long delayed.

So she'd opened the office for him. And once Jess returned, Kerri could hear their voices. Okay, it was a slow day and she had her ear pressed hard to the wall adjoining the office stairwell. But she couldn't quite make out what they were saying. She fully expected them to come down the stairs together and head off to dinner someplace. They'd been seen all over town at various restaurants.

So when Colton came clomping down the stairs by himself, Kerri was surprised. And like any busybody worth her salt, she let her curiosity get the better of her. Was there trouble in paradise?

The gossiping public in Magnolia Harbor would want to know. All of Kerri's friends would want details and facts. Or maybe just the juicy morsels, since facts were often not terribly interesting.

So she hurried out onto the sidewalk with a smile on her face. "Hey, Colton," she said to his back as he was heading toward his pickup. He turned. "Did Jess come back? If not, I can lock up for you." She hoped her voice didn't give away the lie.

"She's back," he said, a little muscle ticking in his jaw. What did that mean? Was he angry at Jess? Or what?

"Oh, okay. Y'all didn't have a disagreement, did you?" she asked, point-blank. "I mean, she wasn't upset that I let you in?"

He shrugged. "I don't know what she's upset about."

Whoa, they *had* argued.

"Well, I imagine she's in a grumpy mood after spending the day with Topher Martin. The word on the street is that he's not the same as he used to be."

"Yeah. I guess." Colton turned and took a few more steps toward his truck before he stopped again. When he turned around, it was as if he was looking at her for the first time. As if he was truly seeing her for once.

A little thrill ran down Kerri's spine. Lord have mercy, he was one fine-looking man. His skin was a deep red-brown, like the wood of a polished cypress knee, and his eyes were tawny gray like Spanish moss. Everything about him screamed South Carolina Low Country.

And this fine-looking man was actually staring at her, his eyebrow rising just so. He put his big ol' hands on his oh-so-slim hips. "So, uh, when's quitting time?" he asked.

Sweet Jesus, was the man about to suggest dinner somewhere? Wow. She looked down at her watch to avoid showing any eagerness, but then she blew it by saying, "In about five minutes." She held her breath and stopped herself from looking up.

This was so wrong. He had a thing for Jess Blackwood. Didn't he? Otherwise he might have noticed her last July, when they'd played on the same softball team and she'd worn her tight-fitting yoga pants.

"So, uh, you doing anything? Maybe we could grab some chops over at Aunt Annie's Kitchen or some shrimp at Rafferty's or something," he said.

She exhaled and met his gaze. She'd be a fool to let this happen. She knew better than to mess with some other woman's man. Assuming, of course, that he was Jess's man. Now that she thought about it, she hadn't seen any solid proof that Colton and Jess had a thing going. He popped into her office from time to time, but she'd never seen any public displays of affection.

Maybe it was just gossip. Maybe they were just friends. Or not.

So instead of saying yes, she folded her arms across her chest and asked, "What's the matter? Did Jess stand you up?"

"I didn't have a date with her," he said in a tight voice. "We're just friends."

Kerri heard the twist in his voice—as if he wanted out of the friend zone and into something more intimate. She should say no. She should turn and walk away from him.

But she didn't. A chance like this came along once in a blue moon. If Jess was too blind to see what she was throwing away, then shame on her.

Kerri gave him her best seductive smile. "I'd love to have a chop over at Annie's Kitchen," she said. "Just give me a moment to close things up."

* * *

Tuesday morning, Jessica sat at her office desk doodling on a legal pad, still too upset by Colton's behavior the previous evening to focus on any work.

His words kept circling her mind: *Let's give them something to talk about.*

She didn't want to give anyone anything to talk about. She'd already been talked about way too much in this town. And ever since her disastrous run-in with rumor and gossip, she'd endeavored never to give anyone anything to hold over her.

She'd been the model of propriety. She'd been polite.

She'd been careful with her friendships and relationships. She'd always tried to tell the truth when she could, and when people resisted the truth or the truth was too brutal, she would say nothing at all.

Except yesterday, when she'd spoken her mind to Colton. And look where that had landed her. She had no clue how she was going to salvage her friendship with him.

Just then Kerri peeked around the door to the stairs.

"Hey," her landlady said. "I made a fresh pot of coffee, and things are slow downstairs. I thought you might like a cup."

Kerri came striding into the office looking like a runway model. She stood almost six feet tall in ballet flats and was rocking one of her shop's cute little sundresses. Accessorized to the max, Kerri was the epitome of classy Southern womanhood with a savvy attitude.

Kerri handed Jessica a cup festooned with daffodils and then sank down into the single side chair.

Jessica took a sip. The coffee was a bold, flavorful roast.

"So," Kerri said, settling back in her chair, "you working on Topher Martin's house?"

Jessica blinked a couple of times. Living in Magnolia Harbor meant everyone knew everyone's business, but the speed with which news traveled still surprised her. "So you know about that?"

"You were apparently seen getting onto Topher Martin's yacht yesterday. And since it's become common knowledge that he wants to run away to Lookout Island and you're an architect..." Her voice trailed off.

"Yeah, I guess it's not hard for people to add up one plus one." *And frequently come up with three or four or more.*

Kerri nodded and stared down at her cup for a long moment, clearly uncomfortable about something. Not wanting to hear any more troubling gossip, Jessica didn't encourage her.

"Um…" Kerri finally said, looking up. "The thing is, I heard about Topher's plans because I went to Annie's place with Colton last night, and—"

"You did?" Jessica sat up straighter in her chair, a ray of sunshine leaking through the cloud that had been hanging over her all morning.

Why hadn't she thought of that before? Maybe the answer to her problem was to find Colton a gorgeous and successful girlfriend. Someone exactly like Kerri Eaton.

"I feel so guilty about it," Kerri continued. "I mean, I'm sure you're going to hear gossip, and I just wanted you to know that it was completely innocent. And really, I felt like I needed to come up here and let you know because…" She didn't finish the sentence.

"You think we've got a thing?" Jessica asked.

"Don't you? I mean, didn't you have some kind of lover's quarrel last night?"

Oh, good grief. When would people stop?

"We did have an argument last night, but it wasn't a lover's quarrel. We don't have a thing." Jessica didn't explain further because anything she said would be fed into the grapevine and come out garbled on the other end. Sometimes it felt as if she could stand on a mountaintop and shout the truth and not a soul would believe her.

"Really? Because, you know, he spent a lot of time telling me how worried he is about you."

"Worried? D—" She swallowed back the cuss word and gripped the arms of her chair.

"Well, maybe not worried. Concerned about things."

"What things?" Jessica leaned forward, irritation flaring into real anger at Colton for running his mouth about her. He knew better.

"I guess he's concerned about this City Hall design competition. He told me that you're going up against some really big firms."

"So what? Everyone has to start somewhere."

The corner of Kerri's mouth twitched. "I guess that's true."

"I'm fine. I know it's a long shot, but you have to take risks to gain rewards, right? And besides, he knows good and well that I just landed the Martin project."

"Whoa, wait," Kerri said, putting her hands out palms forward. "I think you misunderstood. Colton is rooting for you. He just—"

"Spent the whole night talking about me?" Jessica met Kerri's stare.

"Well, not the entire time," Kerri said. "We did talk a little about the chamber of commerce and the general business climate. But otherwise." Kerri's normally straight shoulders slumped. It was clear that her landlady had an unrequited crush on Colton.

Because Colton was an idiot.

"Good grief." Jessica looked away, studying the morning sunshine pouring through her front windows. If she had any skills at matchmaking, this would be the time to whip them out. But alas, she was a dolt when it came to relationships.

"You know, Jess, I'd give my right arm to have a man like that worry about me," Kerri said.

That was probably true. But Jessica liked her right arm a lot and didn't want to give it away for anyone, not even Colton. She turned back toward Kerri. "You're right," she said. "Colton is a great guy. But he's my *friend,* and that's it. So if you want to make a play for him, go right ahead. You have my blessing."

Kerri put her empty cup on the desk and met Jessica's stare. "Really? You're not ticked off that I had dinner with him?"

"I'm not his keeper," Jessica said. "Now, if you don't mind, I'm super busy. I've got that City Hall project to finish."

And by golly, just like that, she had found a way to push Colton out of her mind. If the man was running around town talking about her, then her anger was entirely justified.

# Chapter Four —————————

Late Tuesday afternoon, after prowling around Rose Cottage like a caged beast, Topher screwed up his courage and limped his way down the crushed-shell pathway that bisected Howland House's broad lawn. The path led past an ancient live oak that overlooked Moonlight Bay and a small swimming beach, which would be abandoned this time of day.

Ashley didn't have that many guests this week. So he had a reasonable chance of being left alone while he floundered around in the water. But maybe, if he came out here and swam every day, he'd get stronger. And maybe, by the time his house was finished, he'd be able to climb the stairs to the top of the lighthouse.

The thought made him smile. Once, climbing to the top of the light had been so much fun. Although, now that he thought about it, there had been lots of other fun times out on the island. He and Granddad used to take camping trips out there all the time. On those lazy summer days, they'd sailed all over the inlet, spending nights telling pirate stories around the campfire and eating catfish they'd caught off the pier. Those had been some of the best days of Topher's childhood.

He would get strong enough to climb those stairs, if for no other reason than to prove his newly hired architect wrong. Not that he would ever admit how her words had affected him in the last twenty-four hours.

The funny thing was that she hadn't called out his disability to be cruel. She'd simply noted it down like one of the many observations she'd put in that notebook of hers. Like his frailty was something to be weighed and measured.

Well, screw that.

He skirted the live oak as quickly as he could, not wishing to linger where much sadder memories ran deep. He'd spent a lot of lonely time up in that tree after his mother died. Aunt Mary, Ashley's grandmother, had helped to raise him.

He followed the footpath down a set of concrete stairs to a small sand beach, where he abandoned his cane and towel. Walking along the sand was hard work and required the use of muscles that had atrophied over the last few months.

It was a relief when he finally reached the water's edge. As he waded out into the bay, the water buoyed him up. Feeling momentarily weightless, he could walk along the sandy bottom without nearly as much pain. And when he submerged himself, he discovered that he could swim without any pain at all.

He was out of shape and easily winded, but swimming every day would change that quickly. The discovery lifted his spirits for the first time in ages.

It was getting close to dusk when he finally emerged, the gravity pulling him back to earth. The pain returned, and his legs felt rubbery under him. Even after he'd dried off and rested a few minutes, climbing the three stairs from the beach to the lawn was like hauling himself up every single stair circling the lighthouse.

He blew out a frustrated breath. He wasn't going to recover in a day of swimming. But he was impatient enough to want that. He leaned on his cane and rested, breathing hard as he studied the live oak. The tree called to him, but he resisted.

Instead, he headed back up the path toward the cottage, but a movement in his peripheral vision caught his attention. He stopped and turned his head.

What was that? A shadow against the deeper shadows of the evening? He blinked, his heart still thudding in his chest from his swim. Was it the ghost?

No. There was no such thing. It was only the kid— Ashley's son, Jackie. The kid was sitting under the tree, his knees drawn up against his chest, his forehead pressed against them in a picture of familiar misery.

Topher pulled himself upright, wrapped the towel around his shoulders, and left the footpath. His cane sank into the soft lawn as he hobbled toward the old tree and the sad little boy.

"So, what's the story?" Topher asked when he finally made it across the lawn. The kid had been lurking around the cottage for days, as if he'd wanted to start a conversation but had been too frightened to try it.

Not surprising given the state of Topher's face. But he wasn't about to walk by and leave the kid looking so miserable. Topher had spent his share of miserable days under the canopy of this particular tree.

"Go away," the kid said to his updrawn knees.

"Didn't have a good day at school, then?"

The kid looked up, giving him a daggerlike stare despite

the sheen of tears on his cheeks. "And what would you know about it, anyway?" he asked.

Whoa. Topher expected the kid to give him *the stare*, or maybe run away screaming. But instead the boy met his gaze as if he wasn't at all frightened by Topher's disfigured face.

"I know a lot, actually. I was kind of a nerd in school," Topher said.

"I bet you didn't have people calling you a liar all the time, did you, huh?"

"Um, well…no." He leaned against the oak's lowest branch, the bark abrading his palm. When he'd been Jackie's age, it had taken some doing to swing up onto it. But he'd grown a lot since then. He was tired, but he still managed to pull himself up onto it and straddle it like a horse.

"There's a spot up at the very top of this tree that's like a crow's nest on a ship," he said, choosing to ignore the kid's question.

The kid looked up at him, his face pale in the growing twilight. "You know about that?"

Topher smiled at the bittersweet memories. "Yeah. I do. I used—" He cut himself off.

"What?"

Maybe he shouldn't encourage the kid. Topher knew all about Jackie and his fixation on the ghost of William Teal—the pirate who had lost his life in a shipwreck down the bay hundreds of years ago. So maybe telling the kid about how he used to pretend to be a pirate wouldn't be the right thing to do.

Maybe instead, he should take Granddad's tack and buy the kid a football and show him how to throw it.

"Nothing," Topher said. "I just used to like climbing up there."

The kid turned away, and they sat quietly for a long moment before the boy pushed himself up from the ground. "I gotta go before Mom figures out I'm not upstairs watching TV. It's Tuesday. The Piece Makers are coming."

Jackie headed off across the lawn, leaving him stranded in the tree. Topher had forgotten that it was Tuesday. His cousins Karen and Sandra would be coming over, and they'd find a moment to swoop down on him with a zillion questions about how he was feeling. They would probably have twin coronaries if he ever told them he'd been out here swimming.

Or if they ever found out he'd climbed a tree.

And he'd have no trouble keeping those things a secret from them if he could just find a way to get back down to the ground. The lawn below seemed impossibly far away, but he was not going to be an excuse for Ashley to call in the fire and rescue.

He inhaled, swung his bad leg over the side, closed his eyes, and slipped back to earth. The pain jangled all the way up his spine, but miraculously, he didn't fall on his ass.

* * *

Ashley Scott rarely made caramel cake. It might be a delicious staple of the South, but it took forever to whip the caramel icing—twenty minutes in the stand mixer to get the right frothy consistency.

But Jackie loved caramel cake. And since today marked the end of his summer vacation, she'd made a whole cake just for him. He'd already had a slice after dinner. And there would be plenty to pack in his school lunches for the rest of the week.

Maybe that would improve his mood. Jackie was too

smart for his own good sometimes. And he was also just a little odd, her boy. What with his imaginary pirate friend...who might be a ghost.

Kids teased him, and school wasn't his favorite place, especially at recess or lunchtime. Ashley sometimes wondered what Adam, her late husband, might think of their child. Would her husband, who'd been a man's man, be ashamed of the boy who got perpetually bullied at school?

Probably.

But she wasn't ashamed. She worried about Jackie. And loved him with all her heart, which was why she'd made a double recipe of caramel cake—so Jackie could have his own cake and the ladies of the Piece Makers quilting club could have theirs.

The quilting group met every Tuesday at Howland House, and they'd been getting scratch-made cake every week for decades. The cakes were a tradition that Ashley's grandmother had started when she'd formed the group during World War II. Ashley had taken over the tradition after her husband and grandmother had died within a year of each other.

It seemed impossible that it had been three years since Adam had been killed on deployment. She still cried for him, especially at night, but she'd been learning to live with the loneliness. Besides, her bed-and-breakfast kept her too busy for self-pity most of the time.

Grandmother might not have liked the idea of turning Howland House into an inn, but it had been the only way Ashley could keep the old place in the Howland family. Her married name was Scott, but she'd been born a Howland— a direct descendant of Rose Howland, the woman who had planted the daffodils that had given Jonquil Island its name.

Magnolia Harbor, the largest town on the island, had been founded more than a hundred years after Rose had died. But her daffodils remained.

Ashley checked the oven clock. It was nearly seven. The quilters would be arriving shortly. Their cake now took pride of place in the newly refurbished kitchen, sitting on Grandmother's milk-glass cake stand beside a stack of her china plates and the silver cake server.

Cake had been served on those plates almost every week for eighty years. The sheer longevity of the Tuesday-night meetings made them both a burden and a joy to be a part of. Ashley didn't dare end the tradition, but sometimes she wished the group would meet elsewhere, or maybe give up the old-fashioned practice of hand quilting. They could make a lot more quilts if someone would invest in a long-arm sewing machine capable of machine quilting. The truth was that sometimes Ashley wanted a Tuesday night off.

The sound of the big front door opening pulled Ashley from her dissatisfied thoughts. A moment later, Sandra Jernigan and her sister, Karen Tighe, came into the kitchen. Sandra and Karen, like Grandmother, were members of the Martin family. They had been Grandmother's nieces, which made them Ashley's cousins once removed or something like that.

In any case, Ashley, Sandra, and Karen were part of an extended family that included Topher, who was even more removed, relation-wise. But in this town family counted, especially if your surname was Howland or Martin. The Howlands and the Martins had founded Magnolia Harbor.

"How is he?" Sandra asked the moment she arrived, utterly ignoring the caramel cake that her sister immediately dived into. Sandra didn't have a sweet tooth, but Karen did.

"I assume you're asking about Topher?" Ashley said. Sandra nodded.

"Well, he's still not eating meals with the boarders. But I saw him leave the cottage and come back with a bunch of grocery sacks. I have no idea *what* he's eating, but he's eating something."

"You should have offered to go shopping for—"

"No, Sandra, she shouldn't have offered to shop for him," Karen said, interrupting her sister around a mouthful of cake. "Topher needs tough love."

Karen and Sandra bore a family resemblance if you looked hard enough, but the two of them tried their best not to enhance it. Karen rarely wore a skirt while Sandra was a bit of a fashion plate, although her sense of style was about twenty years out of date.

"The poor dear," Sandra said, giving Karen a glare. "We really need to make an intervention."

"And do what?" Ashley asked. Her cousins were meddling in Topher's life. She was resisting the urge, although clearly the man needed help.

"I don't know," Sandra said, her voice laced with deep and genuine concern. "He's so alone. He's been alone since his father died."

"Before that," Karen said on a long, mournful breath.

Oh boy. Yes, Topher had lived a difficult life, losing his mother at the age of four and his father when he was eighteen, shortly after starting his freshman year at Alabama. Still, he'd managed, and he'd done well for himself until the accident.

Not surprisingly, Sandra and Karen, who had been babying him most of his life, wanted to swathe Topher in Bubble Wrap now that he was hurting.

"He'll be okay," Ashley said, trying to invest her voice

with more conviction than she felt. Topher was desperately injured in both body and spirit. But maybe all he needed was a little time.

Ashley had met Topher only once or twice as a kid, when her father's military service had allowed Daddy to return home to Magnolia Harbor for family celebrations. She remembered Topher as a nerdy kid. Sort of like Jackie, now that she thought about it.

That brought her up sharp because Ashley hadn't been kind to Topher when they were younger. She was four years older and had hung out with their cousins Steven and Timothy. The older kids made a point of excluding Topher from their games, leaving him to play with the little girl cousins.

Melanie, Alicia, and Lindsay had adored Topher. Like him, they were all in their thirties now. Each one had checked in with Ashley over the last few weeks, concerned about him. Apparently Topher was not returning phone calls and seemed to have forgotten that his extended family loved him no matter what.

"I heard from Isaac Solomon down at the marina that Topher took his boat out yesterday," Karen said.

"He did?" Ashley asked. "I guess I didn't notice that he'd left the cottage. I was busy doing back-to-school shopping with Jackie."

"Well, apparently he did. He sailed to Lookout Island with Jessica Blackwood. I called Donna, and she confirmed that he's hired her niece to do a site visit for a house out there."

Ashley brushed an imaginary crumb from her marble countertop. "Well, I guess that's not a surprise. He's been talking about building a house out there since he returned to Magnolia Harbor."

"Yes, but I thought he'd give it up once he was back home with family. We can't let him run away from his problems. And besides, it's not safe for him to live alone out there," Karen said.

Ashley studied the veins in the marble but said nothing.

"Tell me you don't disagree," Sandra said.

"I guess I do agree. But I don't feel right intervening."

"But we must," Sandra said. "Can you imagine him living out there alone during a storm?"

No, Ashley couldn't. But storms had nothing to do with it. She couldn't imagine how anyone would choose isolation over family.

Loneliness was one of Ashley's constant companions. It had been that way even before Adam had died, when he'd been deployed to some godforsaken place and managed to call only every once in a while.

She'd hated the loneliness then. But when Adam had been killed, she hadn't taken a deep dive into self-pity.

No. She'd moved here, where people poked their noses into her business. And then she'd become an innkeeper, with a constant crowd of guests coming and going. She was still lonely, but she wasn't alone.

She understood Topher's grief, but she had no clue how to make him return to the world of the living. She had hoped he would take his meals with the rest of her boarders. But he hadn't. He wouldn't even let the cleaning lady in to tidy up.

"No," she said aloud, looking up. "I wouldn't want him out there in the middle of the bay living alone. Not in a storm or on the calmest summer day."

"Okay, then," Karen said. "We need to put our heads together and figure out a way to stop him."

*Chapter Five*———————

J essica threw herself into the City Hall project, working late into the night on Tuesday and Wednesday. By Thursday afternoon, the proposal was as good as it was going to get. Messing around with it for another twelve hours would only make her crazy. If she filed it today, she'd have time on Friday and over the weekend to generate a few ideas for Topher's castle.

So at half past noon on Thursday, she sent the electronic version of her City Hall design via email to the selection committee's administrator. But she also needed to provide one set of paper drawings, and since she was within walking distance of the old City Hall and in desperate need of stretching her legs, she left the office and walked down to hand deliver the package.

Big mistake.

No sooner had she set foot in the old building on the corner of Tulip and Mimosa than she ran headlong into State Representative Caleb Tate, who was coming down the hall with Councilmember Harry Bauman in tow.

She overheard their conversation—all about sailing—and suspected they were headed off to the yacht club.

PopPop had been a lifelong member of the club, and his connections had helped her land the job as a lifeguard up there the summer of her junior year in high school. But she'd never really belonged to the yacht club set. The kids who hung around the pool were rich and spoiled. Caleb had been one of them.

She'd gotten a bird's eye view of Caleb that summer—enough to know that the Rutledge Raiders' star running back considered himself a gift to all females, whether the females in question were interested or not.

She never had been. But that hadn't stopped him from following her into the deserted women's locker room one afternoon and pressing his unwanted attentions on her.

Thank goodness Mrs. Bauman had arrived unexpectedly. Of course the old biddy had misread the situation and scolded both of them for making out in the locker room. The woman had actually threatened to tell Jessica's parents.

But she'd never made good on that threat. Heck, the way Daddy would sometimes go on and on about the boys on that championship team, he might not have even cared that she was caught red-handed with one of them. And he certainly wouldn't have believed or listened if she'd told him the truth.

Daddy had once been a Rutledge Raider himself. And he was the team's biggest booster. No. He wouldn't have wanted to hear about Caleb's behavior. And in the end, he didn't care about the fact that the football team had started a rumor that had wrecked everything.

When he'd heard those rumors, he'd chosen to believe them.

And it was the height of irony that, months later, the

boy who had attacked her in the locker room against her will was the very same one who had accosted her in the hallway outside her physics class and called her a slut for sleeping around with Colton St. Pierre.

He'd pointed his finger at her while a group of other football players, Topher Martin among them, had stood by and laughed.

And none of them had paid a price for their lies or their cruelty. They'd gotten away with it because they were members of a powerful and entitled group.

Not much had changed. Caleb was still in a position of power over her. He sat on the design selection committee, along with Harry Bauman. And she wanted that commission more than anything.

Harry, an avuncular old gentleman, waved at her as he came down the hall. "Jessica, I hear you've been a busy girl."

What was Harry talking about? What did he think she'd been busy doing? What were people gossiping about today? She hated it when people started conversations this way. It always made her feel left-footed and just a little out of sync.

But she covered her worry by pasting a smile on her lips as she held up the cardboard tube containing her entry into the design competition. "I *have* been busy. Working on my entry for the City Hall design. Thought I'd drop it off myself a day early."

His eyes lit up. "Oh, good." Harry turned toward Caleb. "You remember Jessica Blackwood, don't you? She used to be a lifeguard up at the yacht club."

"I do." Caleb gave her an oily smile as his gaze slid from the top of her head down to her not-very-expensive ballet flats. Why did this man make her feel so small and dirty? "So, do you work for an architectural firm in town?" he asked.

She wanted to spit in his big blue eyes. "I have my own business. And we're doing well. In fact, I just moved my company into new space above Daffy Down Dilly." She delivered this line with forced innocence and enjoyed every moment of his surprised expression.

She had stolen that office space away from him. Bobby Don Ayers down at Berkshire Hathaway had told her Caleb Tate had wanted the office above the boutique and wasn't happy when she'd beaten him to the punch. Score one moral victory for her side.

"Oh, that's wonderful," Harry said. "I'm glad business has been good for you." He turned toward Caleb. "Jessica has been designing a lot of interesting houses in the area."

"Yes, I was the architect of the Akiyama house that was on last year's house and garden tour," she said in her best Southern-lady voice.

"That's the one that looks like a bird taking flight," Harry said. "And speaking of birds, I've heard from several in the neighborhood that Topher Martin has hired you to design a house out on Lookout Island."

"I—"

"Topher?" Caleb interrupted. "Topher is back in Magnolia Harbor?"

"Yes. He is. He's staying at Howland House," Harry said.

"Damn. I need to look that boy up," Caleb said. "I heard he made billions after he gave up football." As if Topher's billions were all that mattered—probably because campaign contributions were Caleb Tate's lifeblood.

"Well, it was nice to see you again," she said, and then edged away from the two men. She couldn't get away from Caleb fast enough. "I'd like to get this into the clerk's office as soon as possible." She managed to sound confident as she held up the cardboard tube containing the architectural drawings.

"Of course," Harry said with a genuine smile. "Good luck. I'm always rooting for the hometown team." He gave her a little wave and headed down the hall.

Caleb straggled behind a bit, turning to look at her in a way that made her want to run away like a scared rabbit. But she held her ground and stared right back at him until he turned around and hurried after Harry.

* * *

Jessica walked down the crushed-shell path of the Howland House garden on Tuesday morning with her portfolio tucked under her arm. Her design concepts for Topher Martin's house were finished, even if they were a bit on the sketchy side.

She'd spent only four days on them, working all weekend and late into the night last night, but she still felt woefully unprepared. And she'd agreed to have this meeting on Topher's territory, cognizant of the steep stairs up to her office above the boutique and still a little guilty for calling him out on his inability to scale the lighthouse stairs.

But she'd taken care of that problem in her design, adding an elevator and turning the lighthouse into a castle-like tower at the corner of the house.

The roses in Ashley Scott's garden were alive with butterflies and bees as she headed toward Rose Cottage. The heavy scent hung in the moist, hot air, making the humidity seem a little worse than it was. Her hands were sweaty, and she wiped them on her graphite-gray sheath dress before knocking on the cottage door.

She told herself she would do fine with this presentation. Her designs were unfinished, but she had made an earnest attempt to capture his vision of a castle at the mouth of the harbor.

The door opened, and for a strange, timeless instant as their gazes met and held, a weird vertigo swept through her. Topher's stare frightened her, but not because of the scars on his face. In truth, the fear was inexplicable. She couldn't even put a name to the disquiet he created, but she pushed through it and forced herself not to look away from him.

She would not let this rich, powerful man intimidate her. Last Thursday she'd stared down Caleb Tate; she could do the same with Topher Martin.

"Hey," he said, setting time in motion again.

Only then did she notice how he'd cleaned himself up. The big, bushy beard had disappeared, replaced with a casually trimmed scruff that showed off the line of his jaw and the blades of his cheekbones. With the beard trimmed back, more of his scars showed through the stubble like silvery swirls across his tanned skin.

Yes, that was different too. He looked sun kissed today, as if he'd been spending more time outside. And his crisply ironed linen shirt exposed a tanned neck and a few masculine hairs at the open neckline.

"Morning," she said.

He turned his back on her and moved into the cottage's sitting room. "Come in," he said gruffly over his shoulder. "If you brought drawings, put them on the table."

He was used to giving commands, wasn't he? She tried not to hold it against him. As the CEO of a successful investment fund, he was probably used to having people jump to his every word.

He strode past the small table into the kitchenette. "Can I get you something to drink?" he asked in a tone that verged on civil.

"No," she said, even though her mouth was dry. But her hands were trembling, and she didn't want to run the risk of spilling water over a long weekend's worth of work.

He kept his back turned as she laid her drawings on the table. "I thought we could start with the elevation," she said, waiting.

He finally turned and stepped closer, bringing his body heat with him, along with the scent of some kind of herbal soap. The aroma was deep and rich...and oddly pleasant. That knocked her sideways. She didn't want to discover anything about Topher Martin that was pleasant.

He leaned over the table and studied the rendering of his castle, showing not the slightest bit of emotion.

Anxiety clutched at Jessica. She'd never had a client respond this way. Usually at this stage, the reaction was mixed. They'd like some things and want changes. But they never stood by stoic and silent and brooding.

"The walls are..." He started but never finished the sentence.

*What?* She waited for him to elaborate, but he didn't, and his silence hung over her like a sword.

Defensiveness sprang up in her like a fountain. "I checked the zoning restrictions for the island, and I'm precluded from putting up a sea wall. So instead, I borrowed the concept of a curtain wall from medieval castle design. Those walls will provide some protection against storm surge without disturbing the marine environment.

"And of course they serve as wind breaks. Which, I believe, is what you said you wanted."

"Oh," he said, but he didn't sound excited or enthusiastic.

"Why don't I show you the plan view," she said, pulling a few more drawings out of her portfolio and laying them on the table. "I've given you a great room with a vaulted ceiling here." She pointed to the room on the drawing. "It's the largest room in the house, with southern windows. They have storm shutters, of course. The master bedroom is here." She tapped on the drawing.

She'd purposefully roughed in some furniture. In the case of the bedroom, she'd drawn a circular bed like the one in the captain's cabin on *Bachelor's Delight*.

"There are two more smaller bedrooms and an elevator in one of the spires to take you to an observation deck." Again she pointed. "With the pool here, the observation deck, and an outside kitchen, I think you'll be able to throw some fabulous parties."

When his silence continued, she ventured a look at him only to discover that he was staring at her, not even focused on the drawings.

And that stare made every synapse in her body fire at the same moment. Was this fear or something else? Something so unwanted it frightened her. How could she find him attractive? How could she be drawn to him?

He'd ruined her life with the stories he'd told of Colton's drug use. He'd stood by the day Caleb Tate had publicly called her a slut. He was gruff and silent and damaged. And he was the kind of domineering person that Momma had married.

She took a small step back, trying to escape the aura that had so utterly captured her attention. "Okay. So I'm getting the impression you don't like these ideas," she managed to croak.

"Where on earth did you get the idea I wanted to throw parties out there?"

"Well, um." She took a deep breath. "I may have drawn some conclusions from your yacht. It looks like the quintessential party boat."

"My yacht?" He seemed utterly surprised.

She nodded. "You know, the black leather, the gold faucets, the red bedspread in the captain's quarters—"

"You looked at the captain's quarters?"

She blushed for no reason at all. "I poked around below decks. Just to get a sense of your style."

His lips pressed together briefly before he asked, "And the castle walls?"

"You said you wanted sea walls. You said you wanted . . ." She swallowed back the rest of her defense and took a deep breath. "Um, look. I'm sorry. You obviously don't like these concepts. Maybe I should go."

She reached for the drawings, intent on putting them away and hiding them forever. But before she could shove any of them into her portfolio, he grabbed her by the wrist.

His fingers were warm and just a little rough. They branded her skin in an oddly gentle way. He'd violated her space, and yet his touch wasn't entirely unwelcome.

Startled by her own reaction, she tried to pull away, but he held her firm for one exquisite moment. "Leave the drawings. But we need to—"

"No!" She pulled her arm out of his grasp as her senses returned. She needed to protect herself. She needed to put distance between them.

He let her go without a struggle, allowing her to pick up the portfolio and run for her life.

# Chapter Six

Topher stood in the doorway of the cottage, watching Jessica run away as if escaping a monster.

Which wasn't far from the truth. His face was certainly hideous enough to be called monstrous, having been rearranged by shattered glass and shards of shrapnel. And he'd acted like a beast. He should never have touched her.

He turned away from the door and returned to the table, where he stared at her renderings for a long moment.

He'd asked for a big wall to keep the winds out, hadn't he? And he'd told her that Granddad wanted a structure that would eclipse Howland House.

She'd certainly given him all of that.

He almost laughed out loud about the party house concept. Maybe he should have told her that *Bachelor's Delight* had been purchased only a few months ago from one of his business partners—a swinger who'd partied like there was no tomorrow.

Erik Sokal would have loved the party deck, but Topher had no desire to hold parties. Unless it was for a pack of children who wanted to swim in the cove, or play pirate in a bunch of dinghies, or sit around a campfire telling ghost stories about the old lighthouse keepers.

No. He didn't like her design because it wasn't him. It was some other person he'd become. Someone he hardly recognized. The real Christopher Martin wanted nothing except to turn back time.

He wanted to escape into those days before Granddad had died. Before he'd wrecked his knee before his sopho-more year at Bama and ended his NFL dreams. Before the deer had appeared in the headlights. Before he'd swerved and ended up wrapped around a guardrail.

He'd had it all once, and now...

He wanted to ball up her drawings and throw them at something or someone. The fury was enough to leave him breathless, but he didn't touch the papers. Let them sit there as a reminder of what he had become.

He closed his eyes and drew a deep breath. Knowing that a house would never return Granddad or his innocence or his health, why was he so set on building one?

Stubbornness?

Maybe.

Maybe he should give it up.

The thought left him hollow. If he gave it up, then what? Would he live out the rest of his days in this cottage with Ashley and Sandra and Karen treating him like an invalid? Would he walk the streets of Magnolia Harbor, becoming a fixture that people would pity?

He grunted a laugh. Maybe he could get a part-time job as a pirate impersonator on the daily cruises that left from the marina. With his bad leg, eye patch, and scars, he could probably scare the crap out of the little ones.

He sank into the easy chair by the fireplace. How had

it come to this? Living a life that belonged in an alternate universe.

No. He pounded his fist on the arm of the chair. He would not become an object of pity or derision. He wanted a house on Lookout Island.

And he wanted Jessica Blackwood as his architect because she'd actually tried to figure out what he wanted. She'd missed by a mile, but she'd paid attention.

And she'd looked him right in the eye.

But how could he ever persuade her to come back to him? He had no clue, except that the first step would probably involve an apology. He picked up his cell phone and dialed her number.

She didn't answer. No surprise there.

When her recorded voice finished its message, he said, "I'm sorry. I'm an asshole. Can we start over? Please? Call me." He disconnected the line and let his head fall back against the easy chair.

Would she call him back?

Probably not.

\* \* \*

Jessica ran through the rose garden as if her life depended on it. She didn't think, just moved in a panic that left her dizzy and shaking by the time she reached the confines of her ancient Volkswagen.

She fired up the engine and cranked the AC to full max, then peeled out of the parking lot, driving like a madwoman as she relived that moment, years ago, when Caleb Tate had cornered her in the locker room. That attack had started with him grabbing her by the wrist.

She didn't drive back to her office. Instead, she found

herself on the road out of town, heading toward the Atlantic Ocean and the house she'd inherited from Momma. The house had belonged to Momma's parents, MeeMaw and PopPop, who had been gone for more than a decade.

She hadn't been consciously going there, but it made sense. The place pulled her heart like a kite on a string because she'd always felt loved there. Not like Granny's house in town, where she'd lived as a child with Momma and Daddy. At Granny's house, she had to be careful not to spill the sugar or slosh the tea. At MeeMaw's house, she baked cookies and went swimming and spent countless hours out on the porch drawing pictures of the ocean that her grandmother stuck up on the refrigerator.

She pulled into the gravel drive, cut the engine, and rested her head on the steering wheel, trying to think of what came next. She'd turned in her City Hall design, and she'd just blown it with her only other client—a client she'd never been sure about. And maybe worst of all, her main go-to friend wanted to change the nature of their relationship.

The confidence she'd shown last Thursday when she'd run into Harry Bauman and Caleb Tate had evaporated. She was in over her head.

She looked up through the windshield at the house she'd inherited. She'd taken a mortgage out on the place for her start-up money. If she didn't make a success of her business, she would probably have to sell the house. And she couldn't bear the thought of that.

Her eyes filled with tears. She was such a screwup.

Her phone rang.

It was Topher. She couldn't talk to him now, in this state, so she sent the call to voice mail, and then, with fingers shaking, she called the only person who might understand why she'd just freaked out.

"Hey," she said when Hillary Barnwell's voice sounded on the phone's tinny speaker. Hillary had been at Longwood Academy with her. And without Hillary's courage and friendship, Jessica might never have survived being banished from her family for something she hadn't done.

"What's wrong?" Hillary asked, her voice low, sober, intense. After all these years, Hillary could still read Jessica's tone of voice, even over the phone.

"I freaked out," Jessica said. "I had a panic attack. I haven't had one of those in years."

"What happened?"

In a shaky voice, Jessica summarized everything that had happened from the moment she'd stepped onto *Bachelor's Delight* until Topher had grabbed her by the wrist.

"And what did you feel? Did he scare you?" Hillary asked when she got to the last of her story.

Oddly, the question stopped Jessica cold. "Yes. No. Yes."

She couldn't quite make herself explain how Topher's touch had been gentle and strong and like a jolt of electricity that branded her. And at the very same time, it had frightened her.

"Look, no one says you have to do anything that makes you feel unsafe," Hillary said.

"That's the thing. I mean, he touched me, but he didn't hurt me. It was just confusing, you know." She didn't give voice to what had really upset her. How in that moment she'd felt a jolt of unwanted attraction.

How could she possibly be attracted to Topher Martin? How could she be attracted to a man who thought it was okay to grab her like that? Down deep, a familiar shame churned in her gut.

She pushed the uncomfortable feeling away and focused on the important thing: She was not stupid enough to be attracted to the myth of the big strong man. But she wasn't ready to talk about the way Topher made her feel, not even to Hillary.

So she changed the subject. "It's not just him, you know. It's...everything."

"What?"

Reluctantly, she told her friend about Colton's suggestion that they give the gossips of Magnolia Harbor something to talk about.

Hillary laughed.

"You're laughing at me? Really?"

"Yeah, but in a good way."

"What's that supposed to mean?"

"Honey, when are you going to realize that Colton St. Pierre checks off every box on the husband-material list."

"Stop." Jessica climbed out of her VW and slammed the door. "I know what you're about to say, but you're wrong. I'm not in love with Colton, and I'm not looking for a husband. I know you've found wedded bliss, but that's not for me."

"Sweetie, do you even know what love is?"

That stopped her. Did she know? Probably not. She'd never really been loved. And she'd never been in love. She'd had a few bed buddies, so she was no longer the little virgin who'd been sent away to a tough-love school for troubled teens. But relationships were complicated.

"Look, this is not about me being in love, okay? It's about me trying to salvage my friendship with Colton. Just the other day, he took my landlady out to dinner, and I'm thinking I should try to encourage that. You know, find *him* a wife. Because once he's married, we could lay the gossip to rest and just be friends."

"Are you out of your mind? You want to start matchmaking?"

"Well, okay, when you put it that way, it's kind of over the top. But if Colton checks off every box on the husband-material list, then he deserves to have a wife, right?"

"Yeah. But—"

"My landlady is single."

"Oh, please. Don't go there."

"I'm serious. She's, like, the best-looking single woman in town. And she's got a business, and she's nice, and she's perfect."

"You're perfect." The piercing wail of an infant interrupted Hillary's well-worn sermon on the subject of Colton St. Pierre. "Damn. The heir is up and needs milk. Hang on a sec," Hillary said.

"How is the darling boy?" Jessica asked.

"He weighs fifteen pounds and he's cutting a tooth." Hillary's voice sounded soft.

Jessica continued into the house, down the hall, and out to the back porch. She sank down into one of the Adirondack chairs and watched the surf as it pounded the shore. She loved the back porch on her grandmother's house.

"I'm back. So, I would not recommend matchmaking," Hillary said, "unless you're matching your own self up with Colton."

"Yeah, you're probably right about the matchmaking part. I'll just let nature take its course on that. Kerri is gorgeous and successful." She blew out a sigh. "And in the meantime, I'm in trouble. I may fail at this business, and I may have to sell MeeMaw's house."

"No, you are not in trouble. You are a strong woman

making a place for yourself in the world and facing challenges you will overcome."

"Right, and I let an overbearing jerk scare me today."

"So go back and face him."

"You think that's wise?"

"My opinion doesn't matter. Look, I don't know the guy. If you think he's going to attack you or hurt you or something like that, then stay far, far away. But if this was just a freak-out panic attack, then you should go face your fear."

Jessica watched the waves for a long time. "Maybe it was bad memories of that time in the locker room. I don't like him much. He was the quarterback of the football team who spread all that gossip about me. And he was friends with the running back who cornered me in the locker room that time and then turned around a few months later and called me a slut in front of half the student body."

"Okay, there is that. So here's the choice. Walk away if he truly makes you feel unsafe. Or you could just make him pay a whole lot for this house he wants."

"He's paying me double my regular rate."

"Oh, honey, you should have asked for more than that."

"You're suggesting revenge?"

"Well, maybe. I prefer to call it justice. You could build him a lemon or something."

"I wouldn't do that."

"Of course you wouldn't. You're the nicest person I know."

Jessica leaned back and let go of a long breath. "I'm really not that nice. On the inside."

"Yes, you are."

"Oh, well, it probably doesn't matter. He hated my design."

"Look, sweetie, I know what you're thinking. I know the voice that comes at you when you're most vulnerable, telling you that you're no damn good, will never be any good, and are destined to fail. But you know that voice is wrong, right?"

"Yeah." She said the word, and she knew Hillary was right, but it didn't change the way she felt.

When she ended her call with Hillary, Jessica decided not to go back to work. She didn't have any projects now that the Martin residence had blown up in her face, and she certainly wasn't in the right frame of mind to think about marketing.

What she needed was a hard run or a long swim, or she could just put on her overalls and start painting the upstairs hallway.

She'd finally decided on a color called "butterfly yellow," which was rich and sunny and reminded her of MeeMaw. She hoped MccMaw wouldn't mind this new coat of paint. As it was, there were some things Jessica had trouble touching or changing about the house. Like the collection of Limoges figurines on the bureau in the master bedroom.

Those little porcelain figures of French aristocrats in their wigs, knee britches, and big, elaborate dresses were about as far away from Jessica's design preferences as knickknacks could get. And yet they had been MeeMaw's treasures, so they stayed on the bureau.

The hallway was merely a passage from one room to another, so it didn't hold a ton of memories. A few weeks ago, Jessica had started patching and sanding the walls, and they were ready for paint.

She got to work, rolling the sunny new color onto the walls, the Zen of the work emptying her brain for a few hours. By the time she'd finished, cleaned her brushes, and showered the paint splatter off her skin and out of her hair, she was in the right frame of mind to listen to the voice message Topher had left hours ago.

She didn't know what to expect when she pushed the playback button. Jerks were good at apologizing. But listening to his voice didn't send shivers of dread up her spine. Maybe she had overreacted.

She needed this job. But she'd have to set limits. She would not tolerate his rudeness or his anger, even if he was going through a bad time in his life.

And she'd need to fully understand where she'd gone off the tracks with the design. Because even though the concepts hadn't been fully fleshed out, she'd been pretty certain that she'd captured what he wanted.

She sucked in a big breath and called him back. Of course she got his voice mail, which was supremely frustrating considering how much courage it had taken to dial his number.

She left a message and then got up from the kitchen table and paced around the room, her mind as flighty as a caged bird.

Maybe this was one of those times when she should just take the bull by the horns and face her demons head-on.

Without thinking too hard about it, she jumped in the car and headed toward Howland House. Twenty minutes later, she opened the garden gate and stepped onto the footpath leading to Rose Cottage. It was after six o'clock, and she was pretty sure Topher would be home. She hurried up the porch steps and knocked on the door.

"He's not there."

Jessica turned to find Ashley standing in the middle

of her rose garden. The innkeeper's body language was anything but welcoming. She'd been cutting flowers and putting them in a wicker basket. But she stood now, with shoulders squared and chin up.

"Your flowers are pretty," Jessica said, trying to be sociable.

"They're for the house. The Piece Makers are meeting tonight."

Oh, great. Jessica checked her watch. She had about an hour before Granny would be arriving for the weekly quilting bee. Did the old biddies gossip about Topher? Did they think she was crazy for helping him build a house in the middle of nowhere?

Probably.

It was a universal truth about her life that, no matter what she did, she could never win widespread approval. She fought the urge to turn and head for the garden gate.

"So, uh, do you know where Topher has gone?" she asked instead.

"He's down at the beach," Ashley said, pointing toward the other end of the inn's expansive lawn.

"He's sunbathing?"

"He's swimming."

"Oh. Thanks," Jessica said, turning in the direction Ashley indicated. She followed the path across the lawn to a set of concrete stairs, which led to a ribbon of sand. The small beach was deserted except for a striped towel with a walking cane and an eye patch lying across it.

She cast her gaze over the bay and found Topher about fifty yards offshore doing a fairly strong freestyle. She leaned against the stairway's metal railing and watched him for a while.

She should go. Trying to win back a client when he was

dripping wet and without his eye patch went too far. She headed back up the stairs.

But something made her stop and look over her shoulder. A strange foreboding, or maybe just one last glimpse. She would never know.

But it was a good thing because something radically changed in his swimming rhythm. He pulled up abruptly, and then his head dropped below the surface.

Decades-old training kicked in. She'd been a swimmer all her life and had earned her certification as a lifeguard at the age of sixteen.

She moved without thought, shucking her ballet flats and grabbing the emergency life ring from its spot on the stair rail. She took the rest of the stairs two at a time and hit the water at speed.

His head bobbed above the waterline again just as her feet splashed into the bay. Hope flared, but his head went down again.

She dived, the water cold against her skin, and her chinos and blouse dragging at her as she swam toward the spot where he'd gone down.

He bobbed again, thrashing.

She corrected her bearing, making sure to approach him from behind. He went down again, but she managed to grab him under the arms, the buoyancy of the water helping her even as he fought her touch.

"Stop fighting me," she yelled into his ear. "Take this." She shoved the life ring into his chest and tried to haul his big body onto it. He resisted her efforts.

"Ow, ow, ow," he screamed.

"What's wrong? What hurts?" she asked.

He didn't answer, but his body posture suggested that one of his legs had cramped up.

There was nothing she could do about that. But she went to plan B. The best way to save a panicked swimmer was to get him to lie back on the flotation device.

She grabbed him around the waist and used the life ring to raise him out of the water. He was utterly incapable of kicking, so she continued to hold him under the arms, letting the life ring buoy him. She began towing him back to shore using a sidestroke.

She was a long way away, and the task seemed daunting, but she focused on making slow, easy strokes. A minute or ten later, as the adrenaline left her system, she registered the warmth of his skin next to hers. He'd stopped resisting her efforts.

Had he lost consciousness? Did she even remember how to give mouth-to-mouth resuscitation? It had been a long time since her training. But she'd done it once on a boy at the yacht club. The EMTs said she'd saved the kid's life.

She turned her head, ready to panic, but she found him looking up at her out of his one good eye. The other was naked.

She hadn't known what she expected to see under his mysterious eye patch. An empty socket? Something so horrible it might make her look away.

But it wasn't like that at all. The cornea of his injured eye was cloudy, and the skin around it puckered with scars. The sight of it didn't horrify her at all.

"You scared me," she said, redoubling her efforts to get them to shore. It still seemed a long way to the beach. She swam laps regularly, but here she had to fight wind and current.

"Shame on you," she continued, looking away from his intense stare. She took another long pull against the water. "Don't you know better than to swim alone?"

"I was trying to get stronger," he said, "so I could climb the lighthouse stairs."

His words hit with the force of a hurricane, rocking her to the core and sending a chill through her body. What if her truthful but ultimately unkind comment about the lighthouse stairs had led to his death?

What then?

*Chapter Seven*———————————

He *was* stupid. Stupid to think he could make himself stronger. Stupid to have come out here in a fit of rage and remorse. Stupid to have pushed the leg farther than it wanted to go. And yes, stupid for swimming so far from shore without anyone there to help him when the crap hit the fan.

Which begged the question: Where the hell had Jessica Blackwood come from? Like an angel of mercy, she'd appeared in his hour of need.

And he'd been so sure that she'd left him forever this morning after he'd let his emotions get away from him.

"Why are you here?" he asked, as the last shred of pain faded away, leaving the offending limb quivering where it trailed in the water.

She didn't reply. Typical.

"Answer me. Why are you here? Why did you come to my aid, especially since I was such a jerk this morning?"

"You were drowning this afternoon," she said in an

infernally logical tone. She had a way of speaking the truth in a blunt, unemotional way. He found it refreshing...and annoying.

He rolled his head, supported by the flotation device. They were still a ways from shore. "Are you okay?"

"I'll get there," she said, swimming with a strong kick.

"I remember the time you saved Randy McGinnis at the yacht club. I was very impressed."

"What?" She turned toward him, her eyes flashing. Why did he get the feeling he'd just pissed her off?

"I never met anyone who saved a life before," he continued. "I guess that's two in your column."

She didn't respond, and he settled back and started to help propel them, using his arms.

"Thanks," she finally muttered.

When they reached shallow water, he rolled off the flotation ring and tested his leg. It was okay. Painful, but what else was new.

"You didn't answer my question. Why are you here?" he asked again, as she stood up beside him and had the temerity to offer her shoulder up under his left arm. He availed himself of it, conscious of how small she was and yet with a backbone as strong as the cane he'd been so desperately trying to jettison from his life.

"Well," she said as they walked out of the water, the unrelenting pull of gravity weighing him down. "I came to see if I could keep you as a client...and to tell you never to touch me again."

He stopped and tried to stand on his own.

"Not now. It's different now."

"How?"

"I don't know. It's just different. I'm not scared of you now."

That was a slap in the face, wasn't it? He'd never scared a woman in his life. "I'm sorry," he said.

"Don't do that again, okay?"

"What? Stupidly swim on my own or—"

"You know."

"Look, whatever the reason, I'm grateful you came back. You saved my life. Now I owe you an enormous debt," he said.

"I don't want you to feel indebted to me."

Her answer was so irritating. Of course she didn't want something like that. Who would? He pressed his lips together as they made their way to his towel. He collapsed onto it, grabbing his eye patch and pulling it over his head and into place before meeting her gaze. He was so pathetically vain.

Jessica stood there before him, her T-shirt and khakis dripping onto the sand. She hugged herself and shivered. Her lips were turning blue, and his shame redoubled.

He jumped up, his leg complaining as he put weight on it. "You're cold," he said, snagging the towel from the beach and shaking out the sand in one motion. He draped it around her shoulders, gripping the edges as he pulled her a fraction closer.

He looked deeply into her eyes. Today they were the color of the bay—an angry gray. "I have this feeling, Jess, that you are here to annoy me for some higher purpose," he said in a gruff voice, too many emotions too close to the surface.

"Higher purpose?" she said in a shivery voice. Her bottom lip trembled, and he pulled the towel closer around her shoulders. He wanted to pull her into his arms and keep her warm.

"Yes," he whispered. "I think you're good for me."

Her eyebrows reached for her hairline. "How? By daring you to climb the steps to the top of the lighthouse? God, I don't like you very much, but I don't want to be the reason you kill yourself."

He stepped back. "I wasn't trying to—"

"I know. You were just being stupid. Were you being stupid that time you told those stories about me? Or when the football team called me a slut in public? Because those stories hurt me. So, let's be clear, I'm not here to save you or redeem you. I'm here to build you a house."

She stood there, the picture of a pissed-off woman, staring at him, water droplets trickling over her pale skin and spiking in her eyelashes. She was trembling, but whether from anger or cold he couldn't tell.

And he was utterly confused by what she'd just said.

"What stories?" he asked.

She shook her head. "The ones about me and Colton."

"What? I didn't make up any stories. I—"

His explanation was cut off when Cousin Sandra hollered from across the lawn. "Topher. Oh, for God's sake, what have you done?"

He looked up.

Sandra flew across the lawn as quickly as her senior legs could carry her. And right behind came Karen in close pursuit. Ashley and Jackie, each loaded down with towels, followed at a slower pace. And behind this vanguard trailed assorted members of Ashley's quilting group.

"Topher, are you all right?" Sandra called. "Jackie came into the kitchen hollering about how you were drowning and Jessica was saving your life."

"I'm fine," he said. "I had a cramp."

"Good God," one of the women bringing up the rear said. "Jessica, how could you have risked your life that way? You should have called 911 or something. Don't you realize that man could have taken you down with him?"

Topher turned toward Jessica with a lifted eyebrow. It was true, what the woman said. In his momentary pain and panic, he had almost taken her down.

"My grandmother," she muttered. "She doesn't think I'm terribly capable."

"She's wrong about that."

He tore his gaze away from her and gave his cousins the best smile he could muster as they came flying down the stairs to the beach. He braced for impact as they showered him with hugs.

\* \* \*

Granny descended upon Jessica like the supreme allied commander of the senior brigade. The old woman took the beach and issued multiple orders while the rest of the Piece Makers sprang into action.

Several of the women took Topher off to Rose Cottage, while Granny and Aunt Donna wrapped her in towels and pulled her up the steps and across the lawn toward Howland House, following after Ashley.

"Honestly, Jessica Ann," Granny said. "I don't know what you were thinking. You could have died out there. Don't you have any sense at all?"

Donna patted her back as they made their way through the rear door, up two flights of stairs, and into Ashley Scott's bedroom on the top floor of the inn.

"Get out of those wet things before you freeze to death," Granny commanded.

"Um..." Jessica looked from Granny to Donna to Ashley.

"I've got something that should fit you," Ashley said,

opening one of her dresser drawers and pulling out a pair of basic gray sweatpants with the word "ARMY" written in black down one leg. A matching gray hoodie sweatshirt followed.

"You're dripping on the floor, Jessica," Granny said. "Are you in shock or something? Get out of those clothes."

It never failed. Her grandmother always managed to make her feel small and stupid. She shucked off the towel and started pulling off her soaked T-shirt.

"Um, why don't we give her a little privacy," Aunt Donna said, grabbing Granny by the arm and pulling her toward the door.

Granny tried to evade Donna's grasp, but Jessica's aunt was having none of that. "I think we all know your thoughts on Jessica's decision to save a drowning man, Barbara. Now, why don't we go downstairs and have a slice of Ashley's German chocolate cake? I'm sure Jessica can manage to change clothes without us."

"I don't like German chocolate cake," Granny said.

But Donna had a height and weight advantage and muscled Granny from the room.

When they were gone, Jessica turned toward Ashley. "I'm sorry," she said.

Ashley laughed. "For what? Saving my cousin's life? Honey, don't let your grandmother get you down. Barbara is one of the sourest people I've ever met. I don't think we'd ever be friends except that she was one of the original members of the Piece Makers, so..." She picked up the sweatpants and held them out. "There's a bathroom down the hall."

Jessica took the clothes and headed toward a small bathroom tucked under the eaves. She closed the door, shucked out of her wet clothes, and toweled off.

"So why *were* you here?" Ashley asked through the door. "I thought you presented your plans this morning."

"You knew about that?"

"I saw you go into the cottage with a portfolio, and I know he's hired you to design a house for him."

As Jessica pulled on sweatpants, the reality of the situation tumbled down on her. No way she was escaping the gossip this time. She may have rescued him, but she had no illusions that she'd end up the hero of this story. Granny would tell everyone what a fool she'd been to jump in the water to save him. Granny would also make sure that the entire community knew that she'd personally warned Jessica not to help Topher build his house because he wasn't able to live on his own. Lord help Jess if Ashley ever found out that her thoughtless comment the other day had pushed Topher out into the bay to swim.

A deep, familiar shame pooled inside her. She could see how all the blame would eventually end up on her shoulders. Because it always did.

"What I'd like to know is why you came back this afternoon," Ashley said.

Jessica pulled the hoodie over her head and stared at her pale face in the bathroom mirror. Should she be honest?

What else could she be? She truly believed in the scripture verse about the truth setting you free.

"The truth is, we had a disagreement," she said. "I came back to try to salvage the situation."

"Oh, well, arguing with Topher isn't surprising. He's been an ogre recently. What did you disagree about?"

"My designs. I didn't give him what he wanted."

"Also not a surprise."

Jessica opened the bathroom door. "Why do you say that?" Jessica asked.

Ashley was leaning against the wall, her arms crossed over her breasts. She looked worried. "Topher wants something he can't have."

"Oh?"

"He wants to go back to when everything was easy. Back when we were kids, my uncle John, Topher's grandfather, had big plans for a house out there on the island where all of us kids could sail and play and have fun. Topher wants to go back to that time, and who the hell wouldn't? But childhood has come and gone, you know?"

"Yeah," Jessica said, even though she didn't understand at all. Topher's childhood sounded idyllic. Not at all like her own, where she'd been required to walk the straight and narrow, speak softly, and behave. But then she'd always known Topher was a spoiled brat.

"Look, I know you mean well," Ashley said in a kind voice. "But even Uncle John never dreamed about living alone on Lookout Island, and after what happened today, surely you can see why it would be foolish for Topher to live out there alone."

A wellspring of familiar guilt bubbled inside her. "Yes," she said in a small voice.

"So I'm pleading with you. If you walk away from this, I might just be able to convince him to give up this ridiculous idea."

It was ridiculous, wasn't it? Building out there would be difficult even if he knew what kind of house he wanted.

And it was even worse than that, wasn't it? Topher knew his quest was crazy. Hadn't he asked her that question last week when they'd sailed out to the island?

And she'd lied to him.

She could walk away, and Ashley Scott might praise

her. It might be wise to get on Ashley's good side because she was a powerful woman in the community.

But no. Acquiescing would be wrong.

If Topher wanted to build a house, he should be able to build it any-darn-where he wanted to. It wasn't anyone's choice but his. And maybe swimming was a good thing for him. Maybe he'd get stronger. Maybe he would be able to climb to the top of the lighthouse one more time.

Or she'd just put a GD elevator in the thing so he could go up there and brood, if that's what he wanted to do.

She met Ashley's intense and worried gaze. "I'm sorry," she said. "I do understand. But I'm not going to walk away from this project. If Topher wants a house, he should have one."

# Chapter Eight————————

Jessica took the long way back to her car, through the Howland House rose garden, intent on swinging by the cottage to tell Topher that she was ready to try again and capture what he wanted in a house.

But her client seemed to be in the middle of a heated argument with his cousins. His angry voice carried all the way out to the garden.

She certainly didn't want to interject herself into that scene. So she beat a hasty retreat.

The next morning, she awoke to a minor plumbing disaster. MeeMaw's house was falling down around her ears, so discovering a leak under the kitchen sink wasn't all that surprising. A week ago, she would have called Colton and asked him to come by and take a look. But that option was now fraught with danger.

So after drinking a strong cup of coffee out on the porch while simultaneously consulting YouTube plumbing videos, she determined that the problem was a leak in the P-trap. She could fix this herself.

She put a Tupperware container under the drip and headed into the office. She'd swing by Wright's Hardware on the way back from work to get the supplies she needed.

She settled in at her desk and pulled up her business plan, a document she hadn't looked at in more than six months. After she'd finished the Akiyama project and it had scored a write-up in a local newspaper, a steady stream of projects had arrived at her doorstep.

But the buzz had died and her prospective clients had dried up. Topher's project would tide her over, but she still needed to think about what came next.

She worked on her plan for an hour, and then, when ten o'clock rolled around, she picked up her phone and called Topher. Of course she got his voice mail.

She left a message, asking him to call her back to schedule a time when they could meet and discuss where the original plans had gone off the track.

She was about to turn back to her business plan when the sound of her front door opening pulled her away. The door closed and rapid footsteps sounded on the stairs.

So it wasn't Topher. No way he could climb stairs like that.

Her office suite was a medium-sized loft without any walls at all. She had plans, once funds became available, to partition the space to make it feel more finished and cozy. But right now Blackwood Designs consisted of her desk, an executive chair, a CAD workstation, a plotter, and a small round conference table with four chairs.

She hadn't hung any artwork or any of her degrees or accolades. In short, her office looked as if she'd moved in a month ago. Which was nothing but the truth.

There wasn't anything she could do about that now, so

she stood up and pasted her best business smile on her face, hoping that the fates had sent her a new client.

But the fates had not done any such thing. Instead, they'd sent her a nightmare.

Caleb Tate reached the landing and turned, his blue eyes running over the space that she'd stolen away from him. What the heck did he want? Was he here to harass her for that?

Or something far worse. A frisson of icy fear climbed up her spine, sending her muscles into fight-or-flight reflex. This full-body terror was nothing like the confusion Topher's touch had unleashed yesterday.

She'd never been in any danger with Topher. The same could not be said about this situation.

"Nice work stealing this space from me," Caleb said, plopping down into the side chair and then propping his feet up on her desk.

She wanted to scream at him, but she sat there breathing hard until she could control her voice. "I didn't steal it," she said, and then regretted the remark. She had to remember that this man sat on the design review committee for the new City Hall. She was required to suck up to him.

Yuck.

Her defensiveness earned her a cold smile that didn't quite reach Caleb's eyes. She sat down and folded her hands in front of her, her knuckles going white with tension.

"Can I help you with something?" she asked.

"Yeah. I'm trying to get in touch with Topher Martin. I thought maybe you had his phone number."

Now, there was an interesting dilemma. A week ago she would have said that Caleb and Topher belonged together like arson and larceny. But now, looking into Caleb's astonishingly handsome face, she wasn't so sure.

"I'm sorry," she said in her best sweet Southern-girl voice. "I don't give out client numbers."

He leaned forward, muscles straining through the expensive-looking worsted of his suit jacket. "Come on, Jess. Topher and I go way back. We're buds."

*Yeah, and if you were still buds, you'd have his number.* But she didn't say that. She smiled. "I'm sorry, it's a policy."

He leaned back, studying her office. "So, how many people do you employ here?"

"It's just me."

"Really? And all that rent you're paying, huh?"

"I've been successful. I just started my business and—"

"I'm not entirely sure the review committee for the City Hall design will be impressed by a one-woman shop." His cruel stare was loaded with subtext.

She got the message. She knew a bully when she saw one. Her own father had sometimes been this way, speaking a silent language full of stares and innuendo. He'd domineered Momma the same way. Using just his words and his disapproval. From what she'd learned over the years, he'd been the same way in business. Lots of people had shown up for his funeral, but he hadn't gotten many glowing eulogies.

"Representative Tate, I know you—"

"You can call me Caleb," he said with another oily smile.

"Caleb. I know that you and Topher were once friends. But I'm sorry. I can't give you his number. For a lot of reasons, he values his privacy. And even if he didn't, it's against my policy."

"Yeah. So, you've seen him, huh?"

"What?"

"Topher. Is he really messed up?"

"He's been injured, yes."

"Tough break." Caleb shook his head. "I just want to send him a get-well card. You understand, right?"

"I can't give you his number."

"I could get it from someone else."

*Then do it.* She didn't say that, either. She just continued to smile, even though the corners of her mouth were starting to ache. "I'm sure you could. Now…" She stood up, hoping the guy would get the message.

He stood up too and looked at his watch. "So, uh, it's almost lunch. You doing anything?"

Oh my goodness. He was hitting on her? Ew. "I'm sorry. I'm busy. Maybe some other time." She inwardly cringed. She could forget about the City Hall project if it required her to suck up to him. And maybe if she didn't win the bid, she'd have a moment when she could get up in his face and tell him in excruciating detail exactly what she thought of him.

He stepped around the desk, coming close enough for her to smell his sweet cologne. The scent made her want to rush right into the bathroom and hurl.

She stepped back. "I think you should go," she said, a tremor in her voice.

He grinned, his teeth so white they had to be caps. "You might want to think things over, Jess. I could be very helpful to you and your business. I have connections."

He turned and strode from the office. It was only when he'd turned his back that she realized he was losing his hair.

\* \* \*

Wednesdays in late August, after school started for the year, were slow at Daffy Down Dilly. So slow that Kerri thought about closing the shop on alternate weekdays.

On the other hand, if she closed midweek, she'd have nothing to do. It wasn't like she had a child to raise or a bunch of hobbies to pursue.

The business had become her life.

So she sat behind the checkout counter reading a copy of *Essence*. She'd already caught up on her bookkeeping, submitted her merchandise order for the fall season, and deep cleaned the entire shop.

She had nothing but the long, lonely winter to look forward to. Maybe she should take those knitting lessons down at A Stitch in Time. It might be fun to design her own knitted apparel.

She glanced toward the window just as a St. Pierre Construction truck pulled into the empty parking spot in front of the store.

Hallelujah and praise the Lord. The day had taken a turn for the better. Colton St. Pierre climbed down from his pickup truck like a vision from out of the pages of her magazines.

The man was as handsome as Derek Jeter. And that was saying something. Kerri was no baseball fan, but Derek had made his way into the celebrity news section of her favorite magazine more than once.

Unlike Derek, Colton needed a wardrobe makeover. She let go of a sappy sigh just thinking about the fun she'd have dressing Colton St. Pierre in something hand tailored.

Too bad the man had a thing for another woman. It didn't even matter that Jess had given Kerri permission to pursue Colton. How was she going to get Colton interested when he only cared about Jess?

A woman could break a heart chasing a man who loved someone else. Kerri had learned that the hard way.

She waited, wondering if she should go out there and tell Colton that Jess wasn't in her office. The woman had left shortly after Caleb Tate had gone up there. Kerri had debated whether she should drop in on her tenant with a cup of coffee just in case Tate got ugly. There was something about that man that made Kerri's skin crawl.

But discretion was the better part of valor. So she'd stayed put and let Jess handle Tate on her own. And she didn't get up now, either.

She turned back to her magazine, but when the little bell above the door rang a moment later, she was nothing short of surprised.

Colton was big and male and sucked up much of the available space and air in her small boutique. The proverbial lightbulb flashed above her head—maybe he'd come to see her and not the woman who rented the office space upstairs.

He moved carefully, as if he might be afraid to knock over the pretty daffodil-themed knickknacks occupying every shelf.

"Is Jessica upstairs?" he asked without preamble.

Well, that was predictable.

"I don't know. Why don't you knock on the door and find out?" she asked.

He turned and took a step toward the door before she took pity on him. "No, she's not up there. She left around lunchtime and hasn't been back yet."

"Oh," he said, turning and jamming his hands into his pockets. He seemed more awkward than disappointed. What was up with that?

"You can wait here for her, if you like. Can I get you a cup of coffee? A Coke?"

He nodded. "A Coke would be great."

She hurried to the workroom and snagged a canned Coke from the small fridge. She stopped at the mirror and gave her hair a once-over. She looked okay. And she was a fool and an idiot for checking.

"Caleb Tate came by to see her a little while ago," Kerri said as she returned to the sales floor.

"What?" Colton seemed agitated by this news.

"He didn't stay long. Maybe five minutes. And she left right after. Maybe ten minutes ago."

He pulled out his phone and punched in a number, and then put it to his ear. A moment later he disconnected the call.

"She didn't answer?" Kerri asked.

He shook his head as he picked up one of the daffodil-print coffee mugs and studied it. What was going on in his head?

And then, out of the bluc, hc said, "You know, Rose Howland didn't plant those daffodils by herself." He was referring to the daffodils that had given Jonquil Island its name. The story was that Rose Howland, mourning for the drowned pirate Captain Teal, had planted the flowers in his memory.

"No?" she asked. She might have batted her eyes at him a little shamelessly.

Colton put down the cup and turned toward Kerri, his Spanish moss–colored eyes sharp. "There's an old family story about how Henri St. Pierre did most of the work."

"Really? Who was he?"

He strolled to the counter, where he leaned forward, invading her space. Her heart rate climbed.

"You don't know your history. I find that amusing

since you've got a shop that trades on the whole daffodil thing."

"I bought this shop from Mildred Sawyer when she retired. I wasn't thinking about history. I was examining her profit-and-loss statements. I have an MBA from Georgia Tech."

He gave her a wide smile. The man was beautiful. Even his teeth. "You like looking at numbers?"

*I like looking at you.* But instead of telling him her innermost thoughts, she said, "I do. Numbers never lie."

He blinked for a moment. "Why do I get the feeling that's a commentary on the human race?"

She shook her head. "Not on the human race, just some people in particular." Like her lying SOB of an ex-husband, whom she'd divorced seven years ago. But who was counting?

"I'm terrible at numbers."

"Really? That surprises me. You've got such a successful business."

"I do. But my books are a mess, and I don't have a degree in anything. I'm strictly seat-of-the-pants."

"So," she said, stifling the urge to lean forward and offer to do his bookkeeping, "tell me about this family history I know nothing about."

He straightened and shrugged his shoulders. "Henri St. Pierre was the only survivor of Captain Teal's pirate ship."

"Oh, you mean the one that sank in the hurricane all those years ago."

"Yep. He swam ashore, and Rose Howland found him, saved his life, and gave him a place to stay."

"But only if he did the hard labor of planting all the daffodils?" Kerri asked.

"Yup."

"What happened to him?"

Colton shrugged. "He lived out his years here. He's buried up on my family's land. At least, that's the legend. There isn't any headstone or anything. And there's an alternate story that he ended up being enslaved at one of the plantations upriver."

"Are you giving me crap for selling daffodil-themed items because Rose Howland was a white woman?" Kerri may not have known about Henri St. Pierre, but she'd always known that the daffodil story was a staple of the white folks' history of the island. But she wasn't selling history; she was using the island's name for her merchandise assortment.

He cocked his head, and his eyes got a little softer. "I'm sorry. That was kind of rude, wasn't it? Giving you crap for selling stuff with daffodils."

"No. It was a fair criticism. But we're living on Jonquil Island."

He nodded. "I know. But it bothers me that Henri St. Pierre's role in our history has been forgotten. Maybe you could give him a little shelf space in your store."

"I'm not sure I want to sell pirate knickknacks."

"OK, but you could add some sweet grass baskets or maybe some other Gullah crafts that help folks remember that black people were brought here to grow rice. Our ancestors farmed this island way before the white folks built their summer homes out here."

"You know, I've been thinking about selling those baskets."

He smiled. "I've got kin who still make sweet grass baskets."

"You do? I'd like to meet them."

He nodded. "I'm sure they wouldn't mind selling you a few for your store." He paused a moment. "Um, look, I'm kind of at loose ends this afternoon. You busy for lunch? We could, you know, share some ideas." His gray eyes sparked with something more than a shared interest in business.

But she chose to ignore that little light in his eyes. She could chalk this lunch up to market research.

Or something.

Hell, Jess had given her the green light, so she didn't need to feel guilty. "I'd love to have lunch with you," she said, her whole body turning to mush when he smiled.

\* \* \*

Last night, when Karen and Sandra descended upon Topher with their worries and their pity and insisted that he stop swimming, he totally lost his temper.

After all the years these two old ladies had looked after him, he had never used language like that in their presence. But he'd shown them, all right. He'd chased them away.

And then he'd picked up a few of the knickknacks that Ashley had used to decorate the cottage and sent them hurtling toward the fireplace surround. And when Ashley had had the temerity to call him on the phone, he'd sent that flying across the room too.

It had exploded into shards of plastic and glass, one of which had left a small nick in his forehead.

He'd howled at that misfortune too, then stumped into the bathroom futilely searching for a Band-Aid. He'd had to sit on the commode pressing a washcloth to his forehead for a solid ten minutes.

By then he'd recovered a little of his sanity. He took a pain pill and went to bed.

In the morning, he'd cleaned up the mess, picking up the pieces of his broken phone.

Now he'd have to go out in public and endure people's stares. But he couldn't live without a phone. And maybe he needed to get some Band-Aids, since he seemed to have developed a knack for wounding himself.

So he took a shower, changed into some almost-clean clothes, and drove to the mainland, where he grabbed lunch at Burger King, stopped at a sports store to buy a football for Jackie, and picked up a phone.

It was late in the afternoon before he got Jessica's message. She wanted to meet. And suddenly the sun came out from behind his personal rain cloud.

He was ready to get to work. Now. So he didn't call her back. He decided he'd drop by her office and get the project back on track. But when he parked in the town lot, near the marina, and looked up her office address on her web page, he was surprised to see that she didn't have an office downtown.

The address was way the hell over on the east side of the island. He groaned in frustration, plugged the address in his GPS, and headed out of town.

Twenty minutes later, he pulled into a gravel drive that led to a house from out of Granddad's dream. It was old, maybe built in the early twentieth century, which would have made it one of the first beach houses on Jonquil Island. It sat up on stilts right behind the primary dune in a grove of palmettos and scrub pine.

As he got out of his car, the scent of the ocean, overlaid with pine needles, greeted him. In the distance, the surf pounded like a bass drum.

The house was a little run-down, paint peeling from the clapboard siding. But it didn't matter. If he had to come up with a vision of something, this would be it.

Except for the stairs. The front door was up a flight of stairs with a slightly loose banister. And the reality, born of pain, slapped him across the face.

He couldn't have a house like this. He'd need one with a ramp or something. It was like having his hopes dashed on the rocks.

He gritted his teeth and hauled his sorry ass all the way up those stupid stairs to the front door and rang the bell.

He waited for a long time—long enough to make him second-guess his decision to come here instead of returning her call. He hated the idea of having to walk back down all those stairs without accomplishing anything.

But just as he was about to turn away, the door opened, and there she stood, looking nothing like a professional architect. In fact, she looked like a really adorable rendition of Rosie the Riveter, in a pair of flip-flops, baggy overalls, a paint-smeared work shirt, and a bright-red bandanna tied around her head.

"Hi," she said, snatching the bandanna from her head, which only exposed a mop of hair that had gone a little curly in the day's humidity.

He liked this version of Jessica better than the one who dressed for success. But it struck him that maybe he'd made a mistake. "Is this your office?" he asked.

"My—oh no." Her big gray eyes widened. "Crap." An embarrassed smile touched her lips. "I mean, I used to have my office here. In the old guest house." She waved vaguely to the left. "But I moved downtown a month ago."

"But your web page said..."

"Oh Lord, I forgot to change the address, didn't I?"

"So is this where you live?"

"Yeah. It used to belong to my grandparents."

"Can I come in?"

She hung on to the doorframe and met his stare. Damn. He'd invaded her space again, hadn't he? He should go.

"I'm sorry, I should have—"

"No, it's fine. Come on in."

*Chapter Nine* ————————————

Once Jessica backed away from the door, Topher came barreling into her house like an invading army. She got out of his way as he limped down the center hall and into the big living room at the back.

"This is"—he paused, looking up at the beams in the ceiling—"amazing."

"Uh, thanks." Good grief, did he like her mausoleum of a house? Was this what he wanted? Well, she could do Carolina Coastal if that was his thing.

He turned toward her, his one bright eye filled with a blue-hot flame that was nothing short of mesmerizing. "This isn't the kind of house I expected you to live in," he said.

"Why not?" she asked.

"I thought you'd live in something ultramodern. Like Yoshi's house."

"That was Mr. Akiyama's vision, not mine. I thought he was crazy at first when he said he wanted a house that looked like a bird taking flight."

"And you don't think I'm crazy?"

Did she? Maybe a little. "Look. Mine is not to wonder why."

He grunted a laugh. "You're BSing me."

Was she? Maybe a little, but she kept her mouth shut.

"You know my family is dead set against what I'm trying to do."

She nodded. "I heard them arguing with you last night. And Ashley tried to talk me out of helping you."

"And you said no?"

She shrugged.

"That's not an answer to my question."

"I did say no. But it's a risk. Ashley could trash my reputation if something happens to you. So be careful, okay?"

"So you care?" One eyebrow arched.

He was pushing it. She met his stare. "I care about my reputation."

He barked a laugh and then strode past her, opening the doors to the back porch and walking right through them.

"This is beautiful," he said when she caught up with him. He turned, gazing out onto the dark-blue waters of the Atlantic Ocean and the white sand of the beachfront. The roar of the surf filled Jessica's head, making it doubly hard to think.

"So, maybe we could schedule a meeting to talk about where my initial design went wrong. And then—"

"Let's do it now."

"Um, well, I'm kind of busy right now."

"Busy doing what?" he asked, turning toward her, his blue eye like a laser.

She stuffed the bandanna into the pocket of her overalls.

"I'm fixing the kitchen sink, if you must know. And really, I think we—"

"You know how to plumb a sink? Really?"

His surprise was so annoying. "Yes," she said, overstating the truth by a mile.

In fact, when she'd arrived home an hour ago, after stopping at the hardware store for a P-trap replacement kit, she'd quickly discovered the difference between YouTube DIY videos and reality.

She'd spent the last half hour futilely trying to get the nut off the pipe. But the wrench was too big for her hands, and the nut had been tightened by someone with a lot of testosterone.

Why, in the name of creation, were nuts, bolts, plumbing, and tools designed for men? One day, some woman would make a bundle redesigning the world so people with small hands could get a grip.

But she wasn't explaining all that to Topher, especially since he was grinning at her. Had she seen him smile like that before?

No. And she hated the fact that the smile made him sort of adorable. Or something.

Well, one thing was certain. He didn't spark fear the way Caleb did. In fact, Caleb had so frightened her that she'd been unable to sit still, which was why she'd come home to get the plumbing fixed.

He turned his back on the ocean and leaned on the railing, folding his arms across his chest. The sea breeze ruffled his long hair and caught in the fabric of his Hawaiian shirt and baggy shorts. He looked a little like a Jimmy Buffett fan in need of directions to a Parrot Head convention.

"Okay, I'll go. Maybe we can meet tomorrow to talk about the house. But there's just one thing, before I leave.

That stuff you said on the beach yesterday. You want to explain what that's about?"

He had to be kidding, right? Had it been so unimportant to him that he didn't even remember? The thought left her chilled to the bone.

"You don't remember the day Caleb Tate pushed me to the floor right outside Mr. Bennett's physics class and called me a slut because I had done it with Colton St. Pierre?"

"Uh, well..."

"Yeah, you don't, do you? And I guess you don't remember how you told the world I was doing drugs with Colton, either," she said, her voice surprisingly low and steady given the sudden swell of anger.

He stood upright, his eyebrow arching. "Weren't you? Doing drugs? I saw you in his car with smoke coming out of the vents. And besides, you got sent away to have his kid. I know that doesn't make you bad, just a kid who made a—"

"What?" The ground under her feet shifted a bit, and she had to grab the railing to keep herself steady. "Where did you get the idea that I had Colton's baby?"

"You mean it's not true?" He seemed really surprised.

"Oh my Lord. Is that what everyone at Rutledge High thought when I left school senior year?"

"Of course they thought that," he said.

"Unbelievable." She whispered the word and shook her head. She was so angry, she might have done or said anything in that moment. But she held all that fury in check.

She'd learned the hard way that getting angry only made things worse for her. It was imperative to keep all that bottled up.

So she turned her back on him, stalked through the great room to the kitchen, where she picked up the big-ass wrench and went to work fixing the sink.

Unfortunately, the damn nut refused to budge no matter how many times she hammered it with the damn tool.

* * *

What the hell had just happened? Topher stood there, perplexed, as his architect ran from the porch and his grasp on the past took a monumental shift.

Holy crap. She hadn't been pregnant? She hadn't been sent away to one of those places for girls in trouble?

Then what the hell *had* happened?

He limped his way across the living room, heading in the direction she'd gone, embarrassment, confusion and…an overwhelming desire to make things right consuming him.

That desire surprised him. It was not merely altruistic. He was smart and realistic enough to know when a woman was starting to get under his skin.

He found Jessica in the kitchen, a big room with 1950s-style paint-splatter linoleum. The cabinets were solid cherry but in desperate need of refinishing, the appliances were definitely from the 1970s, and everything about it screamed antique.

But he loved it at first sight. He could almost imagine the members of her family gathering here to celebrate the Fourth of July on one of South Carolina's hot, humid days.

She was down on the floor, her head poked under the sink, muttering. He might have caught a whispered "damn."

"Can I help?" he asked.

She made a noise that conveyed a mountain of repressed fury.

"So it's not going well?" he asked.

"I'm kind of ticked off right at the moment, so—"

"Kind of?"

She pulled her head out from under the sink and gave him an adorable glare. "What's that supposed to mean?"

"Well, as my old Granddad used to say, you look madder than a mule chewing on bumblebees."

Her mouth twitched. "PopPop used to say that. I used to think it was dumb."

"Yeah, it is. But it's kind of descriptive too."

She nodded, her expression softening.

"Look, obviously I made a big mistake. I'm sorry. Can we talk about this?" He stepped to the edge of the counter and looked down at her.

"About what? The baby I never had or this stupid nut that won't come off?"

"Well, maybe we could start with the nut and work from there."

"Who are you? What happened to the rude, obnoxious guy who took me out to the island a few days ago?"

For some reason that made him smile. He really liked honest and independent Jessica.

He shrugged. "He's feeling a little contrite at the moment. Let me help, okay?"

"You know," she said in a voice laced with annoyance, "you aren't the sort of guy I would associate with DIY projects. You're more of the whip-out-your-cell-phone-and-call-the-plumber type."

He tried not to smile. "You might be surprised at my DIY skills. A man contemplating a life on a deserted island doesn't have the luxury of whipping out his cell phone and calling the plumber."

She gave him a slightly less pissed-off stare. "I'm fine, really," she said, breaking eye contact.

She wasn't being honest now. And he liked her when she was speaking nothing but the truth. So maybe he should just call her on it.

"I know what you're thinking…that if you let someone help you, it diminishes you in some way. But honestly, if you just need help getting a nut loose, I might be of assistance. I promise not to help in any other way."

The corner of her mouth twitched, and that little tell made something ease inside him.

"Okay," she said, one eyebrow arching. "You can help. It will be part of your penance."

"Penance?" he asked.

"Yeah, for starting a bunch of rumors about me."

"Whoa. Wait a sec. I may have repeated some gossip about you, but I never started any."

"No? You didn't tell anyone that you'd seen me in Colton's car that time? I remember that summer when I worked at the yacht club. You cornered me one day and made a point of telling me that Colton was bad for me."

"Because he was. It was only the truth."

"No. You've got that exactly backward. I messed things up for him."

"How?"

"All I ever wanted to do was to befriend him. Because, you know, he was a kid who needed a friend. And I was stupid enough to think that my kindness would help him." Her voice shook.

"He was out of—"

"No," she interrupted. "He got the book thrown at

him because I crossed the color line. Everything else was made-up."

That stopped him because it sounded exactly like the truth. The very ugly truth.

"Okay. I won't argue with you about that. And I apologize for not seeing through the BS before this moment. But why did your family send you away?"

"They sent me to a boarding school, but it wasn't someplace where girls have babies, okay? I can't believe that's what you thought."

"I swear I never told a soul about the night I saw you in Colton's car."

"No?"

He shook his head. "But you and Colton hung out all the time. You were seen by a lot of people."

"That's probably true."

"I still don't get it. Why did they send you away?"

She exhaled and closed her eyes. "They were concerned about my reputation," she said.

"Oh." He had no other words for the irony of her situation.

"So, anyway, you're forgiven," she said, waving her hand in dismissal.

Her words were a sham. She hadn't forgiven him. She just wanted to move the conversation on to a safe topic. And suddenly, he truly wanted to earn her forgiveness. Even if he hadn't started a rumor. There were things he could have done differently. He could have stopped the locker room talk. He could have refused to repeat the things people had said about her.

So he was surely guilty of something, just maybe not what she'd accused him of.

"How can I help?" he asked, the question double-edged.

He'd gladly help her with her plumbing, but he wanted to help her with so much more.

She picked up a big pair of plumber's pliers that were a few sizes too big for her hands. "I've got this wrench, but I—"

"It's not a wrench," he said.

She frowned and stared daggers at him. Whoa, maybe he should avoid mansplaining stuff to her. "Well, whatever it is, I can't get the nut off with it."

Because she could never grip the nut well enough with tiny hands like that.

"You have a toolbox?" he asked, bracing to have her take his head off for asking.

She nodded toward an old-fashioned metal box beside the sink. He squatted down, a motion that caused excruciating pain in his knee. He rooted around for a moment and came up with a sizable plumber's wrench. "Try this," he said, using the edge of the kitchen counter to pull himself back upright.

She took the tool, her slender wrist almost buckling under the heavy weight. She gave him a sober look as she turned the small wheel, opening its jaws.

She poked her head under the cabinet again and snugged the wrench around the nut. And then, with an adorable grunt, she applied pressure.

Lo and behold, the nut loosened.

"Hooray," she said in a rising voice that somehow brought joy to Topher's heart. "I got it free."

"Glad I could be of assistance," he said. Maybe this was a good time to escape. Tomorrow he'd call her and make an appointment, the way he should have done from the start. "Sorry I came to the wrong address. I'll give you a call tomorrow." He headed toward the door.

"Wait," she said to his back.

He turned as she popped up from under the sink, her cheeks flushed. She was so cute he wanted to stay awhile and bask in the glow of her beauty.

"Thank you," she said.

"You're welcome."

"Why don't you come by the office tomorrow, and we can get back on track with the house. I think I have a better idea of what you want now."

Well, that was reassuring because he still wasn't entirely sure. But he loved the idea of spending time with her. "Okay. I just need to know where the office is located."

Her cheeks got a little redder as she crossed the room to an old-fashioned table below an even older wall phone. She pulled a pen out of a cup and found a piece of notepaper.

"I'm sorry I don't have up-to-date cards. I've been so busy obsessing about one of my projects that I've let a lot of basic marketing stuff slide."

When she finished writing, she crossed the kitchen and handed him the scrap of paper, their fingers brushing in the exchange. That tiny touch set off a cascade of reaction that left him gut punched.

"Um…" She hesitated, her gaze drifting down to his Vans and then back up, locking with his one eye. "Be sure to bring your cane because it's a second-story office, above Daffy Down Dilly. So there's a pretty steep staircase."

And right then he saw his opening. But did he dare take it? He'd have to get way out of his comfort zone.

Yes, he would. Because he needed to undo the damage his thoughtless remarks had caused. Hell, he was such a liar. He'd do anything to win her approval. To become her friend. To get into her good graces.

"Um. I have a suggestion. Maybe instead of a meeting at your office, we could have dinner."

"Well..." She probably didn't want to dine with him for so many reasons.

"If we dined at Rafferty's, I could avoid the stairs," he said, working the pity angle even though he hated every minute of it.

She hesitated for a long, uncertain moment before she finally nodded. "Okay, I guess that's reasonable. Let's say six o'clock?"

"I'll see you then." But only after he'd left her house did he fully realize the magnitude of what he'd done. He'd just agreed to have dinner at a public restaurant where he'd be stared at.

# Chapter Ten

$A$shley sat at the weekly meeting of the Jonquil Island Heritage Day Committee drumming her fingers on the tabletop, her mind consumed with Topher and his plans for Lookout Island, and not the upcoming annual commemoration of the hurricane of 1713.

Her attempt to dissuade Jessica Blackwood from continuing with the project had failed. Appealing to the woman's better angles had been a long shot. After all, Topher could afford to pay her a sizable fee. Unfortunately, Topher had enough money to buy just about anything he wanted. Including a loyal architect.

But not everyone was for sale. She just needed to find the right person to stand in his way. But who that person or entity might be was a mystery.

She stared down at the legal pad sitting in front of Reverend St. Pierre, who sat beside her at the table in the large conference room at City Hall. He didn't seem to be paying much attention, either, as Councilmember Bauman droned on about the Heritage Day celebration coming up in mid-September. The preacher was doodling, and she found herself studying his strong, competent left hand as it created intricate Irish designs.

Awareness of Micah St. Pierre as a man, not a minister, suddenly seized her. The thought was inappropriate in the extreme and probably would never have happened if she'd been focused on the meeting and not her current problems.

But then again, she was also not entirely dead. So this fluttery feeling in her chest had to be a sign of something. Maybe, after three years of grieving, she was starting to come out of her funk. It would be easy to believe that, except that just the other day she'd been sorting stuff up in the attic and she'd come across the box filled with Adam's dress uniforms. She'd spent the rest of the day in tears.

"Okay, so everyone knows what they're responsible for in the next week?" Harry said, jolting Ashley back to the meeting's proceedings. Everyone around the table looked up and nodded.

"Okay. See everyone next Wednesday."

People jumped out of their chairs and made separate bee-lines to the door of the main meeting room at City Hall.

Okay, here it was, her chance to gain a little information. She pushed up from the table and headed right toward Harry.

"Hey," she said, coming up to him as he was stuffing papers into a battered briefcase. "You got a minute?"

Harry, who was probably pushing eighty, had a head of white hair and a bushy mustache that had been all the style in the 1970s. He looked down at her from behind his wire-rimmed bifocals. "I've got just a minute. The Braves are playing the Nationals, and I want to catch the end of the game."

"Um, well, I was—" She bit off her words as Micah came up behind her. Wow, the man gave off a lot of body heat.

"Yes?" Harry asked, his bushy eyebrows rising a fraction.

"I was just curious. If I wanted to make it difficult for someone to build a house out on Lookout Island, what would I have to do?"

Micah cleared his throat, and heat climbed up Ashley's cheeks. Was the Rev judging her? Well, so what. She had Topher's best interests at heart.

Harry stroked his mustache for a moment as he thought. "Well, it seems to me that it would be damn—um, sorry, Rev—darned hard to build a house out on that island no matter what."

"I know," Ashley said. "But if I wanted to make sure it couldn't happen?"

Harry continued to stroke his mustache while Ashley resisted the urge to turn around and glare at her spiritual adviser.

"I suppose you could rile up the lighthouse folks," Harry said.

"The lighthouse folks?"

"There's a group working to save the Morris Island lighthouse. They've been quite successful in raising money and getting the property transferred to state ownership and control. I'm not sure they're interested in saving any other lights, but I think the Lookout Island lighthouse may be the only other South Carolina lighthouse in private hands. You could appeal to them or maybe organize a similar group here."

"But could a group like that force the sale of private property?" Ashley asked.

"Forcing a sale wouldn't be impossible. But it might

be difficult. I think the family who owns the Morris Island light was happy to turn the land over to the state."

"Okay. If I didn't want to go that route, what other options might be available?"

Micah cleared his throat a second time. She could almost feel his disapproval like a looming shadow behind her.

"Well, any building would have to meet codes. And I imagine there would be some issues building out there with wastewater and electricity."

"Uh-huh." Unfortunately, Ashley had a feeling Jessica Blackwood knew precisely how to meet those building codes.

"Of course," Harry said, buckling his briefcase, "if you really want to stall development in this town, you call Peggy Fiedler of the Moonlight Bay Conservation Society. She's a thorn in my side. You know, she's even opposed to the renovations we're trying to finance for the historic homes north of town. You'd think a conservation society would want to conserve history by restoring some of the old freeman houses. But since we're talking about inviting history tourists to rent those houses, Peggy is dead set against it. I swear, that woman would rather see all those old houses fall down and the land go back to its pristine state."

Harry hefted his briefcase off the table and looked down at Ashley through his glasses. "But it might be nice to see the old light restored. You thinking about forming a committee to do something like that?"

"Maybe," she said.

"Well, more power to you. Now I gotta run." Harry hurried from the room, and Ashley turned to follow only to find Micah blocking her way.

"What are you up to?" he asked, pinning her with a probing stare.

People could say what they wanted about the Rev. About how his sermons were light on sin and heavy on Christ's message of love. But there were times when he seemed to be able to stare through her skin into her innermost thoughts—the ones she didn't wish to share with anyone. The ones she probably needed forgiveness for.

But this time she had nothing but pure motives. She raised her chin. "You know good and well what happened to Topher yesterday. But he insists on building a house out where no one could rescue him if he got into trouble. I don't object to the house. I object to his running away and putting his life in danger."

"The ends don't justify the means, Ashley. You know that."

Leave it to the Rev to make her feel guilty.

"I know it's not exactly playing fair with him. But the family's desperate to pull him back from the brink. We're all afraid that if he's left alone, he might do something..." Her voice trailed off, unable to actually say the words.

"Do you think he's suicidal?"

"No. Yes. I don't know. He's clearly depressed. But even if he wasn't depressed, he could still die falling down the lighthouse stairs. And who would be there to even know about it? When I think about that happening, I know I have to stop him."

"By riling up the Moonlight Bay Conservation Society?"

"If that's what it takes." She stepped around him and headed toward the door, expecting Micah to say something to her back. His silence was more damning than words could ever be. Guilt made her stop and look over her shoulder.

Did she really need his approval that much?

"You know, instead of judging me, you could try to help.

You were a navy chaplain. You had to deal with injured sailors, didn't you? Maybe you could talk to Topher."

He nodded, his shoulders relaxing a bit. "Okay."

"Thank you," she said, turning away, escaping from his too-intense gaze.

* * *

Jessica arrived at her office early on Thursday morning, feeling good about her plumbing, confused about her client, and furious about the things he'd said to her yesterday afternoon.

He clearly hadn't made up the rumor about her and Colton's love child. He'd heard it from more than one source. If the story was that widespread, surely Aunt Donna had heard it too. Why hadn't anyone said a word about it?

There was only one way to find out, so she called her aunt.

"Hey, darlin'," Aunt Donna said by way of greeting, when she came on the line.

"Does everyone in town think I was sent away to have Colton St. Pierre's baby?" Jessica asked.

Silence greeted her.

"They do, don't they?"

"Well, honey, I'm afraid that rumor got started when your parents sent you off to Longwood Academy. I have no idea where, although I certainly understand how. And believe me, I have done my best to set the record straight, but you know how it can be. I thought it was laid to rest, but then you came back to town and reconnected with Colton. And that just dredged it all up again."

"Why didn't you tell me what people were saying?"

"You didn't know?"

Now she felt like an idiot. How could she have missed this? "No."

"Oh. Well, I reckon that's because you go out of your way to avoid gossip. I'm so sorry, honey. I thought . . . Well, obviously I didn't think at all. I assumed, and you know how that goes."

"Yes, I do."

"And really, you know times have changed. I think the majority of folks in town are rooting for you and Colton to find happiness together."

"Are you?"

"Honey, I am not my sister. All I ever wanted was for you to be happy. And if Colton St. Pierre makes you happy, then I say you go for it."

"Donna, I want you to actively tell people that I didn't have his baby, okay? And then I want you to make it doubly clear that I don't love him. We're friends."

"Honey, gossip doesn't work that way. But you have my word that I'll try my best."

It wasn't nearly enough, but it was all Jessica was going to get. So she let it go and spent the next five minutes making small talk, mostly about her cousins Noah, Ethan, and Abby.

When she finished the call, she pushed her conversation with Donna aside and got to work on her critical to-do list. Now that she had a firm client in hand, she needed to upgrade her office space, get those business cards printed, and fix her web page. She wanted to have another client lined up before Topher's project was completed.

And if, by some miracle, she made it into the final round for the City Hall project, she wanted to make sure her office looked professional. So she hauled out her interior design plans and got to work. She'd just placed an order for Herman Miller room dividers to partition off the conference room and reception space when her phone rang, a gentle reminder that she also needed a business phone system. Running Blackwood Designs from her personal cell phone had to stop.

She checked the caller ID but didn't recognize the Miami, Florida, number. Another potential client? She'd spent the morning drawing down her savings—this call might be the answer to her prayers.

She pressed the connect button and answered with, "Blackwood Designs."

"I'd like to speak with Jessica Blackwood," the deep male voice replied, and she once again kicked herself for not purchasing that phone system sooner.

"This is Jessica," she said, then held her breath.

"Oh. Hi." The voice got a tiny bit friendlier. "This is Damon Brant. You may not remember me, but we met at the Building Resilience Conference about two years ago."

Her breath caught in her throat. Who wouldn't remember Damon Brant? When she'd been working for Costa Designs, she'd attended one of Damon Brant's workshops. She'd been so impressed with what Mr. Brant had said about resilient design and climate change that she'd given him her card and then shamelessly inquired as to whether Brant, Waller, and Palmer Associates, his Florida design firm, was looking for new architects.

Unfortunately, they weren't. Otherwise, returning to Magnolia Harbor when Momma had gotten sick might have been a much bigger sacrifice. Not getting that job turned out to be a classic example of the simple beauty of an unanswered prayer.

If she'd gotten that job, she might not have been able

to return to Magnolia Harbor to nurse her mother in the last months of her life. Those months had been precious. She and Momma had reconciled after too many years of recriminations over what had happened her senior year in high school.

She was glad she'd forgiven Momma.

"Uh, yes, I remember you," Jessica said, pulling herself away from bittersweet memories of her mother's last days.

"Good. Because I remember you too," Brant said, his tone warm. "You sent me no less than five résumés over a six-month period, and I do recall you asking me face-to-face at a conference about job openings in our Miami office."

"I was working at Costa Associates in Charleston at the time. They weren't terribly interested in resilient design. I'm not there anymore. I have my own business designing mostly residential buildings."

"Well, as it turns out, your residential designs have come to our attention," Brant said.

"What?" She was gobsmacked. How on earth could any of her designs have reached Damon Brant's attention? There were a lot of miles between Magnolia Harbor and Miami.

Brant chuckled. "Yoshi Akiyama is an old friend of my managing partner."

"Oh," was all she managed to say.

Mr. Akiyama again. She'd had no idea, when he'd hired her to design his bird house, that he'd be her main source of marketing. The man was connected all over the South. Every single project, including Topher's, had been as a result of that very first house she'd built here on Jonquil Island.

"Yes," Brant said. "Yoshi and Justin Waller were roommates at Georgia Tech. And Yoshi kept telling Justin that we needed to talk to you. Justin was out there in South Carolina last weekend and saw the house for the first time. He said the engineering is solid."

"Thank you." Heat crawled up her face.

"So, we've taken a look at your online portfolio. You're very inventive."

"Uh, thanks."

"Look, I know this is coming from way out of the blue. But BWP is planning to expand our services into residential design, both custom-built homes and design build, and we're looking for architects with that kind of experience. We need a team leader. And I was wondering what it would take to induce you to come down to Miami. We could give you an opportunity to design a lot more houses."

Holy moly. This was like some weird dream come true, only the timing couldn't have been worse. She'd just plunked down a huge chunk of her savings on that Herman Miller furniture. Could she cancel the order?

But did she want to do that?

She honestly didn't know.

"Um, look, you're right. This is from way out of the blue. I've been working to establish my own business, and—"

"I understand. And there's nothing like working for yourself. But you'll never have as much opportunity in South Carolina as you could here in Miami."

"So, what's your time frame? Can I think about this?"

"Of course. We're just putting the plans together for this new division. You've got time, but we'd like to have you down to Miami in the next few weeks so you can see what we're about and why we want you so badly."

She almost said no, and then she thought about Granny

and Daddy and all the people in her life who'd told her what a screwup she was.

Here was validation in the form of someone she respected. She'd be an idiot not to at least consider his offer.

"Okay. But I've got a couple of projects I'm working on now and—"

"No problem. If you decide the fit is good, you can complete anything you're working on. Honestly, Jessica, we're very excited about the possibility of having you. Justin hasn't stopped talking about Yoshi's house."

"All right. I'll consider it."

"Great. I'll have my secretary give you a call in a day or two, and we'll schedule a visit."

When she ended the call, she leaned back in her chair. Should she seriously consider this?

A little voice said yes, so she picked up her phone, called the furniture distributor, and canceled her order.

She could give it a couple of weeks. Maybe this offer from the firm in Miami was exactly what she needed.

Maybe she wasn't cut out to be a businesswoman. She was terrible at the marketing and organization. Maybe getting a job would give her more time to do what she loved best.

It was an exciting thought, until she remembered MeeMaw's house. If she left Jonquil Island, she'd have to leave the old place behind.

She couldn't leave it unoccupied, and it would cost a fortune to renovate it to the point where it was suitable for a vacation rental. The truth was clear. She'd have to sell it. But letting go of that place would break her heart.

\* \* \*

Thursday afternoon, after a day and a half of brooding over his nearly disastrous swimming adventure, Topher decided it was time to figuratively get back on the horse that had thrown him.

He put on his swimsuit and headed out to the beach. He understood the risks, but swimming was improving his health. He promised himself that he'd swim closer to shore, where he could touch the bottom in case he got into trouble. And he wouldn't push himself too far too fast. He was an impatient man, but getting stronger would take time. He couldn't force it and run the risk of new injuries or worse.

He was halfway down to the beach when Jackie streaked past him, running with that loose-jointed ease of the very young. The boy raced toward the old oak tree, head down, in a way that set off alarms. Was he crying? Again?

Damn.

Maybe he'd put off swimming today. Maybe today he'd just play a game of catch.

He returned to the cottage, where he put on a shirt and unwrapped the football he'd picked up yesterday. He tucked it under his arm running-back style, before grabbing his cane and limping off to the tree.

But when he got there, the kid was nowhere in sight. Had he climbed up to the crow's nest? Topher bent upward, trying to see the boy through the leaves. Yes, right there was a patch of white school uniform shirt.

"Hey, kid, I got you a present," he called.

He got no answer. So he stood there, clutching the ball, the familiar texture under his palm. He itched to throw the damn thing. Could he still hurl it seventy yards and hit a target? Probably not.

He leaned his cane against the tree and tossed the ball into the air and caught it. It felt good in his hands. A happy reminder of better days.

"Hey, kid," he called again. "Wanna play catch?"

Crickets...or maybe cicadas. Literally.

He was about to drop the ball onto the ground by the tree's roots for the kid to find, when someone spoke from behind. "I'll play."

Topher turned to find Reverend Micah St. Pierre walking across the lawn toward him. He wasn't dressed for football. In fact, his gray cleric's shirt and dress slacks were almost like a red warning sign.

"I, uh..." Topher stuttered. A man of God was the absolute last person he wanted to play catch with.

"I'll do all the running," the preacher said in a soft voice, then glanced up at the tree right before giving Topher a wink.

Oh. Damn. He was an idiot. The minister hadn't come out here for him. Maybe he should stop thinking the world revolved around him and his pain.

"Sure, I'd love to play catch," Topher said in a big voice. "It's a lot of fun. Did you play football in high school?"

"Nah. But my brothers and I played catch all the time."

Topher threw the ball, a tight spiral that hit the minister right in the chest. Micah St. Pierre caught the ball without a problem. Now came the challenge. If the preacher didn't toss the football accurately, Topher was going to look like an invalid.

Micah reared back and threw, and damn if he didn't put a lot of touch on the ball. It hit Topher in the chest, and he caught it without any problem.

For some stupid reason, the little black cloud that hovered above his head most days scuttled out of the way. He took a deep breath, redolent with the scents of late summer: Ashley's flowers, the bay, and the recently mowed grass.

It was one of those beautiful days when the humidity gave everyone a break—the beginning of the football season. He threw the ball. The minister caught it and threw it back.

They settled into a rhythm, not talking, just throwing and catching. After about five minutes, the branches of the live oak rustled as Jackie left his nest.

Micah winked again and rolled his eyes toward the tree. He threw the ball. Topher caught it and sent it spiraling back.

"Whatcha doin'?" the kid asked. He'd come down to sit on the tree's lowest branch. The one that ran parallel to the ground.

"Having a catch," Micah said. "Wanna try?"

The kid cocked his head, considering. He looked as if he'd had a really good cry up there. His eyes were puffy, and he had a wet stain on his T-shirt, probably snot.

"No. I'm no good at sports," Jackie said.

Topher limped over to the branch. "Well, neither am I. I can't run or jump. And day before yesterday, I discovered that I'm not too good at swimming, either."

The kid shrugged. Topher leaned against the tree limb. Micah stood back, tossing the football up in the air and catching it.

This was the preacher's domain, wasn't it? Topher knew nothing about kids. And yet Micah seemed more interested in playing with the ball.

Topher folded his arms across his chest. "So what's the matter?" he asked.

The kid shrugged.

"Have a bad day at school?" Topher remembered his

own rocky childhood before Granddad had put a football
in his hands.

"No. Not really. I'm just mad."

"About what?"

"Mom."

"Oh."

"She said I couldn't do my Heritage Day project on
Cap'n Bill."

Topher flashed back on his own third-grade Heritage
Day project. Every third grader in Magnolia Harbor had to
do a project that would be displayed in City Hall during
the festival that marked the anniversary of the hurricane
of 1713, the storm that sank the *Bonnie Rose*, Captain
William Teal's pirate ship.

Topher had done a report on hurricanes of the eighteenth
century and why the 1713 storm had been so devastating.
All the rest of the kids had done projects featuring pirates.
This propensity for going geek had been one of many
things that had marked Topher as the bullies' favorite
target in elementary school. Until Granddad had taught
him how to throw a football, he'd been a nobody. Less than
that, really.

So he certainly understood Jackie's problem. "Everyone
does projects on pirates," he said in an encouraging tone.
"What's your mother's problem with that?"

"She thinks it's not healthy for me."

"Why?"

He shrugged. "I wanted to interview him, you know?"

"You wanted to interview William Teal?"

"Yeah. He's here. He's always hanging around this spot."

A shiver ran up Topher's spine. He didn't believe in
ghosts. Much. But even theoretically allowing for the existence of a ghost, Topher could certainly understand why

Ashley didn't want Jackie interviewing one for a school project.

"You know," the preacher said, crossing the lawn as he continued to toss and catch the football. "If you wanted to do something different, you could study Henri St. Pierre. He was a pirate too. Everyone forgets that."

The kid blinked up at the minister, and the tiniest of smiles tipped his mouth. Oh yeah, Jackie and Micah had a special thing going.

Disappointment, like the unrelenting pull of gravity, settled on Topher's shoulders. For an instant he'd thought he might be able to help the kid. But it looked like a far more qualified man had already signed up for the job.

"What's there to know about Henri St. Pierre besides the fact that he didn't drown and he helped Rose Howland plant daffodils?" The kid rolled his eyes. "I'd be laughed out of class if I did a project about a guy who planted flowers." The kid's shoulders slumped again, and the spark vanished from his eyes.

"I wasn't talking about the flowers," Micah said.

"Then what?"

"Well, there's a family story…"

"What kind of story?" Curiosity laced the kid's words.

The preacher smiled and leaned in, speaking in a low whisper. "A story of buried treasure."

"Really?" The boy's eyes grew round.

"Yup."

"Where?"

"Well, that's the hard part. They say Rose Howland wrote letters to her father that have a secret coded map to the treasure."

"Really?"

"Yup."

"Where are these letters?"

"In the library."

"Come on, I don't—"

"I know it sounds far-fetched, but here's the thing. Only direct descendants of Rose Howland are allowed to read the letters. And you, my boy, are a direct descendant."

"Really?" Topher asked, suddenly caught up in Micah's narrative. "Why the restriction?"

Micah shrugged. "I don't know. It's been a bone of contention in my family for years." The minister turned back toward Jackie. "But that means you're the only kid in your class who can read these letters."

"Wow. That's kinda cool. I could read them, then go looking for the treasure. And if I find it, that would be a really great project."

"Exactly," Micah said.

"Oh boy. Can you help me?"

"Well, I'm kind of busy, you know. I'm helping to organize the Heritage Day celebration, and I've got sermons to write and...stuff."

"Oh." Jackie's shoulders slumped again.

"But maybe Topher can help."

What the hell? The damn preacher had just played him.

"Would you?" The boy looked up at him. Damn. Only a real jerk would stand in the way of the excitement on the kid's face. He'd been well and truly trapped.

"Uh, yeah, sure," Topher found himself saying.

"You'll talk to Mom? 'Cause I'm not sure she wants me to do any kind of pirate project?"

Topher nodded again.

"Great. So, uh, can I play?" Jackie nodded toward the football.

"Sure," Micah said, handing Jackie the football. "And

if you really want to know how to throw it, you should ask Topher. He was the quarterback who took the Rutledge Raiders all the way to the South Carolina state championship."

"Really?" The kid looked up at him with that expression he'd once seen on the faces of his classmates at Rutledge High. He hated that awe-filled look.

What was wrong with people anyway? The ability to throw a tight spiral wasn't enough to make a person a hero.

And God only knew he was nobody's hero.

# *Chapter Eleven* —————

On Thursday night at six o'clock, Rafferty's Raw Bar was chock-full of people. Outside, the skies had opened up with a cold rain that foreshadowed the arrival of autumn, so the diners who would normally have used the back deck were now waiting for tables in the main dining room.

The crowd was extra heavy tonight because this weekend was the Last Gasp of Summer Festival, when the yacht club hosted a charity regatta. Sailors from all over the South arrived in town for the races, giving the local economy one last boost before the summer ended.

Jessica scanned the mob, looking for Topher, but he hadn't arrived yet. So she ducked into the entry vestibule and texted him.

*Jessica: I'm at Rafferty's. It's a zoo here. Did you call ahead for a table?*

She waited five minutes before a return text appeared.

*Topher: No. I've been circling, looking for a parking spot.*

Of course. Rafferty's wasn't far from Howland House,

but he wouldn't have walked in this rain. He would have gotten drenched trying to manage an umbrella and a cane at the same time.

Time for plan B. She went back to texting.

*Jessica: Swing by the front. Do you like Chinese?*

*Topher: Chinese? You can get Chinese in Magnolia Harbor?*

*Jessica: Things have changed. Spicy or not?*

*Topher: Not.*

Why did that surprise her? It seemed like a guy who had an eye patch and owned a yacht named *Bachelor's Delight* should be down with super-spicy food. On the other hand, the letter-jacket boy of her memories probably liked his Chinese on the mild side.

And that, in a nutshell, was her problem. She couldn't decide if Topher was the evil jerk she'd painted him to be or a good guy who'd taken a wrong turn on a twisty road.

If he hadn't started the rumors about her, she couldn't really hold him responsible for them, could she? And she couldn't blame him more than anyone else for repeating gossip.

Maybe she should thank him for clueing her in to what people were really saying about her and Colton. Jeez Louise. Did people really think she'd been sent away to have Colton's love child?

And were people still spreading that rumor? Or even worse, was that why everyone seemed so determined to see her and Colton together as a match? Were people trying to write a happy ending to a story that didn't even exist?

She didn't know. But it was doubly disturbing. And really, there was nothing she could do about this gossip. She'd discovered that years ago. The best you could do was ignore the lies people told.

So she decided not to raise the issue with Topher again. She'd let it go.

She dialed the number for Szechuan Garden, the Chinese carryout on Tulip Street, and ordered dumplings, moo shu pork, and beef fried rice. Then she opened her umbrella and stepped out into the downpour.

Topher pulled up a moment later in a brand-new black BMW X3, which was nothing short of her ideal car. But it sure wasn't the sports car she'd expected him to drive.

She hopped into the passenger's side and sucked in the new leather upholstery smell, which was pretty heady stuff until she laid eyes on Topher.

He wasn't wearing a Hawaiian shirt. Tonight he looked like a refugee from Martha's Vineyard in a blue oxford cloth shirt and a pair of Nantucket Reds. If they'd gone through with their plans to dine at Rafferty's, he would have blended right in with the yacht club crowd who'd come for the sailboat races.

"Hi," she said, drawing in a deep breath filled with leather and something else mysterious and spicy.

"So, Chinese?" he asked, lifting his right eyebrow just so.

"Uh, yeah, on Tulip Street." She summarized what she'd ordered and was relieved to discover that he was a huge fan of moo shu pork.

"Does this place have a restaurant?"

"No," she replied. "I was thinking we could take it back to my place and—" She bit off the rest of the sentence when she realized what her words sounded like.

She waited for him to say something snotty, but he remained steadfastly silent. Which only made her gaffe more embarrassing.

"What I meant to say," she said after an interminable moment, "was that every restaurant in town is going to be jam-packed, especially in this rain. So I thought we could eat out on the porch while we talk about your house."

She brought her hands together and interlaced her fingers, suddenly tense and unsure. She busied herself by watching his hands on the steering wheel.

They were beautiful, with long, masculine fingers and nails trimmed all the way back to the quick. They gave the impression of strength and competence. But then, he'd been a quarterback, hadn't he?

"I make you nervous, don't I?" he asked.

She squeezed her hands together and remembered how futile it was to evade Topher Martin's questions. "Yes," she said.

He didn't ask her why. He lapsed into another silence as he drove through the heavy traffic and the downpour.

She fervently wished he would turn on the radio. The silence was so thick she could hardly breathe. She needed to end it. But how? All she managed was an inarticulate "Um."

"What?"

She cast around for something to say that wouldn't get her into too much trouble and said the first thing that popped into her mind. "You might want to be aware that Caleb Tate is trying to reach you."

"I know. He's left messages at the inn."

"He came by yesterday and wanted me to give him your phone number."

He glanced at her, surprise on his face. "You didn't—"

"No. I don't give away client information."

"Thanks."

"So you don't want to talk to him?" she asked, suddenly curious about Topher's relationship with Caleb.

"Who? Caleb? No. He's a jerk." There was a hardness

to Topher's voice that sparked a little flame of hope in her breast. Maybe they had never been friends.

Should she tell him that Caleb did more than try to intimidate her? No. Topher wasn't her protector, and she wasn't gullible enough to fall for the he-man myth. Not that Topher classified as a he-man these days. But he probably still thought of himself that way.

"Well, just so you know, Caleb is hot to get in touch. He's a member of the South Carolina General Assembly now, and he thinks he's entitled to your attention."

"No. He just wants my money." The words were hard as Topher pulled to the curb in front of the carryout place. "I'll get—"

"No," Jessica interrupted. "I'll run in and get it." She opened the door and escaped into the deluge. The cool, moist air cleared her head as she dashed from the SUV to the door.

She needed to get a grip. She was starting to like Topher Martin, and that was unsettling in the extreme.

* * *

The rain beat against the roof of Topher's car and hammered at his conscience. Caleb Tate was an asshole, and he'd done nothing about it back when he'd been captain of the team. Maybe it was time to remedy that failure.

He didn't really remember Caleb calling Jessica a slut, but he did remember a lot of stupid, sleazy things the star running back had done. And his endless locker room talk.

He'd be willing to bet that Caleb was the source of those rumors about Jessica. The thought turned his stomach.

Tonight Caleb was probably up at the yacht club with a lot of Topher's old sailing buddies. They'd be drinking beer and swapping stories. A little part of him missed all that. Not Caleb, but the camaraderie that he'd never have again.

He drummed his fingers on the steering wheel. Would he rather be up there at the club now, getting drunk and telling stories?

No.

He would rather be here, talking to his architect. Trying to figure out why he felt as if she'd been put in his path for some higher purpose. He didn't believe in a higher power. He wasn't religious. He hadn't had a near-death experience that made him grateful for the life that had been spared the night he'd almost killed himself in the Ferrari. Or even after his harrowing experience out in the bay the other day.

And yet Jessica tugged at him, as if there was some mystical string connecting him to her. She was good for him. Hadn't he showered and shaved and dressed up for this dinner? He hadn't dressed up for anyone in months.

He turned in time to watch Jessica dash through the rain to his car. For once he didn't envy the people in his old life. He would much rather be on his way to her place. He couldn't help but stifle a smile at that thought.

He made her uncomfortable. Was it because she blamed him for the rumors? Or because he'd touched her without permission? Or was it something else—the connection that had sparked between them when she'd handed him the scrap of paper with her address written on it?

A deep rush of longing overwhelmed him, and he gripped the steering wheel. It was an established fact that he could be a total jerk. He should work very hard not to add *idiot* to the assessment.

The scent of the rain and moo shu pork followed her into the car. "That smells good," he said, because he didn't know what else to say.

He fired up the engine and headed out onto the beach road. By the time he pulled into her driveway, the silence was like a thick, heavy blanket that might suffocate both of them.

The rain had let up a bit, so he didn't get totally soaked climbing the stairs to her front door. But when they got inside, the lights were out.

"Oh, great," she said with an audible groan. "I'd like to believe this is a widespread power outage, but I'll bet there's a fuse somewhere that's blown." She reached into her purse, withdrew her cell phone, and launched the flashlight app. "But I'm not letting perfectly good moo shu pork go cold while I figure it out.

"You stay here," she instructed. "I'm going to get paper plates and matches. There are candles out on the porch."

"I can make my way to the porch," he said.

She gave him the once-over. That look made him itch. "I'm sorry. I didn't mean—"

"I know the way," he interrupted.

She nodded, and he turned away from her. He headed toward the porch and lowered himself into one of the Adirondack chairs. Rain dripped from the eaves with a relaxing sound, and beyond the curtain of drizzle, the Atlantic crashed against the sand with a rhythmic roar.

He could get used to sitting out here.

She arrived a few minutes later with a tray filled with paper plates, food cartons, and a couple of beers. She lit a bunch of citronella candles, which flickered in the moist breeze. The light cast a golden glow over their corner of the world.

She handed him a beer and then a thick, rigid paper plate heaped with food. "Chopsticks?" she asked.

He nodded, and she handed him one of the disposable

sets that had come with the food. Then she sat down next to him and tucked into her dinner.

They ate in silence until he finished his food and put the empty plate on the floor beside him. "So, I've been thinking about what I want," he said.

"Not a castle, I take it?"

He shook his head. "No. I'm sorry about that. I just..." He looked out toward the ocean. "I don't know. I hadn't thought everything through last week. But I think I have a much clearer picture now."

"Okay. So?"

"The thing is, I like this house. I think this is exactly the kind of place my grandfather wanted to build out there."

"So a Carolina Coastal house, only smaller and not on stilts."

Her words irked him in some deep way. But then again, she'd watched him struggle up the stairs a few moments ago. But he didn't want to focus on that, so he leaned forward and asked, "Why smaller?"

"Well, this house is ridiculously large. Probably six thousand square feet. I rattle around in here. And I'm pretty sure we'll have a zoning limit of five thousand square feet. But even that's kind of large, since it's just going to be you living out there, right?"

"I want a bigger house."

She jumped a little, and he regretted his dictatorial tone. He was out of practice when it came to being in polite company. "I'm sorry, I—"

"No, it's fine," she interrupted. "You're the client. You should get what you want, but there are challenges to building a large off-the-grid house."

"Those challenges weren't a problem with your castle?"

"My castle, as you put it, had only three bedrooms and was maybe three thousand square feet."

He studied her. There was a tiny glob of plum sauce at the corner of her mouth, and he fought the urge to wipe it away. Or maybe lick it away.

Damn. He pushed the idea out of his head and focused on the issue at hand. "Well, the thing is, I want a big house with a wraparound porch."

"How many bedrooms do you want?" she asked.

"I don't know. Five. Six. More."

"So, um, are you planning to raise a family out there or what?"

* * *

Topher barked out a bitter-sounding laugh that suggested he hadn't gotten her intended humor. He turned his gaze beyond the porch railing at the ocean, now a dark-gray shadow as the rainy evening edged toward night. Jessica took this moment to truly study him.

He was a big man, tall, broad shouldered, and unquestionably male in every respect. He commanded her attention even to the smallest detail, the way his lashes outlined his eyelid, the way the scars marred his jaw, the way his lips pressed together. Was he angry?

Or hurt?

Now, there was an odd thought. She'd been so busy being angry with him that the possibility of his hurt had only brushed against her thoughts.

He turned his gaze in her direction, and she caught her breath. Although it was nearly dark, the blue of a summer sky had gotten into his eye, and she lost herself in the endlessness of it.

"You're staring," he said. "Do you think I'm a monster?"

"No. You're handsome, but you can also be rude and selfish and—" She stopped talking before she said anything else. What was wrong with her? She knew better than to speak her mind.

"I *am* selfish," he said. "And you..." He paused for a moment. "You are crazy if you think I'm handsome."

"I'm sorry," she said. "I shouldn't have been so blunt, but your question wasn't fair."

"It didn't stop you from answering."

A raging fire crawled up her face. "I suppose that's true."

"Do you think I'm redeemable?" he asked.

What an odd question. How could he need redemption if he was truly blameless? "I don't know," she said.

"I think you have the power to redeem me," he continued.

Oh, that was a seductive thought, but she knew better. "I think you'd have to take redemption up with God," she said.

Topher snorted a laugh. "I don't believe in God."

She held her tongue. She knew better than to say anything else.

He shook his head and looked away, releasing her from the difficult and bizarre conversation.

She cleared her throat and reached for her best professional-architect voice. "Okay, to summarize, you're good with Carolina Coastal and some number of bedrooms to be determined?"

He pushed up from the chair and moved to the porch railing. He leaned forward on it, the rain from the broken gutter dripping over his fists.

"I want five bedrooms."

"That many?"

"You don't have to know why," he muttered. "I want

them because I want them. I don't need a reason. Remember I'm a selfish asshole," he said like a petulant child.

"Okay."

He turned, looming over her. "And don't think you can soften me up by lying to me."

Now she was annoyed. She stood up and took a step toward him. "I'm not a liar."

"You said I was handsome."

"You are." And she meant it. Yes, he was scarred, but the beautiful boy was still there, tempered by something that was deep and masculine. Something that appealed to her female sensibilities. And she hated to admit it, but there might be something redeemable beyond the surface.

He shook his head. "No. But you're beautiful," he whispered. "That's the truth. Don't try to tell me otherwise." He lifted his hand and stroked the back of his index finger down her cheek. His fingers traced a line of fire over her skin.

He smelled like the trade winds on a summer day, spicy and salty and so delicious that she leaned into him. For a crazy moment, she thought he might kiss her, and she wasn't even frightened by the prospect.

Instead he took a step back. "It's late," he said, even though it wasn't. He turned, heading for the porch door in his uneven gait.

A wave of disappointment crashed over her with the roar of the surf behind. She wouldn't have stopped him. Good grief, she *wanted* him to kiss her.

When he reached the double doors, he stopped and looked over his shoulder. "We'll sail out to the island on Monday, and you'll show me plans for a five-bedroom house with a porch like this one."

He turned and let himself out into the storm.

# Chapter Twelve ──────

Topher awakened on Friday with a growl. He lay in his bed staring up at the ceiling fan, endlessly turning, sending cool air over his hot, sweaty skin.

He didn't want to be awake. His leg hurt, and that only reminded him that he was here, sleeping in, while his old buddies were out on the bay racing their boats.

And even worse, the tourists and sailors would be all over town. Howland House was certainly awash with them, and the swimming beach would probably be busy all day.

But he needed a swim in order to clear his head. This morning his mind was consumed with a bunch of unhelpful thoughts.

Starting with the idea that Jessica might have welcomed his kiss. He rolled up in bed as the back of his neck itched and tingled with a deep-seated embarrassment.

He was unworthy of her. He might not have made up any stories about her all those years ago, but he sure as hell had been willing to believe them. He'd spread the gossip along with everyone else at Rutledge High.

He needed to back off and put her solidly into the box called "business associate."

He stared out the bedroom window. Beyond the Bahama shutters, another glorious late-summer day had dawned. He wished he could be out on the bay sailing, instead of stuck here, thinking forbidden thoughts and longing for things that made his chest ache.

He couldn't woo Jessica. She'd turn him away the way Marla had done after the accident.

No. He'd keep it professional. He'd pay Jessica handsomely for his house and then he'd tell all his friends and business associates what a great job she'd done for him.

Maybe a little positive word of mouth would cancel out all the negative stuff she'd had to endure as a kid.

It wouldn't absolve him from blame for the damage his gossip had caused. And it sure wouldn't do a thing about the longing that suddenly filled his chest. But at least it was an honorable plan. Much better than last night's dangerous and out-of-bounds impulse.

Feeling a little better about himself, he got out of bed, gulped down a few ibuprofens, and headed to the beach, prepared to endure the stares of the other guests.

But the beach was deserted. Evidently, most of the other guests had gone out to sail. The swim improved his mood, and moving his dead leg made it feel better.

When he returned to the cottage, he showered and then decided he would go out for breakfast. He grabbed his cane and walked down Harbor Drive in the direction of Bread, Butter and Beans.

But before he got to the coffeehouse, he found himself walking into the barbershop across the street, where he got himself a shave and a haircut.

By midmorning, after a lazy cappuccino at the coffeehouse, he was feeling so much better about himself that he picked up his dirty clothes and took everything to the Laundromat on Lilac Street.

Later, he was cleaning up the dishes in the kitchenette sink when someone knocked at the cottage door. He opened it to the sight of Jackie Scott, standing there with his freckled face and his big eyes staring up at him with the worshipful gaze football fans used to turn on him.

He hated that look. And he wanted to tell the kid to knock it off, but he held his tongue. There was something fragile about the boy.

"What?" Topher asked.

"You were going to take me to the library. Did you forget?" The accusation in the kid's voice was enough to make him take a step back. It hurt. Down deep. And it raised a fountain of shame.

He met the kid's stare. "Yeah, I did forget," he said.

The kid cocked his head. "So, we aren't going?" Jackie's voice shook a little.

"Of course we're going," he said. "I don't have anything else on my schedule today. Why don't we walk?"

Jackie's smile made the summer sunshine a little brighter.

It took about fifteen minutes at Topher's slow pace to reach the 1940s-vintage redbrick building on Oak Street. Inside, the air smelled leathery, and the well-worn cork floors creaked underfoot as Topher and Jackie made their way to the information desk.

The librarian, a fiftysomething woman, immediately assumed *the stare* as they approached. Topher fought the urge to rage at her. But it had been a mostly good day, and raging would probably spoil it and scare the kid.

So he pulled his punches and said, "Hi. I understand you have some original correspondence from Rose Howland in your collection. My young friend here is doing his Heritage Day project on Rose, and we wondered if we might view the letters."

The woman stood in order to peer down at Jackie. One eyebrow rose, and then she reseated herself, squinting up at Topher. "I'm sorry," she said. "You need to have permission to look at those materials."

"We do," Topher said.

The woman blinked. "I'm sorry. I haven't received any written instructions about the Howland collection."

Topher smiled at the woman, certain it would fold up the left side of his face into something quite horrible. Her eyes shifted to the right as he started to speak. "My young friend here"—he gestured toward Jackie—"is Ashley Scott's son. Which means he's the youngest Howland heir."

The woman stood again in order to look at Jackie. "Is this true?"

The kid nodded and dug into the pocket of his too-big shorts, pulling out something that looked like a credit card. "This belongs to Mom," he said. "She told me I would probably need it. It's her library card. And she told me that it's okay for me and Topher to look at the letters."

Jackie handed the card over, and the librarian examined it closely before shooting another gaze at Jackie and then Topher. "Well, imagine that. Y'all are the first to come looking for those letters in a very long time."

She stood up. "I'll have to keep this until you're finished with the collection." She waved the library card, then stepped from behind the desk and led them to a small room at the back of the building with a single oak desk and a couple of straight-backed chairs. "The original versions of the letters are kept at the main branch of the library in Georgetown. But we do have photocopies."

"If you don't even have the real letters, why all the cloak-and-dagger about getting permission?" Topher asked.

The librarian turned her back and opened a flat file cabinet in the corner, pulling out a large black portfolio. "I have no idea," she said. "I just know that Mary Howland, God rest her soul, made it clear that she didn't want anyone reading these letters. And since Mary Howland gave the money to establish this branch of the library, she got her way."

"But Aunt Mary is dead now," Topher said.

"She's your aunt? Why didn't you say that in the first place?"

"I'm not a Howland, and neither was Aunt Mary. She was born a Martin."

The librarian shrugged. "I know, but she was the matriarch of the Howland family nevertheless."

Arguing with the woman was a futile exercise, so Topher shut up. He waited for the librarian to leave and then turned toward Jackie. "I wonder what your great-grandmother didn't want people to read about in these letters?" he asked in a conspiratorial whisper.

The boy hopped up onto one of the chairs and opened the portfolio. There were a lot of pages in the file, all hand-written in an old-style script that would be hard for the third grader to read. There weren't any transcriptions. Obviously Aunt Mary wanted to keep whatever was in these letters under wraps.

"Can you read handwriting?" Topher asked, as a sudden preternatural shiver worked its way up his spine. What the heck? The library was damned drafty for a warm day in early September.

Topher looked up at the ceiling, searching for a non-existent AC vent while the kid pawed through the pages, pulling one out seemingly at random. "This one. Read this one."

"Why this one?" Topher asked.

The kid focused over Topher's shoulder, and for a moment he thought Jackie was giving him *the stare*. But Jackie had never done that before.

Another shiver worked up Topher's spine. He turned, finding nothing, and then glanced down at the kid. "The captain's here, isn't he?" he asked.

A sly smile tipped Jackie's mouth as he nodded. "The cap'n says you could see him once."

Topher didn't say a word as he took the page from Jackie's hand.

It was a letter from Rose to her father, John Howland—the man who had disowned her when she'd bedded William Teal and produced a child out of wedlock. The letter was dated 1719, six years after the hurricane that had taken William Teal's life. If Topher remembered his history correctly, Captain Teal and Rose Howland's son, Thomas, would have been about seven or eight by this time.

Thomas was the subject of the letter. Rose's father wanted his grandson back at Oak Hall, the family plantation, which had once stood along the banks of the Black River. Rose didn't want to give up her son, and her letter enumerated all the reasons she regarded her father as an unworthy guardian for the young Thomas Howland. At the end of the letter she wrote:

> *You will not force me to leave this island as you forced me to live here in the first instance. I am well here. I have made a home. I am cared for. I am not alone.*
> *And I feel close to the captain here, as I cannot*

*feel close to him any other place, but perhaps in
death. If you make me leave, or take young Thomas
from me, it will be the death of me.*

"Wow," Jackie said. "You think she died because she
had to leave the island and never see Cap'n Bill again?"

"I don't know," he said. It struck him as odd that he
hadn't really thought about what had happened to Rose
after the flowers had been planted. She'd probably ended
up back at Oak Hall because Thomas Howland, the son of
a pirate, had founded the family empire.

Which meant little Jackie was Captain Teal's great-
something-grandson. It was enough to make Topher smile
as he thumbed through the rest of the letters, scanning
them.

"I'm not sure we're going to find any maps to a buried
treasure here," he said.

"It's okay," the kid said. "Just take a picture of this
one." He pointed to the letter he'd pulled from the stack
of pages.

"Sure, why?"

"'Cause it's proof that the ghost exists."

"Um, I'm not sure it exact—"

"It does. She says she doesn't want to leave the island
'cause she's close to him here. I don't think the ghost can
go much farther than the oak tree. I mean, he was here a
minute ago, but kind of thin and transparent."

Topher bit his tongue before he said the word "invisible."
"Um, Jackie, it doesn't exactly say that. It—"

"Just take the picture."

Oh, great. Ashley wasn't going to be happy about
this sudden turn. But Topher took out his cell phone and
snapped a photo of the letter anyway.

* * *

Friday found Jessica sitting at her desk working on Topher's house as she tried, somewhat futilely, to keep her mind from rewinding to that moment last night when he'd touched her cheek.

And ignited a totally unwanted fire within her. She did *not* want to find Topher Martin attractive. She was *not* even the slightest bit curious about what it might be like to kiss him. She did *not* want to have a fling with him.

He was her client. She needed to focus on what he wanted in a house design, and nothing else. So she edited that moment out of her thoughts and focused exclusively on what he'd talked about last night: a large house in a Carolina Coastal style.

She drew inspiration from MeeMaw's house, and that was enough to kick-start her creativity.

The first question was whether Topher could manage an elevated house. He'd certainly made it up the stairs to her door. Twice. So she jettisoned her concerns about that, along with Ashley's warnings, and started her plans with a house up on stilts, with a backup elevator that would run on emergency generator power in a pinch.

Once Topher got up into his house, all the living space would be on one level. It would have a wraparound veranda with a portion screened off that could be used for a parlor or a sleeping porch, which would give him plenty of guest bedroom space in the summers without trying to build a house with a gigantic footprint or even the five bedrooms he wanted. Three would be enough, and one of them would have two built-in bunk beds and could sleep four.

She planned to use Southern cypress, a hardwood that was locally grown and sustainable, and the design would incorporate passive solar heating and cooling, a rainwater collection system, and special windows and hurricane shutters to withstand storms.

She was deep into the details, consulting local flood plain, beach, and residential building codes, when her telephone rang, jolting her back to the real world. She snatched up the phone, hoping that it might be Topher. She was filled with enthusiasm for the project and couldn't wait to share her ideas.

But it was Hillary.

"Hey," she said, connecting the line.

"Hi. I was just checking up on you. I haven't heard from you in a couple of days, and the last time we talked, you were kind of freaked out."

"I'm less freaked out now. But it has been a crazy few days."

"So? What happened?"

Jessica got up from her desk and stretched her legs, moving to the front windows, which provided a view of Harbor Drive. The business district was busy today and would get busier tomorrow, what with all the sailors in town for the boat races.

"For starters, I went back to talk to Topher, and I ended up saving his life."

"What?"

Jessica filled her friend in on Topher's narrowly averted swimming disaster, followed by Ashley's attempted intervention, and then her confrontation with Topher the day he'd dropped by her house unannounced.

"He thought I'd been sent away to have a baby," Jessica said.

"What?"

"I gather that's what everyone thinks."

Hillary laughed.

"You think it's funny?"

"Yeah, sort of, seeing as you were probably the only virgin at Longwood Academy."

Jessica's face heated. "Well, I certainly got an education there."

Hillary chuckled. "Honestly, how could anyone think you'd gotten knocked up? You are the only girl I've ever met who wanted to save yourself for your husband."

"I was a good virgin back then. I'm not so good or virginal now."

"What does Colton say about this gossip?"

"I haven't talked to him about it. I haven't talked to him at all since he suggested that we move out of the friend zone."

"What? Oh my God, you need to talk to him."

"Why? It's all water under the bridge."

"Listen," Hillary said, sobering. "You know how I feel about Colton. I think he's fabulous. He checks off all the boxes any woman would ever want."

"Hillary, how many times do I have to tell you that I'm not interested in having any man in my life? I'm not interested in marriage."

"I know. I know. You don't want to be your mother, married off young and always under the thumb of her man."

"Daddy was a bully."

"I know. And he banished you because you embarrassed him. And I really do understand that this new gossip inflames those old wounds. If your father hadn't sent you away, people would never have thought this wrong thing about you."

Jessica blew out a long breath, the pain close to the surface. Why had Daddy refused to believe her when she'd spoken the truth about Colton? Why had he banished her? Even after she'd graduated from Longwood Academy, he'd forbidden her from coming back home.

He'd given her some BS about wanting to save her reputation, when he'd done nothing but help the gossips trash it. She'd never reconciled with him. He'd died just five years after she'd graduated from Longwood Academy of the same heart defect that had taken his father at a young age.

But all of it was truly water over the dam. She needed to move on. "I don't want to dwell on this," Jessica said in a tight voice.

"I know you don't. But listen to me. This is something you have to talk to Colton about. What if he doesn't know about this rumor? And even if he does, you two need to decide if your friendship is over."

"What do you mean, over?"

"Come on, honey. If he wants out of the friend zone and you don't, that's something you need to talk over. Because regardless of how you settle the question, he's a contractor and you're an architect. Your paths are going to cross. Often."

"I guess you have a point."

"I always do."

* * *

Hillary's advice rattled around in Jessica's brain until quitting time, when she screwed up her courage and gave Colton a call.

He didn't answer the phone, which was unusual, since he was one of those guys whose cell phone was almost surgically attached to his ear. She went back to work for another hour and then called again with the same result.

Was he avoiding her?

Maybe. And it was her own fault for being such a wimp about tackling the ugly, painful parts of their shared past.

She left work around six o'clock, determined to find him and settle things. She swung by his office, but the door was locked. That was strange. Colton usually worked until after seven, unless he was out at one of his job sites.

She decided to go by his house—a place she usually avoided because he lived in the same neighborhood as her grandmother. Every time she was spotted knocking on Colton's door, the whole community seemed to know about it.

Granny never failed to question her if she'd been spotted too often in Colton's company. Good grief, did Granny know about the love child gossip? Probably.

Knowing Granny, the talk had undoubtedly mortified her years ago. And now she was probably terrified that Colton and Jessica would turn the rumor into reality. Her grandmother was not even remotely woke. She wasn't even very tolerant.

Jessica pulled up to Colton's house and was just about to leave the car, when his front door opened and he emerged, wearing a pair of well-washed jeans and a white T-shirt that stretched across his muscled chest.

He looked good. But he wasn't alone.

Kerri Eaton, her hair unusually awry, walked out onto the porch with him. She advanced to the steps. Then she turned and stepped into his arms.

Good grief. The old biddies watching from their parlor windows were getting one heck of a thrill. Kerri and Colton played tonsil hockey for a good minute and a half while his hands roamed all over Kerri's long, lean, shapely body.

When they broke apart, Kerri turned, looking like a

woman who had been satisfied six ways to Sunday. She drifted down the porch steps to her car across the street while Colton watched, his gaze locked on Kerri's swaying backside.

Jessica leaned back into the headrest as the tension in her neck relaxed. A laugh bubbled out of her, and once she started, she couldn't stop. She laughed until tears rolled down her cheeks and her belly started to cramp.

She was still laughing when Colton knocked on the passenger-side window. Jessica unlocked the door, and he climbed in.

"What's so funny?" he asked in a tone that sounded half-outraged, half embarrassed.

That sobered her up. "I'm so glad you and Kerri found each other."

"You're laughing at me, aren't you?" he grumbled.

"No. Yes. Maybe a little. But really, I'm very happy for you. I think Kerri is terrific."

"Yeah, well. After you sent me away last week, I got to thinking that maybe you were right."

"It's my red-letter day," she said, the irony intense. "I can't remember the last time you told me I was right about anything." She rolled her head to give him a serious look.

"Yeah." The word exploded from his mouth. "I know. I'm sorry. I've been pushing you lately. I apologize. It's just that I want you to succeed."

"I want to succeed too," she said. "And I need your friendship for that. In fact, that's why I'm here. I came to have a serious conversation with you about... stuff. But it looks like the crisis has passed."

"About what I said the other day..." His voice trailed off, and he scratched at the back of his head, clearly embarrassed.

"It's okay. I'm glad we're back in the friend zone."

"I guess I was just feeling lonely, you know. Like it was time to think about settling down. And then you were living out there alone in your grandmother's house. And I thought I could..." He shrugged. "I don't know. Take care of you."

"I can take care of myself, thank you."

"Can you? I worry about you."

"Stop. Really. I'm okay. I even replaced the P-trap in the kitchen sink." She didn't say one word about how Topher had helped.

"I knew that sink was going to give you trouble."

"Well, it's fixed now, okay?"

"Good for you."

Silence welled up between them for a moment before he spoke again. "I guess wanting to take care of you isn't exactly the same as having the hots for you."

Colton had a definite way with words. And there was no doubt that he had the hots for Kerri. "So, you going to see Kerri again?"

"Uh. Yeah. I guess."

"You guess? You like her, right?"

He shrugged. "Yeah, I do."

It was typical Colton understatement. Sometimes the man could be so cool that he was hard to read.

"Well, I think she's great."

"Thanks. So I heard you saved Topher Martin's life." He was changing the subject. She decided to let him.

"It wasn't nearly as dramatic as it sounds."

"You still designing his house?"

She nodded. "Yes. And I have other news."

"Oh?"

"This architect from Miami called and offered me a job."

"What? You moving away?" He seemed upset about that.

"I don't know. Maybe. We'll see." For the first time since Damon Brant had called her, she seriously entertained the idea of moving on. Maybe that was the best way to deal with the gossip. She'd thought that stuff was in the past, but clearly it wasn't.

She turned and faced him. "Um, there's something else I need to talk to you about."

"Oh?" He sounded worried.

"Colton, do you know what people are saying about us? About how we had a baby together?"

"Um..." He gave her a funny look.

"So you know about this? Why didn't you tell me?"

He nodded. "Yeah. I know. But it's a very old story. I heard it back when I was in juvie. My daddy came to visit, and he was all over me about getting you pregnant."

"So it wasn't just something people at school were saying?"

"I think Jude heard the story at school and he told Daddy, and Daddy came down to the center and ripped me a new one. He was ready to make me take responsibility for the kid until I told him it was all a lie."

"And he believed you?"

"Of course he did."

Right there was the story of her life. Even Colton's father, who would never win any awards for Father of the Year, had believed his son when he'd told the truth. She pushed the pain away as she stared out the windshield fighting her own personal demons.

"Jess," Colton said softly into the silence, "it's just an old rumor that was laid to rest a long time ago. Who did you hear it from?"

"Topher," she said.

"Oh crap. I'm sorry. He hasn't lived here in a long time."

"Yeah, I guess. And you don't have to be sorry. I keep telling you, none of this was your fault."

"I guess." He didn't sound too sure.

"Well," she said on a very long breath, "I think I know how we can put an end to all this talk about the two of us."

"You do?"

"I think you should sweep Kerri Eaton off her feet with a bunch of public displays of affection like the one I just witnessed. So keep it up."

# Chapter Thirteen —

Friday had been a good day. Maybe the best day since the accident. Topher had gone swimming. He'd cleaned the cottage. He'd walked to town twice. And his leg, while not entirely pain free, was feeling less stiff than it had in weeks.

He made a printout of the photo he'd taken of Rose's letter, but he'd been unable to get a word with Ashley before sending the kid home. As his granddad might have said, Ashley was busier than a one-armed paperhanger with the hives.

The buzz at the inn made him yearn for those old days out at the yacht club. He sat for an hour on the porch until he couldn't sit still a moment longer. He'd never stopped paying his dues to the Jonquil Island Yacht Club. Maybe it was time to show his ugly face there.

So he called to see if he could charm his way into a dinner reservation at the restaurant. He certainly hadn't lost his touch over the phone. Plus the maître d' had known him since he was sixteen and was happy to find him a spot as a longtime member from one of the island's oldest families.

His tie felt like a noose, though, when he climbed the steps into the brick building that had housed the club for eighty years. The place was filled to overflowing with sailors, their cheeks ruddy from a day fighting the wind and an evening downing alcohol.

He made his way through the foyer without anyone recognizing him, although he collected more than a few odd looks. It wasn't until he reached the entrance to the dining room that he ran into Harry Bauman and had to stop and endure the man's *stare.*

The conversation was beyond awkward and involved a few sentences with phrases like "good to see you" and "how was today's sailing."

Five minutes after he'd escaped, he found himself sitting at a corner table hiding behind the menu. This had been a bad idea. Maybe if he'd invited Jessica it would have—

No. It would not have been better. And besides, why would she have wanted to be seen with him here?

He ordered the fried shrimp and pulled out his cell phone when the waiter took away his menu. He didn't have a boatload of email messages the way he once had, when he'd been running CEM Investments. So he pulled up Facebook and cruised the fake news.

"Topher?"

He looked up, bracing for another uncomfortable encounter. Caleb Tate stood by his table dressed in the yacht club formal uniform of gray slacks and blue blazer. The man looked good. Unlike so many of their teammates, he hadn't put on a lot of extra poundage around the middle.

"Hello, Caleb," he said, tamping down the urge to tell

the man to leave him the hell alone. Or better yet, rip him a new one for what he'd said to Jessica all those years ago.

He couldn't say that he really remembered the encounter though. But he sure as hell remembered the pain in Jessica's voice when she'd talked about what had happened. Yeah, they'd both been jerks in high school.

The question of the moment was whether Caleb had evolved.

"I heard you were in town," Caleb said, pulling out the facing chair and making himself comfortable. He waved his half-empty glass of scotch at a passing waiter. He got a deferential nod from the man.

Clearly, Tate was comfortable being the big man on campus, and now that Topher thought about it, Caleb had always loved being the center of attention. Topher, although the captain of the team, had been happy to let Caleb bask in all that stupid adoration.

"It's nice to see you again, man," Caleb said, giving Topher *the stare*.

*Look at me*, Topher wanted to scream. "It's nice to *see* you too," he said, hanging on to civility by a gossamer thread.

The waiter came by with Caleb's drink and put Topher's shrimp in front of him. Caleb settled in, elbows on the table, as Topher dug into his meal. He was surprisingly hungry. Maybe because he'd been out and about today. Or more likely because he'd grown weary of frozen dinners.

"So, I've been trying to get in touch with you. Did you get my messages?" Caleb asked.

"Yeah, I did. But I've been busy. And while we're talking about this, do me a favor and leave my architect alone."

Caleb's gaze narrowed. "Ah, Jessica Blackwood. For a

mousy little thing, she's kind of cute. I bet she's a hot little number in the sack, given what people say about her."

Topher's right hand closed into a fist. So Caleb had not evolved, and it was all he could do not to reach across the table and ram his knuckles into his mouth.

Caleb had always been an asshole. The guy was always talking about girls, boasting of the ones he'd screwed. Back in high school, talk like that was considered the usual fare for the locker room. But Topher had learned his lesson about "locker room" talk.

He'd tolerated it back then because trying to stop the guys from saying stupid things would have been futile. And besides, they were on a run for the championship. It was stupid, of course, but when a team gets on a run like that, you don't do anything to mess up the vibe.

But he hadn't liked that kind of talk when he'd quarterbacked the team, and he sure as hell didn't like it now. Because he had evolved.

He forcibly relaxed his fist. There were better ways to bring jerks like Caleb down. Maybe this was part of his penance.

"Is there something I can help you with?" Topher asked, dropping into a charm offensive. He was definitely off his game, what with the state of his face, but he'd managed to charm the maître d' over the phone. So he still had something left. Besides, he didn't need to be all that charming. Caleb was undoubtedly more interested in his money than his manners.

Caleb leaned forward and spoke in a low, conspiratorial tone. "As a matter of fact, there is. I've been trying to reach you because I wanted to talk to you about our plans for Magnolia Harbor."

"Whose plans?"

"There's a consortium of developers who think this little town can be turned into the next Hilton Head. I thought you might want to get in on the ground floor. There's a lot of money to be made."

Topher had to bite his tongue not to tell the guy he didn't want to see Magnolia Harbor turned into the next Hilton Head. But for Jessica's sake, he played along.

"Really?" he asked. "Tell me all about it."

* * *

Saturday morning was a zoo at Howland House. The inn was filled to overflowing with sailors who needed to be fed and out the door no later than seven. Their boats had to be rigged and sailed all the way out into the bay to the starting line for the races, which began at nine in the morning.

So Ashley, who usually got up at six in the morning, found herself down in the kitchen an hour earlier. Her assistant, Judy McKenzie, was also on the scene early, making up box lunches for everyone. It was an extra service Ashley had added this weekend when almost all of her rooms were taken by sailing enthusiasts.

Ashley's sour mood didn't make the early-morning rush any easier. She made what seemed like endless batches of biscuits, fried up several pounds of bacon and sausage, and boiled up a gigantic pot of oatmeal, all the while waiting for the morning to move on so she could march down to the cottage and give Topher a piece of her mind.

Yesterday evening Jackie had returned from the library brimming with the news that Rose Howland knew all about Captain Bill's ghost. He even had a murky printout of a photo to prove it.

"We're going to go to the library again tomorrow to read more of the letters," Jackie had informed her.

Ashley had been so angry with her cousin that she'd sent Jackie to bed early and marched out to the cottage and banged on the door.

But the cottage had been dark, and further investigation had shown that Topher's BMW was not in the parking lot.

Wow. He'd gone out for the evening—a turn of events that might have encouraged her, but at that moment she'd been doubly enraged. How dare he not be around for her to give him a piece of her mind.

She needed to sit the man down and explain how the ghost was merely Jackie's coping mechanism for having lost his father three years ago. And the sooner Jackie grew out of his fantasy, the better. Her son's therapy sessions were costing Ashley a fortune. The last thing she needed was her cousin, who was having his own issues with fantastical thinking, undoing all of that work.

She slammed the frying pan down on her new eight-burner Vulcan stove and swallowed back a curse. There was no way in hell she was letting Jackie go back to the library with anyone, much less Topher.

She should have known better from the start. She remembered the summer when Topher had insisted he'd seen the ghost and Grandmother had explained about how Topher was sad because his mother had died and his stories about the ghost were just his way of getting added attention.

Jackie was doing the same damn thing.

"We need two more bowls of oatmeal," Judy said, carrying dirty dishes as she came through the swinging door to the dining room. She dumped the dishes into the big sink and turned. "Reverend St. Pierre has made his usual Saturday-morning appearance, and Jackie has come down early."

Ashley moved to the big pot of steel-cut oatmeal she kept going every morning. Funny how oatmeal had been the last thing on her menu when she'd first started this business. But the Rev liked oatmeal, and he popped over for breakfast quite frequently. So she'd started making it every morning. The number of guests who opted for oatmeal instead of the usual eggs and bacon, waffles, or pancakes had been a revelation.

She filled two bowls while Judy loaded a tray with butter, cream, walnuts, raisins, honey, and brown sugar. "I'll take it out there. You watch the biscuits and bacon," Ashley said, putting the bowls on the tray.

"Okay." There was an uncertain tone in Judy's voice. Usually she did the running to and from the dining room.

"I need to give the Rev a piece of my mind."

"Oh?"

Ashley was tempted to tell Judy to mind her own business, but she clamped down on the snippy comment. Her assistant wasn't responsible for her morning funk. But Micah St. Pierre certainly bore some responsibility for it.

She'd asked Micah to *talk* to Topher, not enlist him in some harebrained scheme to help Jackie with his Heritage Day project. The trip to the library may have gotten Topher out of the house, but at what cost?

She pushed through the swinging door and scanned the dining room. The long table was mostly empty, except for a couple of women who were married to sailors participating in today's races. They sat at the near end of the table chatting and lingering over their coffee. At the other end of the table, Micah St. Pierre leaned forward, listening with grave intent to Ashley's son.

As usual, Jackie was chattering away like the proverbial box.

"Really?" Micah said as Ashley approached.

"Yup. Rose wrote it all down in her letters," Jackie said.

"You don't say."

Ashley slammed a bowl of oatmeal down in front of the minister.

He gazed up, piercing her with an amused look. The little smirk annoyed her to no end. "Good morning," he said in an irritatingly cheerful voice, and turned toward his oatmeal.

"Good morning," she said in a curt tone.

"Mom's ticked off," Jackie whispered.

"Is she?" Micah asked, turning his gaze on Jackie.

"I don't think she's happy about discovering that Cap'n Bill is real. But it's okay. I'm not surprised. Topher said she'd be ticked off."

"He did, did he?" Ashley asked, putting her fists on her hips and resisting the urge to grind her teeth.

Jackie nodded. "We're going back this afternoon to read some more of the letters. They won't let us make copies on the machine, which is kinda weird 'cause they're not the real letters. But Topher took a picture of the letter Cap'n Bill wanted me to see."

"So Captain Bill went to the library with you?" Micah asked, his tone deadly serious.

Ashley's head was about to explode. Jackie hadn't given her all these details last night, probably because she'd sent him to bed early. Oh, good Lord, this was much worse than she'd thought.

"Yup," Jackie said with enthusiasm. "And you know what? I think Topher knew the cap'n was there."

"He did not," Ashley said in her best mom voice.

Jackie looked up at her, the picture of childhood innocence. "But he did."

"I'm going to kill that man," Ashley muttered.

"But there weren't any treasure maps," Jackie continued.

"What treasure?" Ashley asked, sinking down into the chair next to the Rev. Breakfast was just about over, so Judy could manage in the kitchen without her for a minute.

"Reverend St. Pierre told us the letters would have a map or something. But we didn't find a map. Topher said there might be clues if we read them all."

"A map?" She looked toward Micah.

He shrugged. "Family legend."

"Family legend?" Her voice cracked.

He nodded as he spooned an inordinate amount of brown sugar into his oatmeal. "Yes. In my family, folks always said that the Howlands didn't want anyone reading those letters because of the treasure."

"You're out of your mind." Ashley turned toward her son. "And you are not reading any more of those letters."

"But, Mom."

"Just because Rose Howland told her father that she felt close to the captain here doesn't mean she was having conversations with his ghost. It's just a grown-up expression. His ship went down out in the inlet during the hurricane and his body was never found. So of course she'd feel closer to him here."

"But, Mom…" Jackie drew the name out into a whine.

She stood up. "I mean it. Find another topic for your project because you're not doing yours on Rose Howland's letters."

* * *

Topher jolted awake to the sound of someone banging on the front door. He pushed up in bed, groping for his cell phone.

It was just shy of seven forty-five in the morning. Damn. He sat there blinking, last night's troubling conversation with Caleb spooling through his mind.

"Dammit, Topher. I know you're in there." A shadow crossed the bedroom window as Ashley's voice pulled him from his thoughts. Man, she sounded pissed off.

He could pretty much guess why.

He rolled out of bed, his bad leg twinging the moment he put weight on it. He usually spent a good five minutes every morning stretching the useless thing before standing up. But he didn't think the woman out on the porch could wait that long.

He limped to the door, opened it, and came face-to-face with one pissed-off mother. "What on earth were you thinking, telling Jackie those letters confirmed the existence of a ghost?"

He squinted in the bright morning sunshine, suddenly weary of being wrongly accused of heinous behavior. Was this how Jessica felt?

He pushed the thought away and met Ashley's stare. "Because the ghost is real?" he said, without a great deal of conviction. But it was kind of fun yanking Ashley's chain.

"Oh my...I can't believe it. You've been *encouraging* him?"

"Uh, well..."

She pointed a finger at his naked chest. She was so angry she hadn't noticed his bed head or the fact that he was standing there in his boxers and nothing else. She was like a wild-eyed mama lion.

And he loved her for that. Because for once she wasn't trying to baby him or pity him. She'd gone back to bullying him, which she'd done quite effectively when he was little.

He listened to her rant and realized it didn't have much to do with him. It was mostly about Jackie's therapy and Adam's death. Angry tears streamed down her cheeks as she poured out her sorrow and anxiety in a giant wave.

He wanted to give her a hug, but he had a feeling she might run away screaming. So he decided to push her a little more.

"Why are you so dead set against believing there might be a ghost?" He shifted his weight off his bad leg and leaned into the doorframe.

"Because there isn't one. And encouraging Jackie to believe in a ghost isn't healthy for him. He's just doing this to get attention. Not unlike—" She bit off the words.

"Not unlike what?" he asked.

She stood there staring at him. "You."

"Me?"

"Yeah. When you were little. That summer I came to visit and you spent most of your time up in the tree telling everyone you had conversations with the pirate."

A shadow memory shifted through his mind. He remembered climbing the tree. He remembered pretending to be a pirate up there in the crow's nest. He remembered conversations.

"Okay. Point taken," he said on a long breath, ready to give up until he had another thought. "But how do you *know* that ghosts don't exist?"

"Because...they don't."

"Are you sure?"

"Of course I am. And don't tell me you saw a ghost. I

know damn well that you made it all up when you were little. You were just a lonely kid."

She had that right. He also didn't remember ever seeing the ghost of Cap'n Bill. But he hated the idea of letting go of the possibility. "Do I have to see a ghost in order to believe they exist?"

"Of course."

"Why? I mean, you believe in God. I know because you go to church every Sunday. Have you ever seen Him?"

"Of course not. It's a matter of faith," she said.

"My point exactly."

"You're crazy, you know that? You're just teasing me. Dishing it out in some weird payback for my vile behavior when I was a bratty little girl."

He refrained from pointing out that she still had her bratty moments. That would not have gone over well. So as usual he said nothing at all.

She put her hands on her hips and scowled at him. "Just stop encouraging Jackie, okay?"

A contrary part of him wanted to push her buttons further, asking her whether he could still encourage him to throw the football or climb the tree. But he didn't. He just nodded.

And then he closed the door gently, even though he wanted to slam the damn thing right in her face.

* * *

Saturday morning dawned cool and clear with a steady sea breeze likely to make the sailors in town happy and the merchants on Harbor Drive, including Kerri Eaton, ecstatic.

Half the customers strolling into Daffy Down Dilly during the day wanted one of Kerri's marked-down sundresses, and the other half were looking for unique Christmas gifts. Her customers were predominantly the wives and daughters of the sailors who'd come for the big regatta.

These people had serious bucks, which explained why the Saturday of the festival weekend was one of Kerri's best-grossing days of the year. It also afforded her an opportunity to move leftover summer merchandise out the door so she could start fresh next spring.

But it was a long-ass day. And by four thirty, when the afternoon crowd finally began to diminish, her feet were beyond tired. Good thing Katia Rivers, the teen who sometimes helped on busy days, would be back from her early dinner soon, and Dottie Peyton, who'd worked at the store on and off for years, was coming in at 5:00 p.m. to give Kerri a break.

During the festival, Kerri usually kept Daffy Down Dilly open until 10:00 p.m., because the restaurants along Harbor Drive would be chockablock with hungry sailors, who would want to go shopping before and after dinner.

She was sitting on a stool behind the counter, waiting for her part-time help, when the St. Pierre construction truck pulled into the parking slot that had just been vacated.

Colton emerged, wearing his maroon golf shirt, the late-afternoon sun burnishing his skin a golden bronze. Kerri's middle hitched, and a wave of yearning seized her. Followed in short order by teeth-gnashing irritation at her own self.

He stood there on the sidewalk, his gaze rising to the windows above the boutique. Jess was up there, working her tail off for the second weekend in a row. Topher Martin must be a nightmare of a client because he'd apparently rejected her first plan and now wanted a second one. Jess had stopped in to borrow some sweetener packets earlier in the day and had grumbled about the short time frame her client had given her. Evidently, Topher wanted to sail off to Lookout Island for a second time on Monday, and Jess needed to have a plan to show him.

Jess had looked exhausted, as if she hadn't been sleeping well. Kerri hoped the sleeplessness was caused by her difficult client and not her decision to give Colton his walking papers.

Because one look at Colton hesitating out there on the sidewalk was enough to underscore the fact that he was having second thoughts about walking away.

No matter what Jess might say, the coast was not clear. Suddenly more than Kerri's feet hurt. Heartache was a bitch. And like the day follows night, she could count on it rising up and grabbing her in the chest if she let her libido run away with her emotions.

She looked away from the window to focus on a customer who had selected the very last daffodil dress, a size sixteen. Hooray, she was officially cleared out of her summer merchandise.

She was ringing up the sale when the bells on the front door chimed. Another customer. It was looking like a red-letter day for the cash register.

She completed the credit card sale, wrapped the dress in tissue, and tucked it into one of her beautiful shopping bags printed with bright-yellow daffodils.

When the customer turned to leave, Colton's deep baritone jolted Kerri. "Hey," he said.

She looked up to find him standing amid her girlie merchandise with hands shoved into his pockets. "I guess you're really busy tonight, huh?" he asked like Captain Obvious.

Lust pooled in Kerri's middle. "Kind of. I'm—" She bit off her words. What the hell was she doing? She'd just been lusting after this man and indulging in self-pity because he liked her tenant more than he liked her. But he hadn't gone upstairs, had he?

He'd come in to talk to her. But did he want her? Or was he trying to make the woman upstairs jealous?

She didn't know. But she didn't actually care. Life was short, and a person had to grab happiness when it walked through the door.

"I've got help coming in a bit," she said. "Did you have something in mind?"

A full frontal grin opened on his face, and his moss-colored eyes ignited as if someone had put a match to his fuse. "Good," he said in that incredible voice, "because Jude gave me a couple of free tickets for tonight's sunset cruise on the schooner *Synchronicity*."

"The sunset cruise?" she asked, her mouth going dry. The sunset cruise was a favorite for lovers and newlyweds. At least one couple every week got engaged during those cruises. In fact, Colton's younger brother, *Synchronicity*'s owner, had taken to advertising his yacht as the perfect place to pop the question.

Damn.

She would have been happy to go back to his place for late-night Netflix. But he'd just upped the ante. And her stupid heart was totally down with the program.

"I'd love to go," she said, making a snap decision for once in her life. Katia and Dottie could manage.

Colton's grin widened. "That's great, because to grab some dinner and make the sailing, we have to leave now."

"Now?"

He checked his watch. "The boat sails at six."

"Just let me call my helpers. They both have keys to the shop."

Kerri ran to the back room, made her phone calls, checked her lipstick in the bathroom mirror, and emerged three minutes later. She posted a note on the front door that said, "back in five minutes," and then boldly took Colton's arm.

And oh boy, the feel of his warm skin and ropy muscles under her palm was enough to set off fireworks hours earlier than expected.

# Chapter Fourteen———

Monday dawned cooler, with a brisk wind that whipped Jessica's hair as she walked down the long pier to where *Bachelor's Delight* was moored.

She'd logged a bunch of hours this weekend working on Topher's house. This trip to the island would solidify a lot of things, but she wasn't entirely sure that sailing out there was a good idea.

For one thing, the bay was choppy this morning, so she'd worn her foul-weather gear. It wasn't going to be the same sunny pleasure cruise it had been the last time.

And for another, she still hadn't forgotten the way Topher had touched her on Thursday night. She wanted him to touch her again, but she didn't want to admit that to anyone, least of all him.

As she walked down the pier, it was fair to say that just the prospect of seeing him again had raised a tempest inside her.

The moment she saw him standing at the bow of his yacht making adjustments to the jib that unwanted awareness almost blew her over. He'd ditched the Hawaiian shirt and the holey jeans in favor of tactical sailing pants and a tight-fitting sailing shirt. His red, white, and blue Helly Hansen foul-weather jacket made him look like a member of the America's Cup team.

He looked up, the wind whipping his much-shorter hair. "Ah, I see you dressed for a sail," he said, his mouth tipping up in a smile that hit her like a gale-force wind.

"It's a little breezy for cruising," she said, stating the obvious.

He made a final adjustment to the jib halyard and swung around one of the shrouds, making his way aft. "The last time we sailed out to the island, I got the impression you were disappointed that I used the engine. So I thought we'd use wind power today." He glanced up, studying the top of the mast, where a small vane marked the direction of the breeze. "We should make pretty good time."

Her heart rate kicked up. It had been years since she'd sailed with PopPop. "I'm a little rusty when it comes to trimming sails."

He chuckled, his eye catching the blue September sky and reflecting it back at her. "*Bachelor's Delight* is fitted out with all the latest technology. It's big, but it's also designed for single-handed sailing."

"Oh."

"But if you'd please untie the mooring lines…" He gave her an utterly adorable look. The very fact that he could manage an angelic look out of a devilish face was disturbing. And he'd asked nicely this time.

She found herself smiling at him as a giddy weightless feeling overtook her. She handed him her big tote bag and hastened to do his bidding.

He didn't unfurl the main sail until they were well into

the channel. But once the sail billowed out, *Bachelor's Delight* proved it was perfectly capable of riding through the chop. This boat wasn't at all like her grandfather's J-22. It was easily twice the size and had a big keel that kept it steady.

Topher also knew how to put the yacht through its paces. The wind was out of the southeast, so the ride to the island was all upwind. That meant he had to make many tacks to get there, and every time the boat turned on its zigzag course, the deck would shift, and Jessica would usually have to move from the leeward to the windward side of the boat.

She wasn't a master sailor, but she'd done enough sailing with PopPop to realize that Topher knew how to read the wind. Someone less skilled would have taken much longer to make the transit from harbor to island. When the lighthouse finally came into view off the port gunwales, she asked, "Why didn't you sail in the regatta?"

"I didn't have a crew. And for a race, I would have needed a navigator and someone to help handle the spinnaker."

"I'm sure you could have found someone down at the yacht club."

He didn't respond to her comment. Instead he shouted, "Ready to come about."

"Ready," she answered. The boat turned, the mainsail boom swinging from port to starboard, while the deck shifted under her. She once again moved from the leeward to the windward side of the boat.

"You didn't answer my question," she said.

"The truth is, I didn't participate because I would have had to register back in July. And I didn't have a sailboat then."

"What?" Her squeaky voice conveyed her surprise.

He gave her a wry grin. "I bought *Bachelor's Delight* right before I decided to return to Magnolia Harbor, about six weeks ago."

"Really?" Her cheeks grew hot even in the chilly breeze.

"It used to belong to one of my business partners," Topher said, his gaze alight with humor. "I had originally planned to live on it while I built the new house. But it's kind of small, and the walk from the slip to the convenience store was long. So I accepted Ashley's offer to rent Rose Cottage for the foreseeable future."

"So the boat's decor is..." Jessica let her voice trail off.

This time he laughed out loud. "No. I didn't choose all that black leather or the red velvet in the captain's cabin."

"Oh no." She buried her hands in her face. "I thought—"

"Yes, I know what you thought. I saw your first set of drawings."

* * *

Was it the wind or a blush that turned her cheeks red? Maybe a little of both. He got no satisfaction from her discomfort. If she'd misunderstood, it had been his fault.

"It's okay," he said. "I realized what had happened the moment I saw your first set of drawings. I didn't blame you for the mistake."

Her cheeks got a little redder, and he had a moment of hope. Was it possible for her to forgive him?

Not for starting a rumor. He hadn't done that. But he was guilty of not thinking about the consequences of repeating all that talk. And he certainly bore some responsibility for not stopping the ugly locker room conversations of guys like Caleb Tate. He hadn't shown any leadership, and he'd been the captain of the team.

"I'm sorry. I jumped to a conclusion, didn't I?" she said. "And it's kind of unforgivable, given my history."

"No. It's easily forgiven."

Something softened in her gaze, and he wondered if she would ever reciprocate the forgiveness. He wanted it more than he'd wanted anything in a long time.

Dammit. What would it feel like to have her in his life? Not just as his architect, but as . . .

He wouldn't let himself finish the thought. A damaged man couldn't afford that kind of thinking.

He broke eye contact and concentrated on sailing. When he'd executed the last tack, putting Lookout Island directly on his lay line, he glanced back at her and asked a safe question. "Tell me about the house you've been working on."

She shook her head, trying to get the hair out of her eyes, but the wind was having none of that. A little curl formed at the corner of her lips as she started talking about her new ideas. This time she wasn't nervous or defensive.

Her words sparked his imagination. As he sailed his yacht toward the island, he could almost see it there: The big veranda, the low, hipped roof, the cupolas. And the other things she talked about: the swimming area off the western side of the island, the breezeway to the lighthouse, the technical details for the electric, septic, and fresh-water systems.

They discussed the house as he made the final approach to the island. Once they had *Bachelor's Delight* moored at the dock, Jessica clambered out of the boat with the grace of a gazelle, and he followed like a clumsy rhino.

"Let's go up to the light," he said, unfolding his aluminum cane.

She turned with a frown. "Don't you want me to pace out the house for you?"

"Later." He headed up the flagstone path toward the lighthouse as fast as his bad leg would allow him. The cane improved his speed, even though he hated using it.

"You're going to try the stairs, aren't you?" she asked from behind.

"Am I that transparent?"

"Yes. Is that why we're here, so you can prove something to me?"

He turned around. "How about proving something to myself?"

She gave him a direct and unsettling stare. The sky was filling with high clouds, and she'd pushed her sunglasses up to the top of her head. Her hair was a windblown mess, which gave her that fresh, girl-next-door vibe that he loved so much.

"Do you need to prove something to yourself?" she asked.

"Of course."

"Why?"

He stood there blinking at her, the question so simple and so impossible at the same time. What was it about this woman?

Was she his tormentor or an angel come in answer to an unspoken prayer? Having no answer for her question or the deeper one plaguing him, he turned around and redoubled his pace to the lighthouse's iron door, which he unlocked and pulled open.

He didn't wait for her as he limped across the slate floor and took the first few stairs spiraling up to the light room at the top, his boat shoes ringing on the cast-iron treads.

The first fifty steps were hard. The last one hundred and

seventeen took the better part of half an hour, with frequent rest stops along the way. Thank God Jessica had the good sense to keep her mouth shut during this ordeal.

When he finally climbed the ladder from the keeping room up to the gallery, the muscles of his left thigh and calf twitched and threatened another leg cramp. He stretched his Achilles tendon and then leaned into the masonry windowsill and gazed westward toward the mainland.

In the time they'd been climbing, the clouds had closed in. Off to the west, a front was approaching.

"Did you check the weather this morning?" she asked.

He nodded. "They were calling for a slight chance of rain."

"That doesn't look slight to me," she said, coming up beside him, her body heat warming his skin. He wanted to reach over and cover her hand with his. Instead, he gripped the masonry a little tighter.

"Are you telling me we need to hurry back down?" He tried to invest his voice with a hint of humor. He wasn't terribly successful.

Silence welled between them for a long moment. "You don't have to prove anything to me," she finally said.

He turned, leaning his left side on the windowsill. Her eyes had gone the color of the clouds scudding in from the west—a gray, stormy color.

"Don't I?" he said, his mouth dry from the slow climb. Gravity was a bitch.

"No. I'm your architect. I'm here to give you your dream house."

Was that it? Probably. They should climb back down and pace off the dimensions of the house. They should talk about wastewater systems and all that. But that wasn't what he wanted.

No surprise there. He was never satisfied. He'd always been striving for something. First it had been the NFL, then it had been a business, then it had been wealth, and then...

It had been speed, in the leather cockpit of a Ferrari on a curvy road.

"We can work on the house in a minute," he said. "Right now, while I'm catching my breath, I want you to tell me the truth."

She stepped away from him. "The truth?"

"Yeah. As odd as it may seem, I'd like to know what really happened sixteen years ago."

She turned her back on him. "I don't want to talk about that, okay?"

"No. It's not okay. The other day you said I needed to do a penance. I'm happy to get down on my knees if that's what it takes. But to truly seek forgiveness, I need to understand how *I* specifically hurt you," he said on a puff of air as he took one painful step toward her.

This time she didn't move back. But her mouth opened a little, her lips round and seductive.

He brushed back a strand of wind-ravished hair with his finger, and then he couldn't help himself. His hand cupped her cool cheek.

"I never intended to hurt anyone. And I goddamn don't want to hurt you now. I've already told you; I think you were put in my path to save me."

* * *

The warmth of his fingers against her skin stunned her for a moment. She stood rooted to the concrete and iron floor, unable to step away, while every nerve in her body jangled.

"Please don't," she said in a desperate voice, her heart shuddering in her chest. She pulled away from him and made a dash toward the ladder to the keeping room.

"Don't run away," he said. "Whatever it is you have to say, it won't offend me."

She stopped and turned. "This isn't about you," she said.

"Okay. I'd still like to hear the story."

"No, you don't want to hear it. And I don't want to tell it." She swung to the first step of the ladder, hoping he would have trouble following her. But he surprised her by moving with astonishing speed.

"Don't run away. I get it. I know."

"You don't know anything."

"I do. I can see it in your eyes. You think you have to keep all those angry thoughts inside. You think if you let them out, no one would ever love you."

His words were like arrows shot right into her heart. How could he possibly know? He was a man who wore his anger for all the world to see. And he was sometimes hard to like, much less love.

Whoa, that stopped her. She blinked up at him, her hands and lips going numb. She didn't love him, but she found him attractive, despite the scars, despite the anger that sometimes raged on the outside.

And that was frightening. She couldn't afford to—

"I'm not here for a bunch of bullshit. I want the truth. Unvarnished," he said. "You owe it to me, especially since you've blamed me for some great harm. Telling me the truth is part of my penance."

She almost laughed at the way he'd turned her words against her. "I forgave you." She continued climbing down the ladder.

"No, you didn't. You said a bunch of polite but

meaningless words so I would stop provoking you. Tell me the truth." His words followed her down to the keeping room. A moment later he came down the ladder, using the handrails to ease his left side.

"Just spit it out," he said, turning toward her. He was out of breath.

She looked away.

"Jessica, look at me."

It was the same tone of voice her father always used when he was angry. The same order. The same words.

She could remember that horrible day when Daddy had called her into his study. Colton hadn't been arrested yet, but the gossip had started and Daddy had gotten wind of it. "How could you have been so stupid?" he'd asked, confirming in one short sentence that he'd believed the lies people were telling about her.

"I didn't do any of those things they're talking about," she'd said, defiantly meeting her father's angry gaze.

"Don't you lie to me," he'd said, and when she'd refused to back down, he'd locked her in her room for an entire day—the day Colton was arrested.

Enraged, Daddy had called Uncle Joe and told his brother-in-law, who was the chief of police at the time, to make Colton's life miserable. And Uncle Joe had taken care of things, arresting Colton for possession of a couple of joints. The criminal justice system had taken care of the rest, sending him away for a year.

The next day, when Daddy told her what he'd done, she'd stood on Granny's precious Persian rug studying the swirling patterns as a tidal wave of remorse hit her. Colton's arrest had always been her fault.

"Look at me," Daddy had demanded.

And when she'd looked up, his cold gray eyes had bored

a hole right into her middle. "Are you ready to tell the truth?" he'd asked.

She'd met his stare and told him the truth. But he didn't believe it.

Three days later, he'd sent her away to a strict boarding school for teens with behavioral problems. On the day she'd left, he'd said, "When you apologize and tell me the truth, you can come home."

"Jessica?" Topher's voice pierced the toxic fog of her memories. "Please look at me."

His tone was nothing like Daddy's now that she thought about it. Her father had demanded. Topher was merely asking. But the words were the same, and it was more than she could bear.

"No," she raged. "No, I won't. I won't look at you just because you demand it. I won't tell lies for you just because you'd prefer to hear them. I won't apologize for anything I did. I just won't."

"I'm not asking you to tell me lies," he said. "I can take the truth. Whatever it is."

His tone was so gentle that she finally met his gaze, stunned by the fact that he was astonishingly handsome, even with the scars marring his face, even with the eye patch. And he wasn't wearing his anger on his sleeve right now. He wasn't staring at her the same way Daddy had stared that day.

"That's better," he said softly. "I like it when you look right at me. It gives me hope or something, because the truth is, not many people look at me anymore. I'm as ugly as sin."

"No—"

"Yes. I am. And it's a kind of armor. Because it means that you could take me to your darkest nightmare and I could endure it because I've already experienced the worst that life can hand out."

"They didn't believe me," she said. "And you know what? They weren't the first or the last ones not to believe me. Sometimes it feels like no one ever believes me. I tell the truth, and it's like . . . I don't know . . . spitting in the wind or something." She shook her head as a knot the size of Alaska lodged in her throat.

"Who didn't believe you?"

"My parents. Daddy." She hauled in a big breath. "He believed all the gossip everyone told about me. And when I insisted that it wasn't true, he called me a liar and sent me away to a school for troubled teens.

"It's worse than that, really. He never let me come back. He insisted that I apologize for things I never did in order to be allowed back into the family."

"Oh my God. I'm so sorry."

"Do you think I should have lied to him?" she asked in an angry tone. A tear escaped her eye and rolled down her cheek. "Because I was so damn stubborn, you know. I was determined to have my truth. And I lost my father because of it. I might have lost my mother too. It took fourteen years before I finally gave in."

"You gave in? Why?"

She nodded as more tears trickled out of her eyes. "It's crazy and complicated. The more important question is why I defied them in the first place."

"No."

"Yes. But it wasn't really defiance. I was trying to prove something. You know, my family was pretty religious. We went to church every Sunday, and I got my weekly dose of how important it was to love. To love everyone.

"And when I got older, I decided I'd love Colton. Not the

way people talked about us. But, you know, I'd make him my friend. Just to prove something. Just to underscore my father's hypocrisy. Because he was good at loving certain people and looking down his nose at others.

"And boy, that backfired on me. For a very long time, I thought hate was more powerful than love."

"Why on earth did you ever come home?"

"Because I don't really believe that. Believing that hate always trumps love is a horrible way to live." Her voice shook, and the tears rolled down her cheeks. "And when Momma got sick..." She looked away, unable to say another word.

When Momma had gotten sick, Jessica had been ready for forgiveness. She'd been through therapy, and she'd been willing to accept the lie for a chance to reconcile.

After fourteen years of standing on principle, accepting the lie seemed so simple. And the reward was salvaging her relationship with Momma and Granny.

But now maybe she wasn't so sure.

She took a shuddering breath and stared out one of the porthole windows. The clouds were gathering on the horizon, and the storm outside matched the one in her chest. "So, the simple answer to your complicated question is that I didn't go away to have Colton's baby. I was sent to a place called Longwood Academy for Girls for the purpose of recovering from my addictions." She let go of a strangled laugh. "I was somewhat notorious there because I was the only student who was still a virgin. I got an education there, but maybe not the one my daddy wanted me to get."

"Didn't anyone at this school realize you didn't belong there?"

"Sure. I never failed a drug test, not even before I was

sent there. But Daddy was determined, not because he really thought I was doing drugs, but because my actions had humiliated him.

"My counselor tried to get my parents to take me back. But they refused. Mrs. Mulgrew was my savior. She helped me apply to college and get a scholarship. Without her, I would never have gotten my degree. As it is, I have a huge amount of student debt I'm still carrying, but I'm luckier than most. I have a professional certification."

"I am so sorry."

She headed toward the stairs, desperate to get away from the pity in his voice. But before she could reach the stairwell, Topher grabbed her by the arm, just as he'd done a few days ago. The touch was much the same as before. Oddly gentle.

And this time it had the opposite effect. Instead of unleashing a panic, it became a lifeline, like the flotation device she'd shoved at Topher a few days ago. His hand on her wrist pulled her up from the depths and saved her from drowning.

In the next instant, she found herself pulled hard against his chest, his warm hand cupping the back of her head, his deep voice rumbling in her ear.

"Oh, Jess, I am so sorry that happened to you. Let me hold you up for a while."

# Chapter Fifteen

Topher held Jessica close as she cried, and his heart broke for her. He knew in some ways what it felt like to be abandoned. His mother had died when he was young, and everyone said he and his dad had taken a long time to get over it.

But Topher didn't remember much of that time. His memories were filled with big family gatherings at Howland House, Aunt Mary's wonderful cakes, sailing with Granddad, camping out on the island. And making his father proud because of his ability to throw a football.

He'd lived a golden life. He'd been loved. Hell, he'd been smothered at times by the women in his family, every one of whom wanted to make up for the mother he'd lost.

He'd told Jessica that he could take anything she could dish, but he wondered. Life had thrown him a horrible curveball. But he'd never been alone.

His family had gathered around him. Not merely Ashley and Karen and Sandra, but all of his cousins. They called him. They badgered him. They pushed him. And yes, they tried to protect him. Because they loved him. No matter what.

Jessica had never been loved unconditionally, had she? In a lot of ways, she'd had a rougher time of it than he ever had. She deserved a few breaks. She deserved to be wrapped up and taken care of.

He held her a little tighter as she cried out her sorrow, burying his fingers in her hair and taking some of her weight on his shaky legs. By the time the storm of her tears had broken, the distant roll of thunder reached him through the thick lighthouse walls.

She lifted her head. Her eyes puffy and tear-swollen, her nose red and runny. She was still beautiful.

He let her go when she stepped out of the embrace and turned, wiping her nose on the back of her hand. He wished he was the kind of guy who carried a handkerchief. It would have been kind of romantic or noble or something to be in a position to supply one.

But he'd never carried a handkerchief in his life, proving once again that he was piss-poor hero material.

Once she'd dried the tears from her cheeks as best she could, she turned toward him, her face a beautiful mess. "Was that thunder I just heard?"

He nodded. "I'm a little worried about the boat. We should probably get back to *Bachelor's Delight* and batten down the hatches. And then we can lie low until the storm passes over."

She glanced back at him like a wounded fawn, not unlike the animal he'd swerved to avoid on the night of his accident.

He recognized that doubtful look. She knew. She understood. He didn't even have to explain. On some deep level, she understood his struggle to live a normal life. He couldn't hide his scars, but she had managed to hide hers. He was trying to escape to this island, but she'd been living on one for years.

The thunder rolled again.

"We should really see about the boat," she said, backing away. Did she realize they were more alike than they were different?

"Yeah, it's going to take me a while going down. Down is harder than up, if you can believe it."

"Do you want me to go ahead?" she asked.

He hated the idea of sending her out into the storm to do something he ought to be able to do for himself. "I'm sorry. I shouldn't have—"

"It's okay. Better for me to go check the mooring lines than to risk damage to your beautiful boat."

"You'll need to tie up the mainsail and take down the jib. Do you know how to do that?"

"I can figure it out," she said, squaring her shoulders in false bravado. "I have a little bit of experience on a sailboat. Don't worry. I'll take care of it." She turned toward the stairwell.

He didn't want her to go alone, and her "little bit" of experience worried him. Now that he'd found her, he didn't want anything bad to happen to her.

Hearing her story made him want to wrap her up in soft cotton and make sure no one ever hurt her again. The feeling was so fierce.

He followed her toward the stairs, issuing instructions. "You'll find a couple of bumpers in the stowage compartment under the seats. Put them between the hull and the dock. And—"

"I'll be fine," she said stoically as she started putting distance between them.

"Be careful," he shouted after her. "If it starts lightning, get off the boat. Okay?"

She didn't answer him.

\* \* \*

By the time Jessica reached *Bachelor's Delight*, the wind had freshened and the clouds had gone dark and ominous. As she was putting out the bumpers between the hull and the dock, the rain began to fall in gray sheets, getting into her eyes even though she'd raised the hood of her foul-weather jacket. She did her best to ignore the occasional flash of lightning, pushing Topher's warning aside. Instead, she counted the beats between the flash and the thunder. The storm, for all its fury, was still miles away.

She had just wrapped the last bungee cord around the mainsail when Topher came limping down the path, moving faster than she thought possible. He clambered aboard and shouted at her in a commanding voice that she immediately resented. "Go back to the light."

She didn't budge as he pulled himself up on the fore-deck and started disconnecting the jib. She'd be damned if she was going to leave him here alone. He could get swept off the deck and drown.

Her heart hammered the whole time Topher stood out there on the slippery deck, while visions of the wind blowing him overboard played in her mind.

But he proved amazingly steady, like the calm eye of a hurricane. Like the strong but gentle man who'd just held her up in her worst of all possible moments.

The myth was so seductive. She could feel desire rising up in her. After so many wounds, so many empty years, was it truly possible to find a soul mate?

No. She didn't believe that crap. He wasn't some long-lost part of herself who could see inside and know her true self. He was just Topher Martin, the one-time captain of the football team.

But this Topher, the scarred man, was a great deal more complicated than the boy had been. And something about him drew her like a moth to a flame.

The analogy was apt because a girl could get burned thinking the thoughts that were filling her head as he stood there defying the wind and the rain.

He finished his task and turned toward the cockpit, spying her there. "Why the hell are you still here?" he yelled into the wind.

She could hardly tell him that she'd been hanging around in case something bad happened to him and he needed to be rescued. So she threw all caution to the wind and said the first outrageous thing that came into her mind. "I was watching you be all manly and stuff."

He stopped moving, that blue eye catching her gaze and holding it as a deep, unwanted surge of awareness flooded her. Oh, she was such an idiot.

"We should get back up to the lighthouse," he said in a gruff voice as he hopped down into the cockpit. "You run ahead. I'll be along in a minute with supplies."

He headed down the ship's ladder.

"Supplies?" she called down to him. She could just see him moving around in the galley.

"That storm looks like it might take a while to pass. Now get your ass back up to the light."

He looked up at her with that single cobalt eye. She'd just been commanded, and as always that tone of voice brought out her inner rebel.

Daddy had done his best to slay that rebel, but she still

lived. It was that rebellious girl inside her that insisted she befriend Colton a second time despite the never-ending gossip, who had walked away from a steady job to risk everything on her own business, who still showed up weekly for tea with Granny in hopes of, one day, getting an apology.

So she didn't hop to Topher's command. She held her ground even though the rain was doing its best to soak through her jacket and an icy trickle was inching down her back.

He was pulling stuff out of the small refrigerator and off a pantry shelf. He turned, seeing her at the top of the ladder. "What the hell? Go get out of the rain."

"But I can help. I'm not some weak female, you know. I've had trouble in my life, but I have survived."

"Me too."

"What?"

"I'm *fine,* dammit. I don't need your help, either."

She blinked. Maybe this wasn't about her following orders. Maybe this was about him feeling competent.

Whoa. She needed to get out of her own way. And his too, evidently.

"Okay. But—"

"What?" He glared.

She refrained from telling him to be careful. But deep inside, she earnestly hoped that he would be. Because she was worried about him.

She *cared* about him.

And that's why she turned and headed up the path to the lighthouse. The rain was coming down horizontally by the time she made it back. The interior was dark now that the storm had closed in.

She was drenched. Completely soaked from the thighs

down and definitely damp even where the jacket was supposed to protect her. A chill crept over her, but she stood by the door waiting for him.

It was a good ten minutes before a gray shape loomed out of the rain, moving with an uneven gait. He was carrying a bright-orange duffel bag over his shoulder, and he looked like a sailor coming home from a long voyage.

"I brought stuff," he said in a breathless voice that telegraphed how hard the climb had been from the dock. He dropped the big bag to the slate floor, and then he pulled off his dripping-wet jacket and limped to the first of the stairs, where he sat down hard.

She didn't say a word. Instead, she tackled the duffel, which turned out to be one of those waterproof bags with a fold-over top and a buckle.

She clawed her way into it with icy fingers and found a couple of blankets on the top and a collection of Clif Bars and soda cans on the bottom.

She pulled a blanket from the bag and wrapped it around her shoulders, then carried the second one over to Topher.

He was soaked, despite his jacket. Water slicked his hair and spiked the lashes of his eye. He stood up as she approached.

His high-performance sailing shirt accentuated the planes and angles of his chest. Maybe he was just getting back to an exercise regimen, but there wasn't an ounce of fat on the man. He had a sinewy, wiry look to him.

The sudden desire to cook him a steak dinner came over her, along with other desires she didn't want to acknowledge. What the heck was wrong with her?

She studied his scars and eye patch while emotions tugged at her. A moment ago, he'd proven that he was strong enough to withstand a storm. Strong enough to hold her up while she poured out every toxic memory and emotion that dwelled behind her protective barriers.

He could seduce her. He could confuse her. He could see through her, and that was frightening.

And yet, when he took a step toward her, bringing much-needed body heat with him, she just wanted to rest her head on his shoulder.

She wanted to surrender to that strength. To the kindness she'd somehow found in the most unlikely of places. To his gentleness.

She stood there, rooted to the floor as he approached. She ought to run as fast as she could, but she couldn't move.

And when he cupped her cheek in his hand, she leaned into the touch, which warmed her from the inside out as no blanket could.

When it finally arrived, his kiss was firm and unhurried. He lingered on her lips for the longest time before delving inside. It was a luscious kiss that made her bones go watery until he backed away and strung smaller kisses across her cheek and down into the hollow of her neck. The brush of beard against skin sent a cascade of shivers down her back.

The touch of his tongue along her collarbone was so deliciously warm that she let go of an inarticulate hum in the back of her throat and buried her nose in his damp hair, where the scent of vanilla and rain leaped from his too-warm skin.

But when she expected him to move on with his seduction, he backed up.

*No! Don't go. Come back to me. Finish the job.* She wanted to scream the words at him, but his kiss had stolen her ability to think, to speak, to do anything but stand there and feel, while the wind battered the lighthouse and the rain drummed on the copper roof way overhead.

* * *

He stopped himself. She wasn't like the other women in his life. The ones who had flocked to him before he'd been injured. Or like Marla, the woman he'd been engaged to when he'd wrecked the Ferrari.

Those women had come to him because he was a football star, because he had money. He'd never had to work to attract a woman. And even though he'd never been a player like some of his business partners, he'd never had to work at seduction.

And that was the thing. He didn't want to seduce Jessica. God only knew, he was the last man on earth she would want to spend time with. No. He wanted her to come to him of her own accord.

It was a stupid thought. An impossible thought. But he was the champion of impossible thoughts these days. Impossible to think he could live out here alone when he'd just proved to himself that maybe he could.

Impossible to build a house like Granddad wanted, and yet Jessica had a vision that his grandfather would have loved. He would build his house. It wasn't so impossible.

So why not think that this woman, who had good reason to blame him and everyone else at Rutledge High for a vicious rumor that had deeply hurt her, could find enough forgiveness to see him?

Not as some kind of monster. But as a man who was beginning to believe that she was the one. The one he'd always been meant to find. What he felt right now was nothing like he'd ever felt for Marla. Marla hadn't been able to look at his scars. She'd walked away when he'd needed her most.

Jessica cocked her head, her gaze fixed on his left side. What was she thinking? Was she like Marla? Did she think he was a monster?

But then she did the unexpected. Jessica traced one of his scars with her finger, her touch electric as it slid over his damaged skin. He flinched back, not in physical pain, but in shock.

"What?" she whispered.

*Don't mock me*, he wanted to say, but only the word "don't" came out of his mouth.

"But they are part of you."

"Not my better parts."

She pulled her hand away, and for an instant he thought she might say something. He yearned for her to say anything that would signal that she wanted the same thing he did.

But she didn't speak. She turned and paced with rigid shoulders back to the duffel bag. "I'm starved," she said, pulling one of the Clif Bars from the sack.

"You want one?" She glanced over her shoulder.

"Yeah." He was hungry, but not for food.

She tossed one of the bars in his direction. He caught it and then retreated to the bottom step, sinking down on the hard iron while he ate.

He waited, watching her fold the duffel into quarters and then use it to insulate her butt from the cold flagstone floor. Would she say anything about what had just happened?

Or would they pretend it hadn't happened at all?

Maybe pretending was better than hearing her say that she wasn't interested. Or that she could never forgive him for repeating stupid stories about her.

But maybe he could make amends in his own way. He could certainly exact revenge on the guy most likely to have started that rumor. He had that much within his power.

And best of all, she would never have to know that he'd been the instrument of Caleb Tate's downfall.

# *Chapter Sixteen* ─────────

The weather on Monday afternoon had turned soggy. So Ashley found herself sitting inside the small seating area of Bread, Butter and Beans across the table from Peggy Fiedler, the executive director of the Moonlight Bay Conservation Society, who looked nothing like Ashley expected.

Peggy wore her gray hair pulled back into a low bun and gazed at Ashley above the rims of a pair of half-moon reading glasses tethered to her neck with a beaded chain.

Her cheeks were round and pink and her eyes, a sharp, lively blue as they inspected Ashley. "So you want me to stop this project," Peggy said in a froggy voice, suggesting that she'd been a lifelong smoker.

"I do. Don't you have concerns? Harry Bauman told me you were opposed to most development," Ashley said.

Peggy laughed, her eyes twinkling. "Did he say that?"

"He said you were a force to be reckoned with." Although Peggy didn't look like anything of the kind. She looked like a sweet grandmother.

"I'll take that as a compliment."

"So? Can you help me?"

"I get the feeling you're not exactly interested in conservation."

"I care about rising sea levels as much as anyone. I also have other reasons for stopping this project." Ashley leaned forward. "For one thing, the house he wants to build is going to be a monstrosity. I found the architectural renderings in the cottage. I took some photos of them." She pulled out her cell phone and handed it to the activist.

Ashley had taken the photos yesterday when she'd sneaked into the cottage after church, while Topher had been playing catch with Jackie on the lawn. Guilt wormed through her.

She'd given up trying to keep Topher and Jackie apart. For one thing, their growing relationship seemed to be good for both of them, their mutual interest in Captain William Teal notwithstanding.

Her guilt intensified while Peggy studied the images on her phone. "This looks like the castle at Disney World."

Ashley nodded and warmed her suddenly cold hands around her coffee cup.

"Why didn't you start with the fact that he wants to build a theme park castle out there?" A note of outrage filled Peggy's voice.

"I know. He's a bit misguided."

"*Misguided?* It's insane."

Ashley put down her coffee cup. "Look, I don't want him to become a laughingstock for building a silly castle out there. The truth is, I care a great deal about Topher. I'm hoping it won't take much opposition to dissuade him."

Peggy gave her another sharp look. "Well, it won't take much to convince people to oppose a project like this. Can you send me the photos?"

"Sure." Ashley picked up her phone and emailed the photos to Peggy, who finished her cappuccino in one big swallow, leaving a milk mustache on her upper lip.

"I'll be in touch," Peggy said, wiping her mouth and reaching for her purse.

"Uh, it might be best if we weren't in touch. You know?" Ashley said.

The woman stood up, slinging her big leather bag over her shoulder. Her twinkly eyes turned icy. "I do know, but you have to realize that your cousin is going to figure out how we got these photos. You can't really avoid being involved."

Ashley's heart squeezed. "I guess."

Peggy gave her a long, hard look, the grandmother vibe vanishing. Ashley wouldn't want to get into a fight with this woman. "Well, the die is cast," Peggy said before she turned and headed through the door, leaving Ashley alone.

She stared into her almost-empty cup for a moment, lost in guilty memories of a time, long ago, when she and Timothy, her oldest cousin, had been mean to Topher. She remembered Grandmother scolding her about how kindness was a virtue.

Was she being unkind? No. Her motives were pure, even if her methods were a little off the straight and narrow. This gambit would work.

It would be just what Topher needed to realize how futile it was to run away from the world. And once he gave up on this idea of building on Lookout Island, maybe she could suggest that he buy a house in town.

She finished her coffee and checked her watch. It was getting toward three in the afternoon, and she needed to get back to the inn. It was still raining as she left the coffeehouse, but not quite as hard as it had been. She opened her umbrella and headed up Tulip Street in the direction of Harbor Drive.

As she walked, the wind kicked up again, and the rain got heavier. Off to the west, the clouds were darkening. The weatherman said to expect thunderstorms all day. She quickened her pace, the wind playing games with her umbrella.

The rain was beginning to fall again in earnest when she reached the traffic light at the intersection across the street from the library. The traffic light caught her, and she was forced to stand there, her feet getting wet, as she waited.

When the light finally changed, she dashed across the street, stepping in ankle-high water that sloshed through her shoes. Just as she reached the other side of the street, her darling child, dressed in his yellow rain slicker, came bouncing through the library doors in the company of Rev. Micah St. Pierre.

"Jackson Howland Scott," she said, rounding on her son, "what in the Sam Hill are you doing here? You told me you were hanging out with Topher this afternoon."

The two culprits stopped in their tracks, hand-in-the-cookie-jar looks on their faces.

She turned on the minister. "And shame on you for encouraging him when you know how I feel about Rose Howland's letters."

Just then, before either of them could explain themselves, a sudden gust hit, tugging at Ashley's umbrella and turning it backward.

"Damn," she swore, struggling to get the umbrella to turn right-side out. But before she could accomplish that, the skies opened in a deluge, and Micah pulled her under the protection of his own big, black golf umbrella.

She found herself way too close to him, just as she

realized that she'd said the word "damn" in his presence. If she were still standing out in the rain, the drops would be turning to steam as they hit her suddenly too-hot cheeks.

She hid her embarrassment behind annoyance. "Do you want to explain yourself?" she asked.

"Uh, well..." the minister began, but he was saved by the wind a second time. Another gust hit them, sending sheets of water sideways, evading even the Rev's gigantic umbrella.

"Uh, let's get under cover," he said.

It seemed like a reasonable idea. So Ashley pulled up the hood on her raincoat and then took off down the street, making a mad dash up to Howland House, about three blocks away.

"Where's Topher?" she asked Jackie when they reached the shelter of the portico.

"Um, well, I kind of didn't tell you the truth."

"You weren't hanging out with Topher?"

Jackie shook his head. "Topher went sailing today. He told me he was going to the island."

"What?" Ashley gazed up at the sky just as lightning jumped from one cloud to another. An ominous crack of thunder followed.

She turned back toward her son as worry of an entirely different kind surged through her. "You are grounded for the foreseeable future. Now, go to your room." She pointed toward the inn's door. "And take off your wet shoes before you track up the floors," she added in her best authoritative-mom voice.

As her son hightailed it to the door, she turned back to the Rev. "And what's your excuse?"

"I didn't know he was supposed to be with Topher," Micah said, also glancing at the storm. "He knocked at my door around noon and said that you had an unexpected appointment. He asked me if I'd accompany him to the library."

"And you took him, when you knew I had expressly forbidden him from reading those letters?" She stared up into the Rev's dark eyes, wanting desperately to be furious with the man but finding it impossible to accomplish.

Micah St. Pierre was a kind and thoughtful man. A better Christian than she would ever be. And he had the most beautiful—

No. She stopped herself from even thinking it. Noticing the minister's good looks was probably a sin, or stupid, or something.

"I'm sorry," he said. "But maybe you should go down to the library and read the letters yourself. They are an interesting glimpse into history."

"Even if this history feeds Jackie's fantasy about the ghost of Captain Teal?"

Micah smiled, folding a dimple into one cleanly shaven cheek. "It's a shame you've lost your faith."

"Since when are ghosts an article of faith?"

"Aren't they?" he asked.

She turned her back on him. "Fine. Be that way. Just quit encouraging him, okay? He needs to give up this fixation on Captain Bill."

"Have you thought, for one minute, that reading real history might help him do that? There isn't anything in the letters that confirms the existence of a ghost."

She turned and tried to glare at him. "Stop. I know you mean well. But I also know you are keenly interested in those letters. And I can't help but feel that you used Jackie to satisfy your own curiosity."

He straightened as if she'd physically assaulted him.

"Oh. Okay," he said, his voice suddenly as hard and cold as the rain pouring down around them. "So it's okay for the Howlands to keep their secrets, but the St. Pierres, who also helped establish this town, are not allowed to be curious about history? Is that it?"

"No. Of course not."

"Oh. Excuse me. Because I thought I heard you imply that." He turned and ran out into the storm as another flash of lightning lit up the gray day, followed almost immediately by a loud *boom*.

Her heart sprang to her throat as she watched the Rev dashing through the storm, the wind whipping his suit jacket as he ran.

She didn't leave her spot until he made it to the rectory's front door. Only then did she hurry inside and up the stairs to Jackie's bedroom to give the child a piece of her mind. Not about Captain Bill, but about the subject of honesty and truthfulness.

After that she placed a call to Harry Bauman, who had contacts with the Coast Guard, alerting him to the fact that Topher might be out on the bay in this heavy weather.

\* \* \*

Jessica didn't know how to read Topher. He'd kissed her. She'd let him. And then he'd retreated to his corner like some grumpy beast and gone quiet.

What did that mean exactly? She didn't know, and she had precious little experience to draw from. She wasn't good at this sort of thing.

Had she failed the kiss test?

That was a little depressing. She'd never failed a kiss test before. In her somewhat limited experience, it usually didn't take guys much to want to take something to the next level.

Topher was the kind of man who got what he wanted. So if he'd backed away, it must mean that he wasn't interested. Which was fine. Because she didn't want to get involved with him.

Much.

If she could have found a private space and a cell phone signal, she might have called Hillary and asked her opinion. The guy had been kind of great when she'd had her meltdown.

And his kiss had been...

Was it hyperbole to say that the earth had moved? No kiss had ever moved her that way.

She sat on the folded duffel, the cold floor still seeping into her backside. If he didn't say something soon, she was going to go crazy.

So she fell back on what she knew best and started babbling about how she was going to restore the light.

They managed to talk about the house for the next few hours while the storm raged. And when it finally began to clear, Topher got up from his perch on the staircase and limped to the door.

"Well, it looks like the worst of it's passed over, although the bay is still choppy and the winds are pretty high."

He checked his watch.

"I'm thinking we should get the weather report. If it's going to be this rough, maybe we should sleep on the boat and go back in the morning."

She swallowed into a suddenly dry throat. Was that his plan? To take her down to the party boat he claimed had been decorated by his business partner and...

He turned, and as if reading her thoughts, he said,

"There's a nice guest cabin down there. We'll be more comfortable, so long as we don't get another thunderstorm."

"Okay," she said, pushing up from the floor.

"And there are a couple of box lunches in the refrigerator. I didn't bring them up here earlier because I didn't have space in the duffel."

So they went back to the boat, ate their lunches, checked the latest weather report, and decided to wait before returning to Magnolia Harbor.

She ended up going to her cabin early, where she tossed and turned all night as the wind buffeted the boat.

# Chapter Seventeen

When Jessica opened her eyes the next morning, sunlight peeped through the porthole and the scent of coffee hung in the air.

Coffee? Where had he come up with coffee? Last night they'd consumed all their food—and had both gone to bed hungry, in more ways than one.

She sat up in the small bed that wasn't nearly as impressive as the one in the captain's cabin.

And then it hit her. Everyone would know they'd been caught out in a storm. Would the Magnolia Harbor grapevine be buzzing about the fact that they'd spent a night out here together? And how did she feel about that?

She didn't know. Maybe a little numb and confused. But she was pretty sure Topher's family would be upset. They didn't want her designing a house for him, and she was willing to bet they would be appalled if they knew he'd kissed her.

But it didn't matter. Tongues would be wagging by the time she got back to town. It was a given, considering her completely undeserved reputation.

She let go of a deep sigh. Maybe she should consider the job offer from Damon Brant. His secretary had followed up, and Jessica was scheduled to make a quick trip to Miami in a few days to meet with him and his partners.

She got up, pulling on her rumpled clothes. Out in the galley, Topher was whistling.

Whistling?

She didn't think of him as the kind of guy who whistled. Did anyone whistle anymore? It seemed like an old-fashioned thing to do. But it sounded happy.

Now, that was a word she wouldn't have applied to the man. He wasn't a happy person, and she supposed he had plenty of reasons not to be.

She jammed her feet into her Keen sandals before she opened the cabin door, which led through a short passageway to the galley.

"You had coffee and didn't tell me?" she said as she entered the small cabin and got her first morning look at him. His hair was kind of a mess, his beard a little scruffier than yesterday, but his blue eye still burned with a fire that ignited a deep yearning right in the middle of her belly.

"Morning, sunshine," he said, his voice a little low and rough. "I found some in one of the cabinets. We don't have any sugar or cream though."

"I can deal," she said, trying not to look him in the eye.

He reached for the electric coffeemaker's carafe and poured the magic elixir of life into a mug that had the boat's name printed on it in navy blue.

Their fingers brushed in the exchange, the jolt of awareness now familiar. She was going down, and she didn't even want to swim hard.

"So, what time is it?" she asked.

"We've overslept. It's after ten o'clock, and the wind has died. So drink up, me hearty. We need to sail back to Magnolia Harbor."

* * *

Topher left the galley, his heart thundering in his chest. His throat thick with emotions he didn't want to have right now. She hadn't said one word about what had happened yesterday.

She'd gone back behind her mask. And he might never see the real Jessica—the angry one, the vulnerable one, the one he wanted to hold, the one he wanted to love—again.

So here he was, standing on the foredeck reconnecting the jib to the halyard and getting ready to rush back to the harbor.

What else could he do? Tell her what was in his heart? Never. She'd run from him like a frightened rabbit.

He shackled the sail to the halyard and made his way aft, where he got busy removing the bungee cords from the mainsail. She joined him a few minutes later, her gaze carefully averted.

She was nimble as she helped him rig the boat, and it made his heart sing to see her moving so easily through the mass of lines and blocks. He could imagine a future, sailing with her. He could imagine...

A lot of things that weren't going to happen.

In less than fifteen minutes, they had the boat shipshape and headed out in the main channel, sailing wing on wing on a run to the harbor. He kept his gaze fixed ahead. He didn't trust himself to look at her.

About ten minutes into their sail, they were hailed by a Coast Guard patrol boat. Topher pulled up and pointed

*Bachelor's Delight* into the wind, stalling their progress while the patrol boat came within hailing distance.

"*Bachelor's Delight*, are you all right?" someone shouted over a megaphone.

"We're fine. We anchored at Lookout Island overnight and weathered the storm there," he shouted back.

"Glad to hear it. There are a lot of people on Jonquil Island worried about you."

"Oh no," Jessica muttered.

"We're fine. We'll be back home shortly."

The sailors aboard the patrol boat waved and headed west, leaving them.

"Look," he said, allowing himself to gaze at her, "I'm sure someone is going to gossip about this, but we both know that we were out on the island for professional reasons."

She cocked her head. Would she mention his kiss or her tears? He waited, hoping, but she didn't. She nodded her agreement instead.

"Good. We're on the same page, then," he said, and set a course for the harbor.

When they reached the marina, she left the boat quickly, without a lot of chitchat. So he was right. She was scared and running for her life. He didn't blame her.

He stood in the cockpit and watched her walk away, knowing himself for a fool. Maybe he should have forced the issue. Maybe if he'd seduced her, she might—

No.

It had to be her choice. Nothing else would do.

He let go of a bitter laugh, remembering something that Erik Sokal, his ex-business partner, had said to him when he'd first seen the scars. Erik, who'd never been terribly sensitive or politically correct, had told Topher it was a good thing he had money. Because women found money attractive.

Yeah. He knew a lot of women like that. But they weren't the ones he wanted in his life. And he certainly didn't want to buy Jessica's affection.

He shook his head and went back to work tidying the boat. When everything was shipshape, he made the long, painful walk down the pier to his car.

It was almost noon by the time he got back to Rose Cottage. He found his spot on the porch and started making calls.

Erik was call number one. His ex-partner came on the line with an enthusiastic greeting. "Hey, man, how are you doing? Have you had a chance to take *Bachelor's Delight* out?"

"Yeah. Just came back from a long sail. She's pretty sweet. Look, I need a favor."

"Whatever it is."

"I know you have contacts with most of the heavy hitters in the real estate sector. I need to figure out what Representative Caleb Tate is up to."

"Oh. Is he up to something?"

"Yes. The other night he told me there was a consortium that's planning a big development out here on Jonquil Island. I got the feeling it was hush-hush. I tried to get details, but he was as vague as a politician can be."

"You want to know who the other players are?"

"I want to know everything. I'm trying to figure out what a state representative is doing up to his neck in a secret development scheme. He seemed to be looking for capital."

"Can I ask why you care?"

"I'm living out here these days, Erik. And Jonquil Island is a paradise. I'd like to keep it that way."

"There was a time when all you cared about was the return on investment."

"I'm a different man now."

"I'm on it. Anything for you, man."

"Keep this inquiry quiet, okay?"

"Sure."

"And I need the information as quick as you can get it."

"Aye, Cap'n," Erik said.

They spent a few more minutes talking about old times and common friends and acquaintances, but Topher abruptly ended the call when Ashley emerged from Howland House's back door and headed across the rose garden looking like a woman on a mission.

He stood up and met her at the porch stairs. "Hey," he said. "In case you've come to give me grief for taking the boat out yesterday, you should know that when the weather got bad, we battened down the hatches and stayed put on the island. I was never in any danger. And I wasn't alone."

"You were with someone?"

Oh God, he'd stepped in it. But he was going to stick with the story. "I sailed out there with Jessica Blackwood."

"Oh, I should have known. The *house*." She said the word as if it was the vilest curse in the universe.

"We were fine. I was fine. Everything was under control." Sort of.

"Okay, but it might surprise you that I didn't come out here to bawl you out or to nag you."

"No?" He managed a smile.

"No. I came out here in desperation."

"Really?" He leaned on the porch rail.

"I have a favor to ask."

He tried not to grin. He'd never had any leverage over his older cousin. If he were a different sort of man, he'd walk away from her. But life was built on favors. He'd done plenty of them, and he'd called in chits when it mattered.

"How can I be of service?" he asked.

She rolled her eyes.

"I mean it. Just ask, Ashley." This time his voice held a note of annoyance.

"Jackie's therapist just called and wanted to switch his appointment to this afternoon. He goes on Wednesdays. Anyway, I'm in the middle of baking a red velvet cake. The ladies are coming and—"

"You need me to drive him to his appointment?"

"I would be so grateful. I would normally ask Sandra or Karen, but both of them are off in Charleston this week for the South Carolina quilters' guild meeting. And I'm peeved at the minister right at the moment."

"Peeved?" She sounded just like Aunt Mary, using that old-fashioned word when pissed-off would have worked just as well.

"Yes. And since Jackie likes you so much, I'm willing to overlook your lapses."

"Gee, thanks," he said, but he managed a smile.

* * *

By the time Jessica went home, showered, and dressed for work, it was after noon. She grabbed some lunch and headed into the office.

Exhausted from her fitful night aboard *Bachelor's Delight*, she almost wished she hadn't moved her office downtown. It would have been nice to spend the day lounging around a home office in her pj's.

Of course, if she moved to Florida, her commute would be much worse. The traffic in Magnolia Harbor could be bad on a summer weekend but not like Miami.

Chalk another point up in the old hometown's favor.

She settled at her desk and started transcribing notes from the conversation she'd had with Topher during the storm. His house was definitely taking shape, and this time it would be a place filled with light and comfort—a place she'd love to visit.

That stopped her. Was it the house or its owner? She stared down at her first sketch of the house, done in pencil. It didn't look like a place where a broken man would go to brood.

But Topher wasn't nearly as broken as he seemed. In fact, it might even be the case that Topher was more whole and complete than she'd ever be.

She focused on the work and was about to transfer her rough sketch into her CAD system when the door to the street opened.

This time more than one set of footsteps came up the stairs, and they didn't take them two at a time.

"Jessica, are you here?" Granny's unmistakable voice floated up from the stairwell.

Goodness, the mountain had come to Mohammad, hadn't it? Jessica had never expected Granny to set foot in her office. Ever.

She pushed up from her desk and met her grandmother at the top of the stairs. Behind Granny, Aunt Donna followed, her face a little red as she climbed.

"I declare," Donna said. "The next time you lease an office, find one with an elevator."

Granny strode past Jessica, into the unfinished room. "Well," she said with an unmistakable sniff, "you haven't really done much with this place, have you?"

"No, Granny," Jessica said as she swallowed back her annoyance and moved toward the conference table. "Come on in and make yourself comfortable. I've got Cokes and water in the fridge. Can I get y'all something?"

"No," Granny said in a grumpy tone as she plopped herself down in a chair. "Sit down, Jessica. We need to talk."

Jessica was tempted to tell Granny to stop issuing orders. It struck her right then that the rebellious girl that had once gotten Colton into trouble hadn't really disappeared. She hadn't been reformed. She hadn't been forgiven. And she hadn't really forgiven anyone for what had happened to her.

No. That wounded child had only been on vacation. She'd returned, and she was angry.

But Jessica was still in charge of that rebellious spirit. So she didn't make a scene. She sat down. But not because Granny had ordered her to do so.

Aunt Donna huffed across the room and sat down too, taking out a Kleenex and mopping her slightly damp forehead and upper lip.

"I suppose you are aware that the whole town is talking about you," Granny said.

Wow, that hadn't taken any time at all. But Jessica pretended innocence. "I have no idea what you mean. I've been busy with—"

"Yes, you obviously have been busy. And I'm sure you know what I'm talking about, so don't pretend you don't. You went out to that island with Christopher Martin, and you didn't come back until the next morning."

Jessica leveled a defiant gaze at her grandmother. "We went out there to take some measurements and to talk about his project. We were caught in a storm. We decided to anchor overnight. What did you want us to do, Granny, capsize?"

"There's no need to get ugly, Jessi—"

"Barbara, let me handle this," Donna interceded.

Granny gave her sister an imperious look but shut her mouth for once. Jessica was two seconds away from telling both of them to get the heck out of her office. The job offer from Damon Brant was looking better by the minute.

Donna put her elbows on the table. "Honey, we're not here to bawl you out."

"No?"

"Absolutely not," Granny said in a tone that almost sounded reasonable.

What the heck? She turned to study her grandmother, and it struck her that their relationship was built on a lie. Jessica had returned to the family fold but only after apologizing for something that had never really happened. While Granny had never apologized for something that had.

"Honey," Donna said in a kindly voice, "just take a big breath. The gossip isn't entirely bad, you know."

Jessica bit her lip and said nothing even though she had a strong desire to cross the bridge and burn it down behind her.

"Of course it's not bad. He's rich, and he's a Martin," Granny said.

"What?" Jessica sat straighter in her chair. What the heck were they talking about anyway?

"We're here to help you land the fish," Donna said.

"Land the fish?"

"Oh, for goodness' sake. Are you stupid?" Granny asked.

"I am not—"

Donna put up a hand. "Of course she's not stupid. But I think we can all agree that you are inexperienced."

"At what?"

"Seduction, my dear," Aunt Donna said.

Jessica was rendered utterly speechless.

"Don't play coy," Granny said. "You know good and well what we mean. Christopher Martin has money, connections, and a family name that means something. You could become the most important woman in this town if you handled this right, and that's saying something considering the way you behaved as a teenager."

Jessica pulled in a breath and pushed another one out. She didn't dare say one word for fear that something truly ugly would come out of her mouth.

"Christopher Martin is a man like your grandfather and your father," Granny continued obliviously. "If you played your cards right, you could be a true Cinderella. You could have it all. And all you'd have to do is overlook the scars. We're here to convince you that his scars are a very small price to pay in return for what he could do for you."

Jessica went cold. At first she wanted to scream at them and tell them that his scars weren't all that bad and certainly nothing she'd ever have to "get over."

And then it hit her like a gale-force wind that Granny was right. Topher was a lot like Daddy. He had money and an important family name. He was used to giving commands. He could get angry and rude at times. He was used to being obeyed. The thought made her tremble as she pushed up from the table.

"I'm really sorry to disappoint you, but Topher is my

client. That's it. I suggest you avoid listening to or repeating the gossip in this town. Now, if you don't mind, I have work to do."

"But, darling, you—"

"I don't want to be Cinderella. It didn't work out for you, did it, Granny? And it certainly didn't work out for Momma. Why on earth would I go looking for the same tarnished nightmare? Now, please leave."

* * *

Later that afternoon, Topher picked up Jackie at school and drove him to the mainland. The kid had nothing much to say during the drive, and Topher felt for him.

He certainly hadn't wanted to get Jackie into hot water with his mother. He wished that Micah St. Pierre had kept his mouth shut about Rose Howland's letters.

After several futile attempts at getting the kid to talk, Topher drove all the way to the mainland in near silence. But as he walked the boy into the medical building for his appointment, Jackie looked up at him and said, "You know, the main public library is just around the corner. One time, we were way early for my appointment, and Mom took me there. You can walk from here."

Topher gave the kid his best parental look, which seemed to bounce off Jackie like bullets off Superman. "Oh no. I'm not going to get you into trouble again."

"I'm not asking you to get me into trouble. You can stay outside and I'll go read some of the letters."

"And you can suddenly read handwriting?"

The kid gave him an adorable look. "Please. Come on, Mom doesn't have to know."

"No."

"We could look at the real letters. The web page says this library has a local history room with all kinds of old books."

"Did you look that up on the internet?"

The kid nodded, proving that he was smarter than the average kid.

"You know I promised your mother not to let you read any more of those letters," Topher said.

"Yeah, I guess. But we don't have to read letters. Maybe they have some old books. I still need a topic for my Heritage Day project."

The kid had a point. "I'll think about it."

They got on the elevator, and the kid looked up at him again. "There's one other thing."

"Yeah."

"The cap'n wants me to visit that library and see what's there."

The elevator doors opened with a *ding*. They exited and strolled down the hallway in silence until they got to the doctor's office.

Topher stopped right outside the door. "So, are you planning to tell the doctor about this?"

"No," the kid said, rolling his eyes. "Dr. Robinson freaks out every time I mention the cap'n's name. I figured that out the first week. So now I come here and tell him I don't ever talk to the cap'n anymore."

"You lie to the doctor?"

The kid shrugged. "Yeah. I guess. Don't tell Mom. She'll kill me if she ever finds out."

"I won't tell your mom. And if you want, we can go to the library and see what kind of books they have on local history. But...no letters. Is that clear?"

An hour later, Topher found himself in the reading room at the public library, bent over an old "commonplace" book that had once belonged to Rose Howland.

And since it wasn't technically one of Rose's letters, he and Jackie were safe. Of course, there was no way to explain how Jackie knew this diary was in the Howland collection—unless you believed in a ghost.

The boy had waltzed right up to the librarian's desk and asked to see Rose Howland's books. And the librarian had asked to see his library card. And that was that.

Kind of creepy. Or supernatural. Or something.

"What does it say?" the boy asked.

Topher studied the pages, which were dark with age, the brown ink fading in spots. But the handwriting, though cramped in places, was familiar.

The book had more than a hundred pages, so they didn't have time to read it from cover to cover. He scanned the pages, many of which seemed to contain copies of several of Shakespeare's sonnets. All of them about love.

Rose was clearly a romantic.

Interspersed with the poetry were notations about her efforts to secure daffodil bulbs. "There's a lot of stuff about daffodils in here," he said aloud. "You could probably do a whole report on that alone." He glanced at Jackie.

The kid wrinkled his nose and shook his head.

Topher turned several more pages containing recipes for rabbit and squirrel stew. Then back to more poetry that he didn't recognize. Followed by a notation about where Henri St. Pierre was planting the daffodils in the autumn of 1720.

And then, on a page dated November 1720, was this notation: *Abimael arrived today in the early morning.*

The words were set apart on a new page. Which was odd, because Rose clearly regarded the paper in this book as precious.

"Do you know anything about a person named Abimael?" Topher asked Jackie.

The boy shook his head. "That's a funny name."

"I think it's Biblical. But I don't remember anyone in the history of Jonquil Island with that name."

"Maybe Abimael was one of Henri St. Pierre's pirate friends. I mean, Abimael kind of sounds like a pirate name, doesn't it?"

"It sounds more like the opening line of *Moby Dick*."

"Huh?"

"Never mind," Topher said. "One day some English teacher will make you read that book and you'll understand. Anyway, I guess we don't want to waste time researching this Abimael character, do we?"

The kid shook his head.

Topher went back to turning pages, skimming endless lines of poetry, recipes, and notations on tides and daffodil planting. And then, a few pages before the writing stopped altogether, there was a hastily scrawled note.

*You will find what you are looking for in the usual place, five paces west of the marker. Take care of what belongs to Abimael.*

Topher read the passage out loud, his heart suddenly racing. "Holy sh—" He caught himself before laying an s-bomb within hearing of tender ears.

"That's it," the boy said, leaning forward to look at the words scrawled across the yellowing paper. "That's like a treasure map, right?"

"It certainly reads like one." Topher took out his cell phone and took a photo of the page.

"Where do you think the marker is? And who did she want to find the book?" Jackie asked.

"Well, she wrote the note in 1721," Topher said. "I'm thinking she must have written it to Henri St. Pierre, since he was the only other person living on the island at that time."

"Okay." The boy frowned.

"Yeah, I know. How did a book that was supposed to be found by Henri St. Pierre end up in the library?"

"Maybe Henri never found the book."

Topher nodded, suddenly captured by the mystery.

"What do you think the marker is?" Jackie asked.

"If you want my first guess, I'd say it's the tree."

The man and the boy locked gazes for a moment.

"Because the ghost hangs out there?" the boy asked.

"Have you got a better reason?"

# *Chapter Eighteen* ————————

Jessica was so angry with Granny and Aunt Donna that she programmed her cell phone to send their calls directly to voice mail. She spent a whole day stewing over the things they'd said while also making plans for her trip to Miami, coming up at the end of the week. She was scheduled to fly out early Thursday morning and would be gone for a couple of days.

Two days away from Magnolia Harbor seemed like a good thing right at the moment.

Everyone was talking about how she'd been marooned with Topher. Half the gossips thought it was wonderfully romantic, and the other half were in a snit because she'd "cheated" on Colton.

Who was, near as she could tell, conducting a stealthy affair with Kerri Eaton. Colton hadn't dropped by the boutique in the last several days. Had he taken it underground, or was he being an idiot and staying away from a woman he clearly had a thing for?

If she were a different sort of person, she might have

started a rumor about them, just to bring them together. But that would have made her the same as Granny and Aunt Donna.

No, Colton would have to manage his own love life. Just like she was managing her own nonexistent one.

The gossips of Magnolia Harbor would be so disappointed to discover that absolutely nothing scandalous had happened on Lookout Island. There had been a kiss, but it hadn't gone anywhere.

And for some reason, Jessica couldn't get that out of her mind. She'd wanted it to go somewhere. But now, thinking over what Granny had said yesterday, she ought to be glad that things turned out the way they had. She certainly didn't want to get involved with a man like her father.

If only she could drive Topher from her mind, but unfortunately she was designing a house for him. So he, and his kiss, were front and center in her thoughts.

She'd just finished the final elevation drawing for Topher's house when her front office door opened.

She tensed, listening for footsteps. It wasn't Granny or Donna, thank goodness. But when Caleb Tate came bounding up the stairs, she almost wished it were.

"Hello, Jessica," he said in a saccharine voice as he crossed the room and captured her side chair without being invited. "I hear you've been a busy girl."

She said nothing as her pulse jumped, pounding at her temples. She wasn't going to feed the gossip. Heck, if she was a stronger person, she'd push him down the stairs and wait ten minutes before calling 911.

The thought was so ugly it stunned her. Was she truly that angry? Maybe. Probably. Her rebellious spirit rose inside her chest, and she pointed her chin at Caleb. "If you don't have business with me, I'd appreciate it if you would leave."

He smiled like a snake in the grass. "Who says I don't have business with you?"

She swallowed hard. "Okay. What can I do for you?"

"It's more a case of what *I* can do for *you*."

"Excuse me?"

He leaned back in his chair, cocking one leg over the opposite knee, taking up his man space. She hated him.

"I'm sure you are aware that I sit on the review committee for the City Hall design competition."

What a jerk. "I am aware of that, yes."

"Well, we've begun to review the submissions. And yours is promising."

"Thank you." She tensed, waiting for the "but."

He smiled again, casting his gaze over her unfinished office space. "You know, I wanted this space. Oh, not for my district office. That's on the mainland. But I have a little side business."

"Uh-huh."

"Just a little business that's in need of capital."

"I don't have any money, Mr. Tate."

"Oh, call me Caleb. We're old friends. I remember you from the yacht club."

A wave of nausea hit her stomach, and she had to grab the arms of her chair to keep the room from spinning. She didn't say anything, but it didn't matter. He wasn't looking for conversation.

"See, the thing is," he continued, "everyone says you have friends in town who *do* have money."

This was about Topher, then. The rumors had brought Caleb here dangling some kind of sweetheart deal, a tit for tat. She remained silent.

He pushed up from the chair. "I think you understand what's needed."

He turned and strolled from her office, leaving her breathless for a solid five minutes before she collected her wits, found her phone, and called her lifeline.

"What?" Hillary said the moment she came on the line.

"I think I've just been offered a bribe."

"Holy... What happened?"

Jessica related the situation, then asked, "What do I do now?"

"Maybe you take the job in Miami?"

She closed her eyes, envisioning a new life far, far away from Caleb Tate and the gossips of Magnolia Harbor.

Yeah, maybe that's what she needed to do. But it was painful to think that the one place on earth where she couldn't stay was her hometown.

And then a vision of Topher came to her, standing out in the rain taking care of his boat, staring down at her as she vented about Daddy, holding her when she cried.

Kissing her.

"Should I tell Topher?" she asked.

"Why would you? He and Caleb Tate deserve each other."

"No," she said in a small voice. "No, I don't think so."

"Holy crap. You've been holding out on me. What exactly happened when you were stranded on that boat? I want to know the whole story."

\* \* \*

A strange lethargy infected Topher on Wednesday. For the first time since he'd gone back to swimming, he woke up in pain and didn't want to move. So he took a pill and slept the morning away.

When he finally dragged himself off to the shower, he was angry—at himself. For backsliding. For taking the pill. But mostly for the aching self-pity that had stolen away his focus. He had a name for this horrible feeling: Jessica.

He didn't want to think about her, but she'd invaded his mind, leaving him with the chastening conclusion that he'd never wanted anything quite as much as he wanted her.

All the successful strategies he'd used in his past life—money, charm, power, his good looks—would never win her. In fact, there was nothing, really, that he could do to make her love him or want him back. And there were no pills that could touch the ache in his heart.

He ate some cold cereal and took up his spot in one of the rockers on the porch, while he called Erik for a status report on Caleb Tate. There was no question about it; the state representative was up to his ass in shady real estate.

He spent the early afternoon making a few calls, talking to some old friends and acquaintances, until Jackie, wearing his school uniform, came racing across the rose garden. The little boy scrambled up onto the porch railing, his cheeks flushed and his eyes alive with youth and innocence.

The pull of gravity lightened a little with the boy's arrival. So maybe Topher would never have the family he'd imagined once. Maybe there would be no kids for him to toss a football with. But this little guy had become his coconspirator, and there was an adventure waiting. The thought lifted his heavy heart.

"Mom's busy doing bookkeeping. She won't come out of her office for hours. We could steal the shovel from the shed."

"Let's do it," he said, pushing himself up from the chair. They purloined the spade and headed out across the grass, the man limping and the boy skipping like a stone over water.

"So what are we going to do with the treasure when we find it?" Jackie asked.

Damn. Topher hadn't really thought about that. What if there was no treasure? Really? Of course there wasn't going to be any treasure. He stopped.

"Look, Jackie, we may never find it, you know?"

"Yeah, I guess."

"Someone may have already found it."

"Yeah, but we might find it."

Oh, such hope. If only he could have hope like that. "Yeah, I guess we could, huh?"

The kid grinned and rushed ahead to the tree.

"Which way is west?" the boy asked.

"That way." Topher pointed toward the bay.

"How big is a pace?"

"Good question. I'm thinking Rose's paces are smaller than mine and bigger than yours."

They stood with their backs against the tree and walked five paces.

"Let's dig," Jackie said.

Topher handed the shovel to the kid. It was almost as big as he was, so he wasn't all that effective even in the sandy soil. After a few minutes Jackie handed the spade back.

"I'm the cap'n. You're the crew," he said. "You dig." He folded his arms across his narrow chest. His school shirt was already dirty, and it occurred to Topher that explaining the dirt might prove difficult. Ashley was going to have Topher's ass in a sling before this escapade was over.

But he was surprised to discover that he didn't care. If Ashley was so sunk in her black-and-white view of the world that she couldn't, for one minute, admit to miracles or pirates or buried treasure, then he felt sorry for her.

He stared down at the boy and decided maybe believing was better than the alternative.

He got to work, digging a three-foot hole but predictably finding nothing. It was a testament to Jackie's wide-eyed innocence that Topher didn't feel immediately discouraged.

"You think someone else found it?" the boy asked, his faith in the treasure palpably real.

"Maybe. Or maybe we didn't go due west. What if we made a trench north and south along this line?" He indicated the direction.

The kid nodded eagerly, and Topher went back to work. He dug for a good twenty minutes—long enough to wonder what failure might do to Jackie's simple faith. Had he made a mistake in following the child's lead?

And then his spade hit something.

"What was that?" The kid's voice almost leaped from his throat.

"Probably a rock," Topher said as he stepped on the spade again. But if it was a rock, it was a big one and made a funny sound against the shovel.

Jackie got down on his knees and started pushing the sand out of the hole with his hands, uncovering a piece of wood that might have been a box once.

The excitement and surprise that washed through Topher almost cauterized his cynicism. Holy crap. They had found something!

Topher got down and helped the boy, his heart pounding in his chest as he dug the cool, sandy soil away from the object, which was a small box about eighteen inches wide and about four inches high.

It wasn't anything like the proverbial treasure chest in pirate movies. The box was flatter and much smaller. And the wood was heavily damaged, falling away in splinters as they tried to excavate it from the soil, leaving only the black corroded hinges and edge details.

"It's falling apart," the boy said in an urgent tone as Topher removed the top portion of the box in several long pieces, revealing several additional objects below.

"What's that?" Jackie asked, pointing to a shiny object that caught the sunlight filtering through the pines.

"It's an inkwell, I think," Topher said, pulling a small cut-glass vial from the hole.

"What's an inkwell?" the kid asked.

He stared up at the child, born in the twenty-first century, and explained about ink and quills. "I think this might have been a writing box."

"What's that?"

"It was a place to keep paper and stuff for writing, and it looks like it had a hinge on the top to provide a slightly angled surface to write on."

"You think this is the box Rose Howland wrote her letters on?"

Damn. The question set Topher back on his heels. What had he just done?

If this was truly an artifact from the eighteenth century, or something that had once been owned and used by Rose Howland, then it deserved to be treated as an archaeological artifact. They should stop digging and start thinking about preserving.

He put the inkwell aside, pulled out his cell phone, and started taking pictures. "I think maybe we should leave this where it is and call someone who knows something about history," he said.

"But...Mom's going to be really unhappy about this."

Topher studied the hole he'd made. He didn't think there was any pirate treasure here. But there was a mystery that needed solving. The only question was whether Ashley wanted to solve it.

"I'm not sure about that. But you can keep it a secret until I talk to her about it."

"Okay. But she can get real mad sometimes."

Topher almost smiled. "I can take it. Don't worry. I'm going to go get a tarp and cover up what we've found for now, and tomorrow I'm going to find someone who knows something about history and archaeology."

"Okay."

"But in the meantime, you should start working on your report. Because I think finding Rose Howland's letter box is cool."

"Not as much fun as finding treasure," the boy said, his voice a little disappointed.

Topher nodded. "I guess that's right," he said, pushing up from the ground and tousling Jackie's mop of hair. Topher had to stop himself from giving the kid a hug.

*Chapter Nineteen*————————

The moo shu pork sitting in the bag on the passenger's seat of her VW made Jessica's mouth water. She'd worked until almost 6:30 p.m. trying to decide what, if anything, to do about Caleb Tate's attempted shakedown.

Hillary thought she should do nothing, but the more Jessica examined the situation and her growing feelings for Topher, the more she felt the need to let Topher know what Caleb was up to.

Deciding to confide in Topher was a big step for her. A few weeks ago, she would have shoved Topher and Caleb into the same pigeonhole. But perspectives change. And Topher had forever changed her opinion of him on Monday when he'd asked her for the truth and then listened to it without judging her.

And then he'd said he was sorry.

It occurred to her that no one, not even Momma or Granny, had ever said they were sorry about what had happened to her. Granny still believed what people had said about her all those years ago. Before she died, Momma had expressed some remorse. But she'd only been sorry about Jessica's refusal to come home earlier.

Until Topher had come along, it seemed like forgiveness was a one-way street.

She left her car and let herself into the garden by the side gate, her heart thumping as she followed the path to his door and knocked. When Topher answered, her already racing pulse went on a wild ride. She hadn't seen him in a couple of days, but it struck her right then that she'd missed him.

He was wearing one of his many Hawaiian shirts, this one green and purple. His jeans were faded blue, almost the color of his eye, and he stood there in his bare feet looking sexy as sin.

He turned his head a bit to the left, presenting his unscarred side, and she almost called him on it. She'd grown accustomed to his face; the scars would never be something she had to overlook or "get over" as Granny had suggested. And she didn't think he had a good side or a bad side. He was who he was.

A whole man. A man who had apologized for something that had probably never been his fault. And boy howdy, she could understand that, couldn't she?

She held up the bag from Szechuan Garden. "I brought moo shu pork."

"You brought me food?" He sounded vaguely incredulous. And then his gaze moved down her body, as if he were drinking her in. The look sent a flash of desire through her.

"Are you all right? Why are you here?" he asked, as if he'd read the crazy emotions and fears running rampant inside her.

"I'm fine," she lied. "But I need to talk to you about something important."

"Okay." He stepped back from the door.

She crossed the threshold and headed toward the small table in the kitchenette, only to pull up short. The drawings of his ill-fated castle still sat on the table.

"You didn't throw those away?" she asked, turning toward him.

He shoved his hands into the pockets of his jeans. "No."

"Why?"

His shoulders rose and fell as he took a breath. "Because I wanted to be reminded of who I am and who I'm not."

She cocked her head. "I don't understand."

"I'm not those drawings. But for a moment I was willing to become that man."

She didn't know what to say, and deep within her a slow fire kindled to life.

He seemed to know that he'd surprised her because he pulled his hands from his pockets and rushed forward, crumpling up the drawings and shoving them into the kitchen trash can.

"There, the evidence of our first failure is gone. So"—he turned and faced her—"what did you want to talk about? Something house-related?"

She placed the bag on the table and shook her head. Now that she was face to face with him, she didn't even know where to begin. So she avoided his gaze and started taking cartons out of the paper sack.

He moved into the kitchen and came back with a couple of plates, which he handed to her. He sat down while she heaped each plate with rice, pancakes, and pork.

"Thanks for bringing food," he said as she handed him his plate. "I'm starved, and I don't have much in the pantry."

She sat down across from him, the aroma of the food

filling the space between them. "I came over because Caleb Tate dropped by the office, and he..." Her voice trailed off as she tried to figure out the right way to frame the problem.

"What?" He spat the word into her silence. "What did he do to you? I swear, if he did anything to hurt you, I'll—" He bit off the rest of his words.

She stared at him. "What? Do you think you're my protector or something?"

His face colored a little. Of course he did. He was a big, strong man. He was injured at the moment, but that did nothing to change his essential nature.

"Caleb didn't hurt me," she said. "He tried to bribe me."

\* \* \*

"What?" Topher barked the question as a surge of anger coursed through him. If Caleb Tate ever touched a hair on Jessica's head, he'd ruin him financially and every other way possible.

He ground his teeth in frustration. He wanted to put his fist through the man's pretty face, but that wasn't possible now that he'd lost his strength. In a physical altercation, Caleb would take him down in a matter of moments.

Hell, Caleb could have taken him down even when he was young and strong and whole. And it made him cringe to think that he'd been such a coward when it came to the team's running back. Topher had avoided confronting Caleb about his nasty locker room talk because he'd been bigger and meaner, and Topher hadn't wanted to screw up the vibe that championship season. In short, he'd been selfish and cowardly—two things he planned to remedy in short order.

No, he couldn't mess up Caleb's face, but he didn't need to do that. He just wanted to.

"He came to my office this morning," Jessica said, pulling Topher from his fury. "He said a lot of things that were, I don't know, vague but kind of threatening. Like if I helped him, he'd make sure I won the contract to design the new City Hall. But if I didn't play nice, he'd make sure I didn't have any chance of winning the bid."

"What does he want?" Topher pushed his plate away. He'd lost his appetite.

"He wants me to urge you to invest in something. I don't know what it is. But he thinks he can use me to get to you, and I'm sure he believes I can help him because of the gossip running rampant in town."

"Dammit. I'm sorry you've gotten mixed up in this."

"It's okay," she said, leaning forward, bracing her elbows on the table. "I just wanted you to know what he was up to. Because I'm not taking his bribe and I don't think you should invest in anything he's involved with. As for the City Hall project, well…" She paused a moment, looking away from him, her shoulders hunched. "The truth is I never had any real chance to win that bid. So it's not that important."

That was a load of BS. If she didn't have a chance to win the contract, why the hell was Caleb dangling a bribe? And besides, he could read her body language. That City Hall project was damned important to her.

He was tempted to demand her honesty the way he'd done on Monday. But he held back because he didn't want to reduce her to tears again. Besides, right this minute, he was too stunned by her bravery.

The irony was rich. People were forever calling him a hero just because he was the quarterback of a team that had won a state football championship. But here, sitting across from him, was someone who had saved lives, who'd endured great pain, and who was as scrupulously honest as the day was long.

His admiration for her swelled.

She wouldn't have to worry about Caleb for much longer. Topher was well on his way to making that problem disappear. And tomorrow, just to make certain she was protected, he'd make a large contribution to the City Hall building fund and demand a seat at the table.

She would win that contract. And he would never let her know what he'd done. She might never love him, but he would take care of her the way her family should have done years ago.

"I'm really sorry," she said, turning back to meet his gaze. "None of this would have happened except for the unrelenting gossip about me."

"You don't have to apologize. And what gossip are you talking about?"

She slumped back in her chair, studying the ceiling, as a truly adorable blush seeped up her cheeks. "It's nothing."

"Obviously that's not true. It's got to be something if Caleb thinks he can get to me through you."

Her gaze shifted, and those oddly colored eyes of hers seemed to have gone toward the green side of blue. What did that color mean? Anger? Surprise? Desire?

Oh please, let it be desire.

"It's stupid," she said.

"Okay. But people act on stupid stuff all the time. Trust me, I've seen fortunes lost because of stupidity."

"Okay," she said on a long breath. "It's like this. Since we got caught out in the storm, there are a lot of folks who think we're an item. And there are a bunch of people who are ticked off at me for dumping Colton."

Her words hit him like a two-by-four. "What?"

"I told you it was stupid. Two people go out to discuss a house project, get caught in a storm, and *poof,* the whole town starts making up ridiculous stories."

"Are they so ridiculous?" he blurted, and immediately regretted the words.

She turned away again, inspecting the fireplace in the sitting room as if it needed a makeover, while the pink in her cheeks blossomed into a red the color of Ashley's roses.

What should he say now? He had no clue. He was in alien territory. Never had he been the object of rumor or innuendo, and if he had been, he would have put his firm's publicist on the case and spun the message.

"I just want to be clear," Jessica said after a tense moment. "Colton and I are not a thing. In fact, I happen to know that he's got a thing of his own going with someone, but I'm not going to gossip about it."

"Hooray for Colton," Topher said in a slightly acerbic tone.

She pushed her chair back, the legs scraping against the wood floors. "Well, I guess I should be going. I've delivered my message. I think I'll just…"

He stood up and closed the distance before she could make it to the door. "I didn't mean to make us the object of gossip," he said.

"I know. We can blame the weather for that." She tried to step around him, but he blocked her, and then, as gently as he could, he cupped her face.

She didn't pull away, thank God.

"Jessica," he murmured, leaning in. "I enjoyed the kiss. Is it beyond reason to hope that something like that might happen again?"

Those big eyes turned in his direction, darkening, telling him everything he needed to know.

He resisted the urge to crush her to him. And maybe it was a good thing that his days of carrying women into his bedroom were over.

She reached out and touched his scars. This time he forced himself not to flinch. And then a miracle happened. She rocked up on tiptoes and kissed his cheek, where the damage was at its worst.

Her mouth trailed along the ruined skin, linking kisses and heat all the way to his left ear, which was missing most of the lobe. The damaged nerves along his face jangled, and he winced.

She drew back. "Did that hurt?"

"No. It's numb there. So it tingles a bit."

"Oh." Her eyes got round, and he wanted to erase the shock in them, so he swooped in and kissed her.

She tasted like hope, like a spring day, like coming home. Like it used to feel sometimes when he'd spend his summer days out on the island with Granddad.

She was everything good in the world. She hugged him tight, and he prayed to God she would never let go.

\* \* \*

His lips had a plummy taste, like the moo shu sauce but so much deeper and richer and lustier. How could she square the deep desire with his almost reverent gentleness?

It seemed illogical, but then she'd stopped thinking. Her barriers came down. She let him in, and he swept her away.

Someone should call out the rescue squad or the National Guard, because this had the makings of disaster. He'd started a fire, and she was ready to let it burn.

Maybe it would burn down the house he wanted to build. Maybe it would cauterize her wounds. Or maybe it would just destroy everything in its path.

It was anyone's guess, but she was tired of trying to do the right thing. She was tired of always being blamed for stuff she never dared to do.

For once she was letting the rebel out, and she didn't care what people thought.

She followed him to the bedroom. They took off their clothes in utter silence. It seemed as if there ought to be conversation, or banter, or at least some words.

And yet the silence was fine. It was a defense against saying too much, or too little, or the wrong thing.

He was still beautifully built, despite the scars marring his knee. And she was pretty sure that he'd been with lots of women who had curvier figures and longer legs and bigger breasts. So she didn't ask him what he was thinking.

She just lay down with him and let him rock her world.

* * *

When Jessica awoke, the room was awash in the glow from the fireplace. Sometime in the last hours, while she'd been sleeping, Topher must have gotten up and turned on the gas.

How could she have fallen asleep and missed any minute of this encounter? But then again, the afterglow had been so peaceful.

She wanted more, which was unexpected and new. She wasn't terribly experienced in relationships, but she'd never wanted more before. Usually she couldn't wait to leave.

She rose onto an elbow and studied Topher. He'd lost the eye patch, and in the soft light, his scars weren't noticeable. He was utterly beautiful at rest. The usual tension in his face had disappeared. She was tempted to wake him up, and she wondered if he might object if she stayed all night.

Not that she could. The gossip would be...

Oh, good grief. What had she been thinking? The gossip was going to be horrible.

She checked her watch. And then it was like her higher brain functions finally kicked in. It was almost three in the morning and she couldn't stay.

She shouldn't stay.

She got out of bed and tiptoed around the room collecting pieces of clothing.

"Don't go," he said from the bed, his voice rough and sexy.

"I'm sorry," she said as she found her underwear where she'd dropped it on the floor. "I had a really good time, but I need to go."

"Why?"

"I have a meeting in Miami this afternoon. My flight leaves in about six hours, and I haven't even packed for it."

He sat up in bed. "You have a meeting? A new client?"

"It's a job interview." She found her pants and pulled them on.

"You're looking for a job?"

"No. But this opportunity fell in my lap. A firm that specializes in resilient design is trying to recruit me."

"Oh. And when were you going to tell me this?"

He sounded angry, and she stomped on the urge to tell him it was none of his business. After last night, it probably was. Sort of. Not that she'd made any commitments. Thank goodness.

"I'm sorry," she said. "I guess I should have told you last night. But—"

"Yeah, you should have."

Now he sounded entitled, and that ticked her off. She finished buttoning up her blouse. "I'm sorry," she said. "To be honest, this job interview is a blessing given what Caleb Tate is trying to do to me. To you. If I take this job, I don't need to worry about the City Hall project."

"Oh." Now he sounded wounded, and she hated that even more.

"Look, I told you. I'm sorry. I had a really good time and I'd like to stay, but I need to go."

She turned and jogged through the sitting room and out into a September night, lit up with moonlight that sparkled on the bay. What a perfect night for romance. Too bad she had somewhere else to be.

But maybe that was a good thing. Granny's words from that day when she'd visited the office haunted Jessica as she hurried through the garden to the parking lot.

*Christopher Martin is a man like your father.*

The words played on an endless loop in Jessica's mind as she drove herself home. She had enjoyed the evening, but maybe it was best to leave it at that.

She wanted nothing to do with Granny's vision of her perfect Cinderella future.

* * *

Topher didn't sleep the rest of the night. At six o'clock, he dragged himself from the bed and went out for a swim and then spent another couple of hours down at the local YMCA.

He sweated out his frustration, but he didn't excise Jessica from his mind or his heart.

A hollow place had opened in his chest unlike the depression that had been his companion the last few months. He should have told her how he felt last night. He should have spoken what was in his heart.

But maybe it was better that he hadn't. Especially if she'd been planning to leave Magnolia Harbor all along.

He returned to the cottage in the early afternoon and spoke briefly with a professor from the College of Charleston, who'd been recommended as an expert in local eighteenth-century history. They chatted for a bit about the artifacts he'd found out by the oak tree, and Professor Hawkins gave him instructions on how to protect the dig until she could take a look at it on Saturday.

"We don't get artifacts turning up from the early-eighteenth century very often," she'd said.

At least someone besides Jackie was excited about the hole behind Howland House because Ashley was decidedly unamused.

After he'd finished with Dr. Hawkins, Topher called Harry Bauman and made arrangements to wire a sizable contribution to the City Hall building fund. Once the money cleared, he'd make his request to have a say on the design committee. Maybe if Jessica won that bid, she'd stay in Magnolia Harbor. And if she stayed, maybe there was some hope for him.

But then again, he'd be living out on Lookout Island in his retreat. And she'd be here in town, building a life for herself.

It wasn't even two o'clock when he'd finished all the items on his to-do list. He found his usual spot in the rocking chair on the porch. And like some old has-been, he sat there brooding for the next few hours.

Would Jessica contact him while she was away?

No. She wouldn't.

Should he follow her to Florida?

No. Not unasked.

As he rocked, he thought about the things he might do to keep her here. And he jettisoned the ideas one by one. Nothing he could do. No deal he could make. No strings he could pull would ever make her love him.

Maybe it was better if she went away so he didn't have to see her ever again.

He suddenly understood Rose Howland's letter. Oh yes, he was like her in so many ways. And when Jessica was gone, he'd retreat to his island and keep watch in his lighthouse. And Jessica would be with him.

Always.

# Chapter Twenty ———————

A cool rain fell on Friday morning as Kerri Eaton opened Daffy Down Dilly. It was supposed to rain all day today and tomorrow, which would keep the weekend crowd down and affect her bottom line. She depended on these early-fall weekends to meet her sales goals for the year.

The rain soured her already foul mood. She was beyond irritated at every gossip in Magnolia Harbor who was wagging their tongue about how Jess Blackwood had dumped Colton for Topher Martin.

Just last night, at her weekly girls' night out, Kerri's girlfriends had done nothing but talk about how Jess was some kind of schemer who'd dropped Colton the minute Topher had returned to Magnolia Harbor. Everyone agreed that it had to be Topher's money; otherwise why would Jess choose a guy with a face like that?

Really? The gossip was cruel. And it ticked off Kerri because it was unfair to Jess. She'd even said something to her girlfriends, which had soured the evening.

Everyone accused her of being blind because Jess was her tenant.

It had taken all of Kerri's restraint not to get up in her friends' faces and tell them how, on Saturday—two days before Jess got caught in that storm with Topher—Colton had taken her on a sunset cruise that had ended at his place.

But Kerri could hardly do that seeing as Colton had ghosted her since then. Almost a whole week without any word from him.

Kerri didn't want to add any fuel to that fire. Or humiliate herself. Or any such thing. She didn't want to become the topic of the moment the way Jess had.

In fact, Kerri was rethinking a lot of things. She'd done her share of telling tales about people. But it wasn't so much fun when the stories hit close to home.

She flipped over the closed sign and made herself a cup of coffee. Rainy Friday mornings in September were the bane of her existence.

There wouldn't be many customers, so she faced a long morning ahead, trying hard not to think about Colton or the romantic memories of Saturday's cruise.

*Synchronicity* had taken passengers down the inlet to a spot where they could watch the sun set over the bay. The weather had been perfect, with an easy breeze that had caught the boat's many sails and carried them all the way down the bay without the use of the engines.

There had also been a couple of times when Jude St. Pierre, *Synchronicity*'s captain, had asked his brother to help with the rigging. Man oh man, Colton was sexy as hell just standing on her sidewalk. But when he'd climbed out onto the mast at the front of the boat in order to help rig one of the big sails, she'd been blown away, her heart racing. But not nearly as fast as it had later in the evening, at his place.

She was falling for him. The fact that she was ticked off at him was a surefire indication that he'd gotten under her skin.

She finished her first cup of the day and headed back to the break room. She'd just poured her second cup when the little bell at the front of the store jangled.

She checked the clock; it was a little after eleven. She'd been here for an hour, and this was her first customer.

She headed to the front of the store and came to a stop. Colton stood there amid her trinkets.

"Do you know where Jessica is?" he asked before she could say a word.

Well, damn. And here she thought the man had finally come to his senses and had arrived to light her fire on this chilly rain-swept day.

"I just got here an hour ago. Why would I know anything about Jess's whereabouts?" Kerri said in a snippy tone.

He turned, running his hand through his damp hair, water dripping from his rain jacket to her floor. A coil of fury and desire knotted in her stomach.

"I need to talk to her about something important, and she's not at home or her office. I checked. The door is locked."

"Did you call her?"

"Yeah. No answer. I'm worried about her."

"Well, I can't help you. I'm just her landlady."

He didn't seem to be listening. Instead he paced like a caged panther, dripping water everywhere.

Kerri made a snap decision. She could fall in love with him, but she wasn't going to let herself. He'd been dishonest with her. He had a jones for someone else. And that made him exactly like the last guy who'd darkened her door.

"I think you should leave," she said, coming to the only conclusion she could. She needed to get that man out of her system. He was trouble.

He turned, a surprised look on his face. "What's gotten into you?"

"I'm standing here right in front of you and you haven't even said good morning. You take me for granted, which is bad enough. But you've been dishonest with me."

"What? How?"

"You let me think that there was no one else in your life. And clearly there is."

He stood there looking slightly thunderstruck. "But there isn't."

"No? You come in here telling me you're worried about Jess. You treat me like I'm invisible. What do you expect me to think? Colton, you need to take a good long look in the mirror."

"Uh." His mouth dropped open.

"I mean it. If you care about Jess Blackwood, then why the hell did you take me out on Saturday?"

"But—"

"Think about it, Colton. I don't like being used to make some other woman jealous. And what is it? Are you worried now because everyone says she's got a thing for Topher Martin? Or—"

"Topher Martin? Are you out of your mind? She hates that guy."

Kerri blew out a breath. "We're not talking about her. Okay?"

"Wait. I thought we were."

"No. We're talking about the way you came in here and

treated me like I was nothing. What is it? Are you sorry you took me on that cruise?"

He frowned. "Uh, no. I mean, I didn't call because I was busy. Jude needed—"

"I don't care what you've been doing. Honestly."

"But—"

"I just want you to leave now. It's clear that I don't mean very much to you. And while it was fun, I think we're done now, okay?"

"What the hell?"

"Go. Now," she said, trying very hard not to bellow or scream or shriek. That would have been uncool, and Kerri always kept her cool.

"Yes, ma'am. And I am sorry I darkened your door." He turned and strode from the store, inadvertently knocking one of her daffodil teacups to the floor in his wake. The cup shattered into a million pieces.

Sort of like Kerri's heart. She burst into tears and went running for the broom and dustpan. By the time she'd swept up the shards and mopped up the water he'd tracked in, she'd regained her composure.

Barely.

But she'd pull it together eventually. She was strong enough to weather this setback. And besides, she had plenty of practice nursing a broken heart.

* * *

On Saturday morning, Ashley found herself sitting at her dining room table next to her troublesome cousin. The Rev sat across the table from them like a referee.

"Honestly, Topher, if we weren't related, I'd wring your neck." Ashley gave Topher one of her I'm-fed-up-with-you glares. It didn't have much of an impact on him, probably because he'd become Jackie's favorite relative. Like the crazy uncle every kid loves.

Sort of like Uncle John, Topher's grandfather, now that she thought about it.

And even though Topher had specifically defied her instructions by taking Jackie to the library, she couldn't complain about that since Jackie was going to have the absolute best Heritage Day project ever.

No other kid had ever uncovered an archaeological site in his backyard. So Topher had her exactly where he wanted her.

And it was annoying.

Jackie sat next to the Rev, kicking his legs under the table as he gobbled down a second helping of pancakes.

She cast her gaze from Jackie to the Rev, who was also packing away her cooking. The rush of pleasure at seeing her food consumed took the edge off her irritation.

She was proud of Jackie, furious at Topher and Micah for disregarding her wishes, and worried about the historian who was scheduled to arrive at any minute.

There had been a reason Grandmother had put restrictions on who could look at Rose Howland's letters and diary. And Ashley had a sick feeling the reason might be buried in the backyard.

"Is there more bacon?" the Rev asked, turning his dark-brown stare on her. It never failed to unsettle her.

"Sorry. That's the last of it," she said, folding her arms across her chest.

His mouth twitched in reaction to her body language. "I can see you're not having a very good day," he said.

"No, I'm not."

"Come on, Mom. This is an adventure."

Right.

"So"—the Rev turned toward Topher—"this diary y'all found. What exactly did it say, again?"

Topher pulled out his cell phone and showed Micah the photo he'd taken of the page in Rose Howland's common book that contained the directions to the "treasure."

"Good God," Micah said, his whole body stiffening as he studied the photo, using his fingers to make the image larger.

"What?" Topher asked.

"I know who Abimael is."

"Please don't tell me he was a member of Captain Teal's crew," Ashley said, picking up the coffee carafe and pouring herself a third cup—or was it a fourth? She'd lost count. She needed to cut back. In fact, her hands were a little shaky even as she poured.

"He wasn't a pirate," Micah said. "He was—"

The doorbell rang, interrupting the conversation. "That will be the historian," Ashley said, pushing up from the table and running after Jackie, who beat her to the door.

Laurie Hawkins, a thirtysomething professor with the joint College of Charleston–Clemson University Historic Preservation Project, stood on her doorstep, head tilted back, studying Howland House's facade.

"Early 1800s, I would guess," the woman said. She had chin-length black hair and wore a pair of tortoiseshell glasses. In her jeans and a College of Charleston T-shirt, the woman didn't fit Ashley's idea of a college professor.

"Professor Hawkins?" Ashley asked.

The woman shifted her gaze and met Ashley's stare. "Hi," she said. "Mrs. Scott, I presume. You must be Jackie, the boy who found the treasure," she added, squatting down to meet Jackie on his level.

"I am," Jackie said with a wide smile.

The professor looked up, meeting Ashley's gaze. "Nice house you have, Mrs. Scott."

"Ashley," she said. "And yes, Howland House was built in 1827. But there was a much older house on the property before that. Not far from where Jackie made his discovery."

"I'm excited. I can't wait to see it." The professor's childlike enthusiasm was contagious.

In short order, they all went out to the site by the old oak tree, where Professor Hawkins brought out a paint-brush and some tiny trowels and began sifting through the sand.

"It's definitely an eighteenth-century writing desk," she said as she lifted out a piece of the rotting wood, her hands covered in neoprene gloves.

"Why would Rose bury something like that?" Ashley asked.

"The more important question was who she was burying it for," Micah said.

"I think we can assume it was for Henri St. Pierre," Topher said.

Laurie turned around. "I don't know the history of the people who lived here. Who were Rose and Henri?"

Ashley gave the professor the short version of the history. "So it was just Rose and Henri living on the island," Ashley said when she'd finished with the basic details. "I can't imagine why Rose would have buried a writing desk."

"Maybe it was intended as a legacy," Micah said.

"For whom?"

"Abimael."

"Who's Abimael?" the professor asked.

"In her diary, the woman who buried this desk said it was for someone named Abimael, but we don't know who that person is," Ashley said.

"No. We do know who he was," Micah said. "He was Henri St. Pierre's son, and one of my ancestors."

Everyone turned toward the Rev. "Oh my goodness. Why didn't you—"

"I was about to tell you that when the professor arrived."

"Oh. Wow. So I guess that means Rose and Henri weren't the only ones living on the island back in the 1720s," Ashley said.

Micah cleared his throat. "Well, Thomas Howland Teal lived here with his mother. And then Abimael, when he was born some years later."

"Oh, look," Laurie said, interrupting the conversation that had suddenly taken an unexpected turn.

Ashley shifted her gaze to the hole in the ground where the professor was digging. A moment later the woman pulled up a small heart-shaped brooch of tarnished metal.

"It's a Georgian heart," the professor said.

"Oh boy. I knew there would be jewels," Jackie said.

The historian laughed as she met Jackie's excited gaze. "Well, I suppose so. But not valuable ones. The garnets crowning the heart aren't worth that much. But whoever put this here treasured it, I'm sure. A heart brooch like this was a token of love."

"From the cap'n to Rose?" the boy asked.

"No," Micah said. "I'm thinking maybe it was from Rose to Abimael."

Ashley turned. "What? Why—"

"Ashley, Abimael and Henri ended up at Oak Hall. There are records of them living there in deeds of property and wills and such. We also know that Abimael was Thomas

Howland's most trusted slave. He was well educated and worked side by side with Thomas to build an empire.

"It's only a guess, but I think we know now why your grandmother didn't want anyone to read Rose's letters. I think Thomas Howland Teal and Abimael St. Pierre were half brothers."

# Chapter Twenty-One

On Saturday morning, after a long two days of travel and meetings, Jessica got up and dressed for tea with Granny, making a point to put on one of her pinkest dresses.

It was a tiny rebellion against her grandmother. One she'd been subconsciously waging for the better part of a year. But today she picked the hottest pink dress in her closet.

She had a lot to say to Granny, starting with the fact that she'd just been offered a dream job in Miami with a salary and benefits that were nothing short of amazing. Damon Brant wanted her, and he was determined to make her an offer she couldn't refuse.

In fact, Jessica had halfway accepted the job Thursday night during dinner at a swanky restaurant. But Damon had told her to think it over for a few days before saying yes. "Giving up your own business to go work for someone else is a big step," he'd told her. "Make sure it's what you really want to do."

It had been what she'd wanted to do on Thursday night,

but today, as she sat down in her own little office space to get a few hours of work done before going to Granny's house, her certainty had evaporated.

If only Caleb Tate hadn't tried to intimidate her. If only the people in town hadn't told lies about her. If only . . .

Yeah, Magnolia Harbor would be a perfect place to live if it weren't for the past.

At two o'clock she left her office and made the short walk down Harbor Drive to the historic section of town. It was a gray day, with rain in the forecast, but a crew was busy hanging the Heritage Day banner across the main street anyway. The big weekend was coming up in mid-September.

The festivities would start the Friday after next, with the winners of the third-grade history project being announced. On Saturday, there would be historical demonstrations at the park, pirate cruises down to the spot where Captain Teal's ship had been sunk in the hurricane of 1713, a craft fair at the high school, and a dinghy regatta.

And just for fun, every restaurant in town would offer a special drink with the word "hurricane" in its name.

The whole campy event would be topped off with a swanky ball at the yacht club, where only the most important people were invited.

Momma and Daddy used to go to the Heritage Day ball. Jessica had never possessed any desire to attend, which was fine because she'd never been invited. To this day Granny regarded her disinterest in the social event of the year as slightly blasphemous.

As Jessica made the turn onto Tulip Street, her attention was drawn to a neon green flyer that had been taped to one of the streetlamps. The large-print headline stopped her in her tracks.

STOP THE DESTRUCTION OF LOOKOUT ISLAND.

Jessica pulled the flyer away and read the small print. Evidently, the Moonlight Bay Conservation Society was on the warpath, and Topher was in their sights. The flyer claimed that Christopher Martin, billionaire and friend to corporations everywhere, was planning to build a gargantuan eyesore on the island. The Conservation Society was determined to stop this rape of the land and invited concerned citizens to a town hall meeting at Grace Methodist Church next Saturday to discuss the efforts of State Representative Caleb Tate, who was ready to introduce legislation that would prohibit the development of Lookout Island in perpetuity.

"Damn him," Jessica whispered out loud. She almost jumped at her own audacity in using that kind of language. But she was furious. This flyer felt personal. The house she planned was not a monstrosity, but more important, Topher wasn't a callous billionaire. And no one was going to rape the environment.

Tate had to be behind this. The man must be desperate for cash, and he was squeezing Topher where it would hurt the most.

He was a despicable human being.

She folded the paper and headed off to Granny's house. She was still out of sorts when her grandmother opened the door.

"Why do you wear pink?" Granny asked instead of greeting her like a member of the family.

Jessica squared her shoulders and looked her grandmother in the eye. "Because I like pink. It's my favorite color." Then she walked right past Granny, invading the older woman's space as she made her way to the living room and the tea tray that awaited her.

She was suddenly weary of the role she'd been playing since her return to Magnolia Harbor. She didn't want to be a nice, polite Southern girl. She wanted to be herself, warts and all.

She sat down on the camelback sofa and stared at the Lenox tea service, fighting the urge to pick up the teapot and hurl it across the room.

Granny sat down facing her, a strange, sly look in her eyes. "Darling, I am so pleased that you've come to your senses."

"About what?" she asked as she picked up the teapot and started pouring, her hands surprisingly steady considering her state of mind.

"About Christopher Martin."

This time Jessica didn't slosh the tea, which she regarded as a minor victory. She calmly handed a cup and saucer to her grandmother.

"I have no idea what you're talking about," she said.

"I'm talking about last Wednesday night, when your car was seen at Howland House well into the wee hours."

She picked up her own cup and saucer, pot poised. She wasn't surprised by this news. For once the gossips had their facts right. And she didn't even care.

If people wanted to talk about how she'd slept with Topher, then they could just have at it.

"I hope," Granny continued, "that this puts the whole Colton St. Pierre phase to rest. Because, really dear, he—"

"Stop. Not another word." She put the teapot down without pouring herself a cup.

"But—"

"I don't know what people are saying. But Colton and I were never a thing. And it's time for you to realize that."

"But, darling, when you came back home you said—"

"Yes. I remember what I said. And I lied to you. And you know what, Granny, that's the first time I lied. All the rest of the time—you know, when you and Momma and Daddy wouldn't let me come home—I was telling the truth. Colton has always been my friend. And if you can't stand that, then I guess you'll just have to sit on it.

"And as for Topher. I have no intention of trying to land that fish, as Aunt Donna put it."

"Are you out of your mind? You could have that man if you wanted him. I know he's not as handsome as—"

"Stop. Just. Stop."

Something snapped inside Jessica, and a poisonous pool of rage flowed up from the deep well she'd been hiding for all these years.

She stood up. "I'm done," she said, her voice calm.

"What do you mean?"

"I'm done coming over here every Saturday and enduring your endless criticism. If you want me in your life, you'll apologize."

"For what?"

Really? She didn't even know? "Granny, you always lived with Momma and Daddy and me, so it's not as if you weren't around when Daddy decided I wasn't worthy of being a member of this family. He chose not to believe me when I told the truth. And the only way to get back into this family was to tell a lie.

"I don't want to do that anymore. What I want is your apology. And you know what, even if I *had* done something bad with Colton, I'd want your forgiveness. But if I can't even get an apology, how could I ever hope for forgiveness?"

She headed toward the door.

"Jessica, you come back here."

She stopped and spoke without turning. "No. If you want to have a relationship with me, you know where to find me. You know what you have to do. Just apologize. That's nothing more or less than Daddy wanted from me."

She took a few more steps toward the door and stopped again, turning this time. "And one other thing. You should know that I've been offered a job in Miami, and I'm seriously considering it. So don't wait too long. I might be gone soon."

\* \* \*

Professor Hawkins spent four hours excavating the "treasure" Topher and Jackie had discovered. The woman was so meticulous that the little boy quickly lost interest when he discovered there were no more jewels in the small hole. Eventually, Jackie had scampered off to climb the tree.

The Reverend also left early, excusing himself to finish tomorrow's sermon. And Ashley left soon after that, needing to take care of her house guests.

Professor Hawkins widened the hole in the hope that more artifacts would be found, but nothing else turned up. She took half an hour to study a pile of ballast stones near the tree and confirmed the family's suspicion that they had once been the foundation of Rose Howland's cabin.

"I know it doesn't seem like much, but it's quite a find," she said.

"I'm not sure the powers that be will be so happy about it though," Topher said as he walked her back to her car.

The only salvageable portion of the box had been the brass hinges, but the inkwell and brooch were now safely in Professor Hawkins's possession. She would take them back to Charleston and confirm the dates.

And then Ashley would have to decide what to do with the artifacts. By rights they should be donated to the museum the town was planning as part of the new City Hall.

Topher had only just learned the scope of the project, and he now understood why Jessica wanted to win the bid. The building would be large and include government offices as well as a museum and community meeting rooms.

Rose Howland's letters should be displayed in the museum, and the truth about Rose and Henri needed to be further researched and ultimately revealed. It was time for people to accept the true history and not the story the Howlands had wanted told. The truth was that Rose Howland had defied her father at every turn.

Topher said goodbye to the professor and made his way back to the cottage, his mind turning toward Jessica now that it wasn't otherwise occupied.

Had she returned from Miami?

Had she had a good time there?

Had she gone partying at some trendy place in South Beach? He could almost imagine her dressed in something sparkly, even though she usually dressed conservatively.

Boy, he'd love to buy her something expensive.

Damn. The itch was there, and he wanted to scratch it. But he had no hold on her.

So instead of calling her, he settled into his rocking chair with John Grisham's latest book. He'd have to get used to this new life he was living.

An hour later, his phone rang. It was probably Erik, calling about the latest land deal, which was proving more expensive than either of them liked. But when he saw the caller ID, his heart soared. It was *her.*

An insane joy bubbled up inside him as he connected

the call. "Hey," he said, sounding exactly like the besotted idiot he'd become.

"Hi." Her voice sounded tense.

"What's the matter?"

"We've got a problem with the house."

"Oh. What?"

"It's kind of complicated. I thought maybe…" She stopped speaking midsentence, sounding awkward.

"What?"

"Well, I thought we could meet for dinner or something to talk about it. But, um…"

"What, dammit?" He ground his teeth as a familiar frustration surfaced.

"Sorry. I just don't want to be seen meeting you at Rose Cottage—or any of the restaurants in town for that matter."

"Why not?"

"Well, if you must know, I don't want to feed the gossip mill."

"Oh. What are people saying now?"

"Someone saw my car in the Howland House parking lot after midnight on Wednesday."

"And drew a reasonable conclusion?"

She let go of a long breath that hissed in his ear. "I guess. But gossip is gossip even if it's true. I keep telling myself I don't care what people are saying, but I do. Is that screwed up?"

"No."

"So," she said into his silence, "maybe we could meet somewhere discreet or—"

"I'll bring food over to your place."

There was a small hesitation before she said, "Okay."

"Before you hang up. What's the problem?"

"Just a complication. But I'd rather talk to you face to face about it."

"Oh." He didn't know whether to relax or to worry. Maybe a little of both. "I'll be there around six, okay? Chops from Annie's work for you?"

"That's fine. See you then." And she hung up without one word about what had happened on Wednesday.

He might as well have been speaking to his architect.

* * *

Topher rang the doorbell precisely at 6:00 p.m., sending a flight of butterflies through Jessica's middle. She hadn't exactly been looking forward to this meeting, but she hadn't been dreading it, either.

The truth was complicated. She didn't want to lose her focus because of some man in her life. She didn't want to become dependent the way Momma had. She needed her independence the way some people needed air to breathe.

And Topher was a threat to that. A big, beautiful, sexy threat.

She opened the door to find him with a bag from Aunt Annie's Kitchen in one hand and a bouquet of bright-pink roses that had probably come from Ashley's garden in the other.

He looked more adorable than threatening standing there in a blue Tommy Bahama shirt, his hair still shower-damp, his spicy scent mingling with the barbecue. He'd trimmed his beard back again, to the thinnest of scruffs, almost as if he didn't care what she thought about his scars.

Her heart skidded sideways. The truth was that she didn't care. Did that mean he was willing to overlook her imperfections?

He thrust out the bouquet like an awkward teenager. "For you," he said.

"From Ashley's garden?"

He nodded. "But I cut them myself. I have thorn scratches to prove it."

She took the flowers, their scent lingering between them. "Come on in. I'll get a vase for these and dishes for the food."

He followed her down the hall into the dining room, where he put down the paper sack. "Can I help?"

She shook her head and escaped into the kitchen for a moment, taking care of the flowers and then stacking a couple of plates, silverware, napkins, and two Heinekens on a tray.

They sat down at one end of the long dinner table, two lonely people huddling in a corner of a table big enough for a family of ten or more. She dug into the paper bag and pulled out the polystyrene containers of the chops, okra and tomatoes, and hush puppies. She arranged the food on two plates. He popped the top on his beer but didn't say a word until Jessica placed his plate in front of him.

"So, what's the problem with the house?" he asked.

Thank goodness. She didn't want to talk about last Wednesday. She wanted to pretend it hadn't happened. Not because people were gossiping. Not because of the look in Granny's eye this afternoon that had so enraged her.

But because she didn't trust her own heart. Because she wanted it to happen again. And she feared that if it did, she'd lose her way and her focus. She'd belong to him, and she didn't want to belong to anyone.

So she pushed all that difficult emotional stuff away to tell him about the flyers she'd seen on Harbor Drive.

"The handbills suggest that Caleb has joined forces

with the Conservation Society. They claim that he's about to introduce legislation that would stop all development on Lookout Island."

She looked down at her food. "I'm so sorry. I can't shake the feeling that this is somehow my fault. I mean, if—"

"How on earth is this your fault?"

She looked up, and he pinned her with his endless blue stare. "I don't know. I just feel..." She shrugged.

"Okay, let's make something clear. This is not your fault. Any more than the rumors Caleb started were your fault."

"We don't know for certain that Caleb started those rumors about me."

"No, that's true. It could have been anyone who didn't like the idea of a white girl having a black friend." Topher paused for a moment before cocking his head and speaking again. "Can I tell you a secret?"

The bottom of her stomach dropped. She wanted his secrets, but at the same time she was scared to death of them.

"Don't worry," he said, as if he could read her mind. "It's not one of *those* secrets. It's a historical secret."

"A historical secret?"

He nodded and then launched into a tale about how he had been roped into helping Ashley's little boy with his Heritage Day project, and they'd uncovered Rose Howland's diary, which seemed to suggest that Rose had been in love with Henri St. Pierre.

"You're kidding," she said, shocked in spite of herself.

He shrugged. "I don't know if we'll ever prove it. But there's enough circumstantial evidence to suggest that the Howlands and the St. Pierres are both descendants of our town mother. Although, in fairness, the Howlands should be using the surname of Teal."

"So Rose had a thing for pirates," she said, and then blushed, because it struck her right then that Topher could do a darn good impression of a pirate with his eye patch and slightly shaggy hair.

"I guess so," he said. "Should we let the secret out and see what the old biddies do with it?"

She stared at him. The idea was so incredibly seductive and so terribly wrong. "No. Let's not."

"Yeah. Probably wise to keep it a secret until we can verify it. And then it won't be gossip; it will be the truth," he said.

The truth. It was what she'd always wanted. But the truth was way more complicated than she'd ever fully realized. People could get hurt when you told the truth.

She focused on her food, cutting and chewing. She wanted to tell him how she felt, but it scared her silly. She didn't need or want a man in her life. She didn't want to give up her freedom.

When she ran out of food to eat, she said, "You know, Caleb probably has the power to take the island away from you."

"First he'd have to get enough votes in the assembly, and then he'd have to come up with the money to purchase the property from me. Those are pretty high hurdles."

Topher said this with such conviction that it blew her mind. He wasn't the slightest bit worried about Caleb. It seemed to underscore the truth about him.

"So what do you propose we do? Stand by and wait for him to raise the money?"

"There isn't much we can do about it."

"We could gate-crash their meeting and present our designs," she said. "Show them that we aren't planning on raping the environment."

He cleared his throat. "The flyers certainly used colorful language about that, didn't they?" he said. "But I think it would be crazy to go to their meeting."

"Really, why?"

"You can't win those people over by arguing with them."

"But we have to."

"No. We don't."

"But when they see how we plan to build the house, I'm sure they'll—"

"No amount of green design will appease them."

"So what? You just want to give up?"

"Did I say I was giving up? No. I'll just steamroller them."

She stared him down. This. This was what scared her about Topher. He had the power to do as he pleased and never pay any consequences.

"I'm not sure that's the right approach. I mean, the flyers paint you as some kind of eccentric billionaire who never gave one thought to protecting the environment. Are you willing to stand by and let them assassinate your character like that?"

The corner of his lip curled just a tiny bit. "I don't care about my reputation. That's one of the big differences between you and me."

And that was the problem.

She cared. No matter what. She would always care. Her reputation was everything. Without it, she'd have no business. Heck, her business up to this point had been built entirely on Yoshi Akiyama's word of mouth. If she squandered her reputation, those good vibes would disappear.

"Well," she said in a tight voice, "I won't stand by and let people accuse me of designing some kind of monstrosity. That's the word the flyer used. I have to defend myself."

* * *

Topher laid his knife and fork across the plate and looked into Jessica's eyes. They were the color of graphite today, filled with a determination he admired.

He wanted to tell her to save her breath. Caleb was nothing but a paper tiger who was about to discover that all his plans and schemes had been built on quicksand. It would be enjoyable watching the a-hole going down in flames.

But looking into the outrage on Jessica's face, he had a momentary doubt. Was it enough to simply bring the bastard down? Maybe she needed this confrontation.

But it was so risky. He hated the idea of her going into that meeting and facing down those people. She could get hurt. And he wanted to protect her.

But not by divulging his plans. It was clear now that she'd be annoyed at him for taking away her chance to square off against Caleb. No. He wouldn't tell her the truth. He'd just make sure the fight ended the right way. And he'd stand up beside her, just in case things got ugly.

It would be like that time with the pliers. He wouldn't fight her battle. He'd just back her up and give her the right tools to ensure victory.

"Okay," he said. "You've convinced me. I'll show up at the meeting with you."

"You will?"

He nodded.

"Thanks. I think it's important." She looked away.

Uh-oh, here came the bad news. He steeled himself. He'd already decided not to attempt any more seductions. It would only prolong his misery.

"There's something else I need to tell you," she said.

Something withered inside his chest. He could hope.

He could make the bad guys disappear. He could save the island. But he could never make her love him.

So he didn't wait for her to deliver the bad news. He simply cut to the chase. "I can guess," he said. "You're going to take the job in Miami."

"Well, I haven't said yes yet, but I'm leaning in that direction."

He pushed up from his place at the table. "Good for you," he said. "Now I need to go."

"Please, don't feel you have to leave. I can—"

"But I do have to go. I have things to do."

"Oh. So you're okay with me leaving town?"

"Of course I am. I think this job in Miami is perfect for you. I think you should follow your dreams. But you promised me a house."

"And I will deliver one, assuming Caleb Tate and the Conservation Society don't get in the way."

"I'm sure we can get around them." Thank God. He'd at least have that much. He could spend time with her until his house was completed. For a moment he almost wished the zoning board would give him a lot of trouble, just to stretch out the process.

"Now I need to go." He headed down the hall to the front door, silently cursing the limp that made him so slow. He needed to get away from her before he did something stupid and destructive.

When he reached the door, she said, "Your house is my first priority for the next week, regardless of what I decide about this job offer. I hope to have the plans near completion so I can file for a building permit in a week or so."

"Good."

"And I should have something pretty final to bring with me to the meeting on Saturday." She paused a moment. "I guess I'll see you then?" Was there a note of yearning in her tone?

No. He wasn't going to fool himself. It was bad enough standing by while she ran away to Miami.

"I'll be there," he said, and escaped down the stairs as fast as his bad leg would take him.

# *Chapter Twenty-Two* ———

"Come on, kiddo, it's time to go, or we'll be late for your baseball game," Ashley said, tapping on Jackie's bedroom door. It was Saturday afternoon, a week after Professor Hawkins's visit, and the boy had been up in his bedroom brooding most of the morning.

She knocked again, determined to preserve his privacy but losing her patience.

Crickets.

So much for privacy. She opened the door, but the room was empty.

She checked her watch. She had exactly fifteen minutes to get Jackie to his fall league baseball game. Jackie wasn't a standout athlete, but he made up for that by being a veritable font of baseball information and statistics.

He had a growing baseball card collection and would sometimes spend an hour or more talking baseball with the Rev. Those conversations were a little frightening because Ashley didn't understand a word of them, especially when they started talking about ERA and RBI.

"Jackie?" she called, hurrying down the hall to the bathroom. "Are you in there? We have to go."

No answer. She turned around and headed into her own room, where he sometimes watched television. Also empty.

She returned to her son's room, a frisson of worry niggling at her. Was he still angry about the edits she'd made to his history project?

Ashley had allowed Jackie to do his project on Rose Howland's letters and diary. In fact, earlier in the week, she'd helped him make a poster-board presentation with photos from the dig and quotes from Professor Hawkins about what they'd found. She was pretty sure Jackie would ace the assignment, maybe even win the prize that was given out at the Heritage Day celebration next week.

But she'd put her foot down when Jackie had wanted to tell everyone about Abimael St. Pierre and how Rose Howland was probably his mother.

"Why can't I say that?" he'd asked in that tone of outrage he sometimes used. "It's the truth."

"You don't know it's the truth," she'd said.

"But the cap'n says it's true."

At that moment she'd truly wanted to kill the captain, except the man was either already dead or a figment of Jackie's imagination.

"It's not history. It's speculation," she'd said. "You can't put speculation in your history project. Do you know what that means?"

"It means it might not be true. But it's not speckilation if the captain says it's true."

There'd been no arguing with Jackie's single-minded logic, so she'd pulled the *I'm the Mommy* defense and simply ordered him to amend his project.

She'd even stood over him while he'd copied the edited version onto fresh paper, omitting the parts about how Rose taught Henri to read and how they had loved each other.

When he'd finished the written portion, they'd glued it to the poster board, and that had been the end of it. Except that Jackie had been surly about the whole thing ever since.

And now he was MIA on a baseball day.

She stood in the middle of his empty room, worry creeping through her. She shook it off. He was probably out back, tossing a football with Topher. The two of them had become thick as thieves.

She headed down the stairs, through the back door, and across the garden, but Jackie and Topher were not on the lawn. There was no sign of either of them, so she headed up the porch steps and banged like a madwoman on the cottage's front door.

Topher opened it. "What have I done now?" he asked.

There was a note of resignation in his voice that she found momentarily alarming. She also noted the dark circles under his eyes, as if he hadn't slept well.

The poor man. He'd been doing better recently, but it certainly looked as if he'd taken a step backward. On the other hand, the sitting room behind him looked tidy, and there were papers on the table that seemed to indicate he was working on something business-related. He was dressed in khakis and a golf shirt, as if he were planning to attend a business-casual meeting or something. She wondered if maybe he had decided to go back to work.

"You haven't done anything," she said, slightly breathless. "Have you seen Jackie?"

"This afternoon?" He straightened a bit.

She nodded. "He's hiding, and we have a fall league baseball game."

He frowned. "I haven't seen him all morning. He's probably up the tree," he said, stepping through the door. "When I wanted to hide, that's where I'd go. And believe me, I ran away from home multiple times."

"You ran away? Why did I not know that?"

He stepped off the porch and headed down the path across the lawn. He was walking much better now, without his cane and with a much less perceptible limp. Ashley followed him.

"Well, for one thing, you didn't live here as a kid," Topher said as they headed down the footpath. "And for another, I was the only one who thought I was running away. Sandra, Karen, and Aunt Mary probably thought I came over here to mooch cake. But trust me, I showed up on Aunt Mary's doorstep every time Dad locked himself in the bedroom. He had a bad time after my mother died. I missed Mom too, but until recently I didn't fully understand how lost my father was."

They reached the tree, and Topher hollered, "Come on, Jackie, you don't want to miss your baseball game, do you?"

Silence. It hung heavy on the hot September day. Jackie must have been staying very still because not a leaf rustled.

Topher surprised Ashley then. He hoisted himself up on the lowest branch, showing a great deal more strength than she thought he possessed.

"Topher, no, you can't go climbing—"

"Watch me," he said as he straightened up on the branch and started to ascend the tree, which rustled as he climbed. A moment later, long after he'd disappeared into the tree's crown of evergreen leaves, he called down to her.

"He's not here, Ashley."

"Oh my God. Where could he be?"

"Hang on, I'm coming down. We'll find him."

But she didn't wait. "I'm going to run across the street to see if he's with the Rev," she shouted, then turned and fled through the garden to the side gate that opened on the street right across from the rectory.

She hurried to the minister's door, trying to swallow back mounting panic as she pressed the bell. Jackie loved his baseball games. He wouldn't miss one.

Micah came to the door dressed in his cleric's garb. And it struck her the moment she set eyes on him that she hadn't seen him since last Sunday at church. And before that it had been a week ago, when the professor had come to examine Jackie's treasure.

Was he worried about what might happen when the town discovered that the Howlands and the St. Pierres were branches of the same family tree? Or was he worried that she might never let anyone discover that truth?

"What's wrong?" he asked before she could even open her mouth.

"Is Jackie here?" she asked.

He shook his head, a look of deep concern coming over his face.

"Oh God." She sagged against the doorframe. "I think I've lost him. And I think it's because I refused to let him tell the truth. I haven't seen him since breakfast, and I have no idea where he went. Oh, crap. I can't lose him. He's my everything."

Micah stepped forward and wrapped her up in one of his big hugs. "You haven't lost him. Don't worry. I'm sure he'll turn up."

"Oh, Micah, I can't lose him." She pressed her head

against his big chest as tears sprang to her eyes. "Maybe I should have believed him about the captain."

"Hush," the minister said, briefly cupping the back of her head. "Maybe you should have, but you aren't going to lose him. You're a good mother. Now, dry your eyes. We need to go look for him. And I promise you, we'll find him safe and sound."

\* \* \*

Jessica pulled into the full parking lot at Grace Methodist Church on Saturday evening. Peggy Fiedler certainly had a large following of people ready to believe the worst about Topher.

A surge of annoyance flooded through her. How dare the woman? If she'd had an issue with Topher's house, why not come directly to them and talk about it instead of stirring people up and holding a big, one-sided town meeting?

She took a big breath, her annoyance morphing into anger. That little burn in her gut was useful. She could draw on that flame and use it to stand up for Topher and his dream.

She found a parking space at the far end of the lot, got out of the VW, and scanned the cars, looking for Topher's BMW. But it wasn't there. She checked her watch: fifteen minutes before the meeting was scheduled to start. Was he going to abandon her?

They'd had several phone calls over the week as she'd put the finishing touches on the architectural plans needed for his building permit. He had tried to talk her out of coming here several times, but each time she'd insisted, he'd promised to come and stand with her against the crowd.

She pulled her cell phone from her purse and messaged him: *Where are you?*

She got no response, which didn't surprise her. Facing down a crowd of people would be hard for him. She'd made it clear that she didn't need him. She could do this on her own.

And it was something she needed to do. Not just to face Caleb Tate but to stand up for herself and her design. And to protect Topher if it came down to that.

Not just because he was her client.

He'd become much more than that. And he could become even more if she would allow it. But she refused to fall in love with him.

She picked up her portfolio, containing a couple of foam-core boards with the newly completed elevation drawings for his house. It was everything he'd talked about. A house up on stilts with four bedrooms, a wrap-around porch, and a flat Carolina Coastal roofline that would make it look a lot like a keeper's cottage. Sited next to the lighthouse, it would look as if it had been there for decades.

She headed into the church and turned down the hallway to the Sunday school wing. As she approached the meeting room, the hum of voices grew louder.

She hesitated in the doorway, looking for a bright Hawaiian shirt, but the crowd was awash in neutral colors.

The room was crowded with people she didn't recognize. Only a handful of year-round Magnolia Harbor residents: Bernice Cobb, the nurse practitioner at the local clinic; Wally Faulkner, one of the town's many charter boat captains; Lewis Harland, who worked for Colton St. Pierre; and Bobby Don Ayers, the real estate broker, sat near the front of the room.

Who were the rest of these people? Vacation homeowners? Activists from the mainland?

She glanced toward the front of the room, where Peggy Fiedler was having a conversation with Representative Tate. Peggy couldn't have been more than five feet tall and had to crane her neck to look up at the big man who'd once played football for the Rutledge Raiders and the University of South Carolina.

Tate was smiling down at the activist like a cobra, hypnotizing his prey. Didn't Peggy realize that Caleb was a pro-development legislator? He didn't exactly have a sterling record on topics like climate change.

Had Peggy been bribed? It was a troubling thought.

She checked her phone again. Nothing from Topher, and maybe that was a good thing. There were a lot of strangers in this room who would probably stare at him.

"Hey," a deep voice said from behind.

She turned to find Colton St. Pierre, dressed as always in his khakis and maroon St. Pierre Construction golf shirt.

She'd spoken with him a week ago Friday, when she'd returned his phone calls. He'd been frantic to reach her when she'd been in Miami to let her know about the toxic flyers the Conservation Society had been putting up all over town. By the time they'd spoken, she'd already seen them. But since that conversation, she hadn't seen or spoken to Colton at all.

"Hi," she said. "How's it going with Kerri?"

He frowned. "Not good. She's mad at me."

"Why?"

"I don't know. Maybe because everyone says you're cheating on me and she thinks we're a thing."

"What?"

His gaze bored into her. "I know you've heard the gossip around town."

She sighed heavily. It might be nice to live in a big

city where a person could find anonymity. "I have. And I'm sorry."

"About what? Sleeping with Topher?"

She blinked. "Are you jealous?" The words popped out of her mouth without thought. No, it wasn't possible for Colton to be jealous. He and Kerri were sleeping together. Right?

"So you're here to defend Topher Martin?" Colton asked, ignoring her comment, thank goodness.

"I'm here to defend my design." What she'd said was the truth, but not the whole truth. Defending Topher was on her list, especially since it looked as if he might be a no-show. Someone had to defend him.

"I figured you'd say something like that." Colton seemed angry or depressed or something as he turned his back on her and took a few steps down the hallway.

"What's the matter?" she asked, following him. "Did Kerri really dump you?"

"Yeah. But I probably deserved it. I'm a screwup. You should—"

"Stop. You're not. You—"

"No. I am. And it's worse than that, really."

"What? Tell me."

He turned around and stared at her. The look on his face spelled disaster, and she suddenly wished she hadn't invited him to speak his mind. Even before he opened his mouth, some sixth sense told her he was about to say something awful.

"I really need to know the truth. Are you and Topher Martin a thing?"

"No. We—" She bit off the words of explanation and said, "No," a little more firmly the second time.

"But you could be?"

Boy, Colton could read her like an open book. "I don't think he's my kind of guy, and—"

"Stop."

"What?"

"He's a good guy. He was always pretty straight up with me, you know? He once told me that I needed to be careful with you."

"What? When?"

"Years ago. Before I was arrested. Before I even knew what that meant. And I—"

"When exactly did this conversation happen?"

"That summer you were a lifeguard at the yacht club. I was waiting for you to get off work one day, and he just got into my car and told me that I needed to be careful with you. He told me you were an amazing person. I gather you'd just saved some kid's life. And you know what? He was right. You are an amazing person, and I..." He blew out a breath.

"Colton, what's the matter?"

"Look, I don't want to lay something heavy on you. But I want you to know the truth. Because, you know, Kerri made me think, and you deserve the truth."

"About what?"

"It was never Topher Martin who started those rumors about us."

"Of course it wasn't. It was most probably Caleb. He's such a—"

"No! It wasn't him, either. It was me."

She lost the ability to breathe for a long moment.

"It was all me," he said. "I told the lies."

"Why?" The word came out as a whisper.

He shrugged. "I was trying to make myself more important, you know? It was a big deal that a girl like you had decided to be my friend. So I told a story to Jamal Kingwood."

She blinked, trying to remember who the hell Jamal Kingwood was.

"He was the center for the Raiders. I was kind of jealous of that, you know? He was a big man on campus. Whatever. So I bragged to him about taking you down to Dead Man's Cove. He must have repeated it to other members of the team."

Jessica had to rest her hand on the wall as the room started to spin. *Don't faint.* She desperately sucked in air as Colton continued.

"I'm sorry to lay this on you now. But I guess I've been carrying it around for so long. And I needed to get it off my chest. The thing is, you never owed me anything. It was never your fault. And I sure as hell wouldn't want to be the reason you couldn't forgive Topher Martin, if it turns out that you really care about the guy."

# Chapter Twenty-Three

Damn, damn, damn. Topher was running late. The afternoon had been a nightmare, searching for Jackie high and low and even checking with the police about the possibility of an Amber Alert.

And then, just thirty minutes ago, Micah's sister-in-law had called to say that the boy had been found wandering around Jude St. Pierre's property. Topher had no idea how the boy had gotten that far away from town, or why he was out there in the wilderness north of Magnolia Harbor in the area some peopled called Gullah Town.

But Topher would have to wait for his answers because he needed to be at Grace Church. By the time he arrived, the parking lot was filled to overflowing. Even the handicapped spots were taken, so Topher had to park down the street. It took him forever to walk back to the church and find the meeting room, where things were already under way.

He stood in the doorway, looking for a seat, but they were all taken. He didn't see Jessica right away, but the room was large and packed. She might be hiding in the back.

He turned his attention to the grandmotherly woman who stood at the front of the room making a PowerPoint presentation. Her slides, in a garish shade of kelly green, flashed on a screen at the corner of the room. She was giving a long spiel about the mission of the Moonlight Bay Conservation Society.

Behind her, Caleb Tate sprawled in a folding chair. When their eyes met, the politician straightened and had the audacity to give Topher a cheesy smile.

What? Did the jerk think he'd won, just because Topher was here? He could think again. Topher didn't plan to say a word. He was here to support Jessica and nothing else.

Just then the woman changed the slide, and a grainy photograph of Jessica's first design flashed on the screen. It was the elevation drawing of the stupid castle he'd asked for.

Rage coursed through him. Someone with access to the cottage had taken these photos. Ashley? Karen? Sandra? Any one of them could have taken the photograph while he'd been off swimming or tossing the football with Jackie.

If he had to bet, he'd say Ashley was the culprit, just because she had more opportunity to snoop around the cottage than either of his older cousins. But what had possessed his family to hand those photos over to the Conservation Society?

He didn't have to guess too hard. They had always been dead set against him moving out to Lookout Island.

The speaker took out a laser pointer and began pointing out the features of his castle: the spires, the castle wall, the swimming pool, and the damned party deck.

It was more than embarrassing. It was infuriating.

He was about to break his self-imposed rule and stop the proceedings, when a voice from the back piped up.

"Excuse me, Ms. Fiedler," Jessica said, her voice surprisingly loud and firm without a microphone. She'd been in the last row, obscured from his view by a big guy in the row in front of her. But she was standing now and heading down the aisle as she spoke. "Everything you just said is untrue."

The speaker turned toward Jessica, a frown folding down over her intense gaze. "Who are you?"

Jessica advanced to the middle of the room. "I'm Jessica Blackwood, Christopher Martin's architect."

The crowd gasped and murmured. Topher balled his fists. If anyone said a negative word about Jessica, he would explode. He wasn't going to let her be hurt by these people.

"You designed this crap?" the speaker said, pointing an accusing finger at her.

\* \* \*

Jessica stared Peggy Fiedler down as an unwanted memory filled her mind of Daddy pointing an accusing finger at her. "I won't tolerate a liar in this house," he'd said.

And here she was again, standing up for the truth when no one wanted to believe her. The crowd began to murmur in an ominous tone, and her knees and hands started to shake.

Had the truth ever set anyone free? Or had it only hurt people? Colton's truth hurt terribly. She wished he'd never spoken it out loud.

Of course, the truth she'd come to speak wasn't nearly as earthshaking, but the audience didn't want to hear it. They wanted someone to be against. They wanted to stop Topher no matter what the truth.

But the little rebel who had always lived down inside of Jessica refused to give up.

"I designed the castle," she said. "And you're right, it's a monstrosity. It's not my best work. But Mr. Martin rejected that idea weeks ago. There isn't going to be a castle on Lookout Island."

"You designed this ridiculous house?" Caleb stood up from the folding chair where he'd been lounging. "Really?" His voice dripped with sarcasm. "This is something the City Hall design selection committee will be interested to know."

Well, the City Hall project was already a dead deal because she'd refused Caleb's bribe. It struck her that maybe she should tell the truth about Caleb and his attempted shakedown. But she wasn't brave enough to say that out loud. Besides, the audience wouldn't believe her—she had no proof. And damaging Caleb wasn't her goal.

She'd come here to defend her design and to clear the way so that Topher could build his house. The rest might be important in the long run but not in the moment.

"I have the information about the final house plans here. I'll be filing for a building permit next week. It seems to me y'all should take a look at the final plans, not a concept that was rejected."

"I'm going to ask you to please sit down," Peggy Fiedler said. "This isn't your meeting. It's mine."

"No," Jessica said, her tone defiant. "This is an open meeting, and people here deserve the truth about the house Mr. Martin is planning to build."

"If you don't sit down, I'm going to call security," the grandmotherly woman said in a voice that brooked no argument.

Jessica's heart redlined. The very last thing she wanted

was a scuffle with the law. She could just imagine what the gossips would do with that. But these people needed to hear the truth. She cast her gaze around the room and realized Topher was standing by the door, dressed in khakis, a white golf shirt, and a blue blazer.

His presence gave her courage. So she hurried forward and put the foam-core board with her elevation drawing onto an easel at the front of the room. "Here are the drawings."

"No one gave you permission to put that up there," Peggy said. "Take that down."

A young man in the front row charged the easel and literally ripped the board out of Jessica's hands.

Jessica turned to the crowd. "Don't you want to know the truth? Are you happy to let these people tell you what to believe?"

"Everyone here knows that Christopher Martin's investment company has significant holdings in various enterprises with very poor environmental records. He's not a friend of the climate. And he doesn't need to build a house on an island with a historic lighthouse. Your plans are irrelevant," Peggy said.

Jessica glanced at Topher, hoping he would counter the woman's words. But he continued to lean against the doorframe, his arms crossed over his chest.

"No one has cared about the lighthouse in years," Jessica said. "Y'all were happy to let it fall into ruin until right this minute. So this looks more like a vendetta against Mr. Martin than a meeting designed to rationally discuss the house he wants to build. You should all know that we're happy to entertain changes that will mitigate environmental impacts." She scowled at the man who'd taken her drawings away.

"I've asked you nicely to sit down or leave. We all understand that Mr. Martin is paying you to say these things. But here's the truth for you—we are not for sale." Peggy finished speaking and turned toward Caleb, who continued to grin like a jackal. "Perhaps Representative Tate would like to say a few words about his legislation that would protect Lookout Island in perpetuity."

Tate strolled to the podium, giving Jessica an odious look before he seized the microphone. "I would love to talk about my bill. But before we leave the subject of Topher Martin, ya'll should know that he's in the room right now."

"What?" Peggy scowled out at the audience.

"Right there." Caleb pointed. "Christopher Martin is the man standing by the door. The one with the scars."

\* \* \*

More than a hundred eyes turned in Topher's direction, the vast majority filled with hatred and raw disgust. People would believe anything, and he certainly had a villain's face.

That was the thing. He'd never aspired to be a hero. The truth was far more complicated. The speaker was right. He *had* invested in all sorts of start-up and high-tech businesses over the years. He hadn't given much thought to the moral consequences of those investments; he'd just read those companies' spreadsheets and bet on the ones that looked like winners. He'd won more than he'd lost, and that had given him power and prestige. But it hadn't made him a good person.

"Save the island!" the woman at the podium yelled, and like automatons, the people in the room chanted with her, drowning out anyone who might have spoken the truth about the house he wanted to build.

He hated watching Jessica try to argue with this mob. He wanted to march across the room and rescue her, but that would have been the wrong move because she was doing fine all on her own. She didn't need to be rescued. She didn't need him.

So he pushed away from the doorframe and started to turn away. But right then one of the people sitting in the front row, a broad-shouldered man wearing a blue suit, his gray hair shaved marine style, calmly stood, walked right up to Caleb, and pulled the microphone out of his hands.

"Now, y'all just pipe down," he said in a broad drawl, waving at the people to sit. "Most of y'all aren't from around here, but I do appreciate your interest in saving our island. My name is Bobby Don Ayers, and I'm in real estate."

The man had a commanding way about him that said ex-military. The shouting crowd paused in their chant long enough for him to speak again.

"I make my living managing vacation properties. And here's the thing. I agree with y'all that we don't want too much development in our town. We're not like Hilton Head, thank goodness." He turned his gaze on Caleb when he said this. The politician seemed stunned that anyone would try to take his soapbox away.

"And that's the funny thing, y'all," he said, turning back to the crowd. "Because there's a consortium of investors that have been trying to buy up a lot of sensitive land around here. They're trying to do a deal to build some kind of big golf course with a huge hotel and a gated community, you know. Like they have down in Hilton Head."

"Steve, call security," Caleb said, pointing to the guy

who'd ripped the drawings out of Jessica's hands a minute ago. Steve whipped out a phone and started to dial.

"Let me cut to the point," Bobby Don said. "I looked into this consortium, and it appears that Representative Tate is one of the investors. Imagine that, our own representative, who's been up here crying crocodile tears about development, is himself trying to change our little community.

"And y'all know what? There's one person who's single-handedly trying to stop Representative Tate."

The crowd hushed, and Bobby Don gestured in Topher's direction. "That would be Mr. Martin over there, who's been buying up every parcel of environmentally sensitive land for the last couple of weeks and paying an exorbitant amount of money to do it. So much, in fact, that it makes no economic sense, unless he's on a mission to stop development in this town."

Another somewhat louder murmur spread through the crowd. "So I'm just wondering if maybe this meeting is some kind of personal vendetta aimed at the one man standing in the way of all this development our representative says he's so opposed to."

Bobby Don turned to glare at Caleb and then turned back to the crowd, which was starting to buzz. "Now, y'all, I wouldn't judge a book by its cover. So if y'all are looking for the hero in this room, it would be Mr. Martin over there." Bobby Don shifted his gaze, pinning Topher where he stood. "And, Topher, those of us who actually live here still remember that time you took the Rutledge Raiders to the state championship. We've always been with you four-square." Bobby Don put down the microphone, and the meeting erupted into confusion.

Topher, his emotions pushed beyond his capacity to name them, left the room, walking as fast as he could.

He hadn't wanted anyone to know what he and Erik had been doing over the last week, jumping in and snapping up land just to keep it out of the hands of Caleb and his people. Damn. He'd wanted to bring Caleb down in stealth mode.

He limped down the hall, his leg complaining as he contemplated the long walk back to the car. If the crowd came after him with torches and pitchforks, he'd be overrun.

But one glance back told him that Bobby Don Ayers was running interference for him. No one was getting out of that room, except for the one person who'd stood up in his defense.

Jessica.

Dammit, couldn't she just go away? Couldn't she just leave him alone? He didn't want to talk to her right now. He'd never wanted her to know what he was up to.

"Wait," she called after him. "Is what Bobby Don said true?"

"Yeah."

"And you didn't tell me?"

"No."

"Why the heck not?"

Her words penetrated his chest like a bullet. "Because I wanted you to have your moment."

"You what?"

"Your moment. Confronting Caleb. Standing up to him for the whole town to see."

"You orchestrated this?"

"Hardly. But—"

"I quit," she said. "I don't want to design your house."

"What?" Panic rushed through him. "Why?"

"Because I'm fed up with people who lie to me. All I've ever done is tell the truth."

"I'm sorry. It wasn't a lie. It was—"

"It was a lie. You didn't tell me what you were doing. You let me go in there blind and uninformed." Her voice broke. "I'm done with you. Hell, I'm done with everyone in this town."

She turned and ran down the hall faster than he could ever hope to catch her.

She had finally walked away from him. It was inevitable, but now that it had happened, he didn't think he would ever recover.

* * *

As Jessica walked away, her cousin Ethan Cuthbert, a deputy with the Magnolia Harbor Police, came running toward her.

"Representative Tate's people just called. Where's the problem?" he asked.

Ethan was a third-generation policeman and Uncle Joe's grandson. As Jessica walked past him, she said, "Don't run. The problem is leaving the building."

She continued on, half running while her breath caught in her throat. By the time she found her VW and hit the road, numbness had overtaken her.

Fifteen minutes later, she arrived home and wearily climbed the steps to her front door, and then up to MeeMaw's bedroom on the second story.

And that's when the full weight of the evening's revelations descended upon her. All those years of guilt and remorse and regret. All the self-recriminations because of what had happened to Colton when Uncle Joe had arrested him.

All of that old anger tangled together with a new fury over Topher's dishonesty about his plans for Caleb Tate.

The maelstrom swept her away into a rage. She picked up one of MeeMaw's ugly porcelain figurines and smashed it against the wall. Then another. And another. Until there weren't any porcelain figurines left on the bureau.

And then she stood there staring down at the mess she'd made, breathing hard until the tears came. They came like a raging storm, and it was all she could do to throw herself onto MeeMaw's bed and sob until she couldn't sob anymore.

She felt so utterly alone, lying there hugging her grandmother's pillow. MeeMaw would be furious about what she'd just done. Those figurines were her beloved grandmother's most prized possessions. And Jessica had just destroyed all of them.

She'd be bawled out. She'd be called names. She'd be sent to her room and locked in. She'd be...

No.

MeeMaw and PopPop had never punished her like that. MeeMaw would have pulled her into a hug and asked her why she was so angry.

She had reasons to be furious. So many reasons. And they all started with Daddy. She'd always been angry at him, even before he'd called her a liar and sent her away. In Granny's house, where she'd lived with Momma and Daddy, approval came only if she followed the rules.

When she turned sixteen, she'd started to challenge those rules. When she'd turned seventeen, she'd simply defied them and made friends with Colton St. Pierre.

So maybe Daddy had a reason to send her away. In his perfect world, she'd been a big problem, a troubled teenager, even though she wasn't doing drugs or having sex. But she mouthed off and she told him exactly what she thought about his politics and his intolerance.

And the sad part was that all she'd ever wanted was his attention and approval. He could have changed everything if he'd just given her a hug.

She squeezed her grandmother's pillow and cried her heart out. There was no one left in this world who loved her the way MeeMaw and PopPop had. And she wished, with all her heart, that MeeMaw was here right now, to rock her to sleep.

# Chapter Twenty-Four———

Topher hardly slept a wink on Saturday night. His mind kept replaying the moment when Jessica had realized that he'd failed to tell her the truth.

He could understand why she might be annoyed at him. But her reaction had seemed oddly over the top. He kept wondering if he could have done things differently. If he could have changed the outcome.

Sadly, he knew the answer. Nothing he could have done would have changed things. And now she'd abandoned his house. He wondered if he could call her and ask for her plans. Maybe he could find someone...

No.

He sat out on the porch in the early morning. It was shaping up to be another beautiful summer day, even though the calendar had turned to September. It was only 7:00 a.m., but up at the big house, he could see the activity through the kitchen windows.

The faint scent of bacon wafted from that general

direction. Maybe he should go scarf down some breakfast. He was hungry.

But he didn't have the energy. He just wanted to sit here and be miserable. Ironically, he was miserable about feeling miserable. The sun shone down, but inside it was raining buckets, and he tried to tell himself that he liked it that way.

But, in truth he was tired of the rain.

He closed his eyes, the bacon tickling his nose. He might have dozed for a minute because when he came back to consciousness, Jackie was sitting up on the porch rail, wearing a nice pair of blue slacks and a clean white golf shirt. It was Sunday; the kid was dressed for church.

"You were snoring," the kid said.

Good thing he hadn't been drooling too, because Jackie always called it the way he saw it. Topher sat up in his chair and ran his hands through his hair. He was exhausted.

"You want to tell me why you ran away yesterday?" Topher asked.

"I was on a mission from the cap'n."

Topher stared at the kid for a long moment. Maybe Ashley was right to be concerned about Jackie's obsession with Captain Teal. It was one thing to pretend there was a benign presence haunting the inn and another for an eight-year-old to leave home on a mission that took him miles away from safety.

Topher decided not to bawl the kid out. That wouldn't help him understand the problem. So he asked, "What kind of mission?"

"I'm not sure I should tell you."

Oh, the kid was good. Either that or the captain was coaching him. Now, that was a creepy thought, but Topher chose to employ reverse psychology. "Okay. Don't tell me," he said.

Jackie hopped down from the porch rail and leaned back on it. "The truth is that the cap'n needs us to right a wrong."

"Oh really? What wrong?"

"I'm not sure. But it's his unfinished business."

"Oh, so he can go into the light?"

"Right."

"So, what? Do you think he wants everyone to know that Rose and Henri were in love?"

"Maybe."

"So why did you have to go to Gullah Town for that?"

"I needed to find Henri St. Pierre's grave."

"What? Why?" Topher almost grabbed the kid by the shoulders.

"Don't yell at me. I knew you wouldn't understand. But it's okay; the Rev does." The kid turned and scampered away, back toward the main house.

Damn. Topher needed to tell Ashley about this, but she was going to freak out. Hell, she'd probably blame him for this turn of events. Maybe he should consult Micah first, just to see what Jackie had told the minister.

Topher stepped down from the porch and let himself out the side gate. He hobbled across the street and up to the rectory's door.

The minister, also dressed for church in a somber gray suit and cleric's collar, answered the door.

"I'm sure Sunday mornings are busy for you, but have you got five minutes?" Topher asked.

The minister checked his watch. "I've got fifteen. What's up?" He opened the door and ushered Topher into his living room. The place was oddly empty, as if the man didn't have much in the way of possessions or maybe hadn't fully unpacked.

Topher sat down on the sofa and told the minister about his conversation with Jackie.

Micah nodded. "Jackie told me much the same thing last night. And I had to explain to him that Henri's final resting place is probably in the black cemetery up at Oak Hall. The family story is that Henri was captured and enslaved. I don't think that's the truth. I think he followed Rose and Abimael when John Howland forced them to return to Oak Hall."

"Okay. But what about Jackie walking all the way to your brother's property? How did he even know where it was?"

"I have no explanation for how or why the child turned up there."

"What should we do about this?"

The minister shrugged. "I don't know. Ashley is determined to treat this as a psychological issue."

"And you agree?"

"Jackie isn't my child."

"So you don't agree. Do you believe in the ghost?" Topher asked, surprising even himself.

Micah shrugged. "I believe there are many things in this world that can't be explained. And not just ghosts. There are miracles around us every day."

"Yeah." Topher stood up.

"You sound as if you don't believe in miracles."

"No. I think I might be more inclined to believe in ghosts." He limped toward the door.

"That's sad, you know."

Topher turned and stared. "Being realistic about things is better."

Micah shook his head. "I don't think so."

"But I've never been religious."

"I'm not talking about religion. I'm talking about faith."

"Same thing."

"I heard about what happened last night at the meeting," the minister said as Topher reached the door.

He turned. "I'm not surprised given the way gossip runs in this town."

"You did a good thing," the minister said.

"So what?"

"More than one, actually. I know you're worried about Jackie, but he's going to be okay. And you're part of the reason. In addition to listening to him, you gave him something to believe in for a while. But what do you believe in?"

Topher blinked. This was why he shied away from conversations with holy men. They always asked existential questions.

"I'm sure you're busy, and I—"

"Did you run into Colton at the meeting?" Micah asked abruptly.

"No. I didn't see him there."

"Well, maybe he left early. But I know he planned to be up there. He was going to talk to Jessica because of all the gossip about you."

"About me?"

Micah nodded. "About you and Jessica. Colton thought it might be a good time for him to tell the truth."

"The truth about what?"

"That he's the one who started the rumors about Jessica all those years ago. He didn't want the lie to get in the way of . . . you know . . . things."

Holy crap. Colton? All this time it had been Colton? Jessica must have been furious. Of course, that explained a lot about last night. "I don't believe it."

"I know. It's hard to fathom. But he was really messed up at the time, and I guess he wanted to build himself up. So he made up a story involving a white girl. Not the smartest thing in the world to do."

"So that's why she was so angry last night."

"Probably so. What do you plan to do about it?"

"Uh. Nothing."

"Why not?"

Topher had nothing to say.

"Come on, Topher. You're talking to a minister here. And I've been watching you for some time now. Any fool can see that Jessica Blackwood has gotten under your skin. Have you told her how you feel?"

"Why would she even want someone like me?"

"Well, I could think of a few reasons, but maybe you should ask her. It's usually the best way to find stuff out. Now, I really do have to go. I've got a sermon to give. And wouldn't you know, it's on the topic of forgiveness. Sometimes the Lord is so sneaky-mysterious it blows my mind."

* * *

Jessica awakened on Sunday morning with her head pounding and her eyes puffy. She crawled out of bed and stood over the broken shards of her grandmother's figurines, feeling empty and guilty at the same time.

She needed to hide the evidence of her crime, so she went down to the kitchen and brought back a broom and dustpan. When she'd swept up the mess and deposited it in the trash can, she stood in the middle of the kitchen trying to figure out what came next.

Obviously, she was going to tell Damon Brant that she'd

take the job in Miami. But just as obviously, she didn't want to let go of this house.

Even though it was falling down and as empty as her heart, it still represented the best years of her life. She truly did understand Topher's wish to resurrect his grandfather by building his house out on the island.

She was luckier because she didn't have to build anything. She could live inside this memory. All she had to do was stay in Magnolia Harbor.

But maybe it was time to go. There wasn't anything left here but this one good thing. Maybe it was time to say goodbye to the house and MeeMaw and PopPop.

That's what she'd do next. She'd go visit them for the last time. So she dragged herself into the bathroom and took a long shower before putting on a Sunday dress. Then she headed out to Heavenly Rest Church, where her grandparents had worshipped all their lives.

MeeMaw and PopPop had been laid to rest in the little graveyard beside the church. Jessica arrived well before the ten o'clock services and stood staring down at her grandparents' shared headstone for a long time, remembering them. PopPop had shown her how to sail. MeeMaw had always had time to build sandcastles. She couldn't think of one time either of them had ever said an angry word to her.

"I'm sorry about the figurines," she whispered out loud, just as the organ music swelled from the little church in the grove of live oaks.

Members of the congregation had been streaming into the sanctuary for a while, and the music drew her up the steps and into one of the pews in the back.

She hadn't been inside Heavenly Rest except for MeeMaw's and PopPop's funerals years ago. Granny was a Methodist, and that's where she'd always worshipped. Momma had been laid to rest in a grave beside Daddy in the cemetery clear across town.

Heavenly Rest was the oldest church on the island, and it was small and a little dark inside. But it had a peacefulness to it that soothed Jessica's aching heart. She settled back and lost herself in the worship service.

The Gospel reading from Luke was the one where Jesus teaches his disciples how to pray the Lord's Prayer. It was a familiar one, even though the King James Version was a bit more flowery than the passage she'd learned in Methodist Sunday school.

Reverend St. Pierre ascended to the pulpit and began his sermon in a strong voice that carried all the way back to where Jessica sat.

"The Gospel reading today is about more than the power of prayer," he said. "It's about forgiveness. Think about the words Jesus taught his followers to use: *Forgive our trespasses as we forgive those who trespass against us.*

"What was He telling us? Was He saying that all we have to do is ask, and poof, we're forgiven? No. That's not it. In this passage, Jesus says that we have to work for forgiveness, and not with empty apologies. To be forgiven, we have to forgive.

"To find love, we must love. To find comfort, we must comfort. To find truth, we must tell the truth. And so it goes. Imagine a world where everyone was ready to forgive, where everyone opened their door and gave their daily bread to a stranger. Where everyone told the truth and loved their neighbor.

"That would be a world worth actively praying for. This is what we say every week when we recite the Lord's

Prayer. This is what we are hoping to find and what we pledge to create right here on earth, every day."

Oh dear Lord. This message was so simple and so beautiful and something her therapist back in Charleston had been trying to tell her for years.

It wasn't enough for her to apologize for things she hadn't done. To bury her pain so she could come back to her family.

That wasn't forgiveness. That was living a lie.

Forgiveness was forgiving. And not because it let any of them off the hook for the damage they'd done. But because all of that forgiveness would be good for her own self.

Jessica was glad she'd come home and spent some time with Momma before she died, but she'd come expecting an apology. That wasn't the way it worked. You couldn't really count on the people who had hurt you for that kind of thing.

You just had to truly move on. Forgive them and hope they'd see the light.

And she'd been wrong this morning. There was something left here in Magnolia Harbor. There was her business. There was Colton, who needed and wanted forgiveness. And there was Granny, who needed it but didn't really understand.

She could forgive Granny but forgiving her didn't mean she had to go to tea every Saturday and hold her tongue when Granny said cruel things.

She didn't have to be with Granny if that was the way Granny chose to be. And she didn't have to run away, either.

And that brought her back to the most important thing. The thing she'd been running from the most.

Topher.

She didn't need to forgive him. She needed to apologize.

He was the walking embodiment of a real hero. He hadn't gone looking for glory. He hadn't intended for her to find out what he'd done to save the town, but that wasn't the same as lying to her. He wasn't out there tooting his own horn like Caleb Tate.

No. He'd never been that way.

He'd pulled her aside years ago and told her to be careful. He'd pulled Colton aside and told him to take care. He hadn't done that out of judgment. He'd done those things because he'd cared.

Because he understood what Reverend St. Pierre had just said better than she did.

She'd been so wrong about him. Topher wasn't at all like Daddy. He'd never judged her. And when she'd really needed someone's shoulder to cry on, he'd been there, like MeeMaw and PopPop. When she'd needed a lifeline, he'd pulled her up out of the depths.

All Topher had ever done was respect her.

He'd done more than that the night they'd been together. He'd loved her that night. He hadn't said one word, but he'd been speaking with his heart.

Micah was right. To get love, you give it. And how could she do anything but love Topher Martin, when he'd been loving her, silently and from afar, these last few weeks?

* * *

Topher took a shower and put on his best Tommy Bahama shirt before he drove all the way out to Jessica's place.

If it hadn't been Sunday, he might have stopped at the florist shop for some roses or something. Although roses hadn't really done the trick the last time he'd tried that approach.

Her yellow VW bug wasn't in the drive when he arrived at her house. He checked his watch. It was only nine thirty. Where the hell was she, anyway?

And then it occurred to him that Jessica was exactly the kind of woman who went to church every Sunday. But which church?

He had no clue.

It would be hours before she got back, and that irritated the crap out of him. But he sucked back his annoyance.

Maybe the universe was sending him a message about his lack of patience. Maybe the wait would do him good.

So he got out of his car and took a long walk on the beach. Sand walking was tough, but it built muscle.

What the heck was he going to say to her when she finally got home?

He'd never been very poetic, and he was even worse at expressing his feelings. And if he managed to surmount both of those impediments, what the hell would he say?

Would he just blurt out the words?

That would be stupid. She'd laugh at him. She'd walk away. No. She'd run.

There was no way to slice or dice this. He either manned up and said the words out loud or he forgot about the whole thing.

Where was she? Had she volunteered to hand out coffee during fellowship hour? Or was she off doing something else?

He hated the idea of her being off having fun while he was here pacing around like an idiot.

But all of that angst was nothing compared to the way his heart pounded the moment her little yellow Bug turned into the drive.

"Topher?" she said as she got out of the VW. God, she was so beautiful this morning, wearing a pretty pink dress, her changeable eyes on the blue side this morning.

His mouth went dry and his hands went cold and every stupid word he'd rehearsed left his brain. He didn't want to talk. He wanted to hold her. He wanted to love her. To keep her here. With him.

If he ever spoke these words out loud, she'd run for the hills. She didn't want to be possessed. And yet he wanted to possess her.

She walked toward him in slow motion, a funny, unreadable expression on her face. What was that about? Last night she'd been so angry.

But maybe not now. The thought gave him a wild and crazy hope.

"I went looking for you at Rose Cottage."

"What?"

"After church. I waited for almost an hour. I was worried that you might have decided to go back to your life in Columbia before the accident."

"Uh, no. I've been here since early. Waiting for you."

"You have?"

"Look—" They both spoke at the same time.

"You go first," he said, ever the coward.

"I'm sorry about last night," she said, and then shook her head as if she had also been rehearsing a bunch of words. She took a deep breath and blew it out, her bangs lifting adorably. She truly was exactly like the spunky girl next door.

"Let me start again," she said. "I'm sorry for every bad thing I ever thought about you. All of it was wrong. Everything. You never judged me. You never lied about me. You never told stories about me. And I'm so ashamed that I thought those things about you. I want to apologize for all of it."

"You don't need—"

"Yes. I do. I confused you with someone else."

"Who? Caleb?"

"Yes. No. Yes." She laughed and rolled her eyes. "I lumped you in with all those boys, Caleb included. So yes. But that's not who I confused you with."

"No? Then who?"

"I know this is going to sound crazy. But I confused you with my father."

The pieces of the jigsaw puzzle suddenly slid into place. Fred Blackwood had been a member of the Rutledge Raiders booster committee. And he'd been the typical high school football fanatic. And if Topher remembered correctly, her father had once played for the Raiders. "So you have a thing against football players?" he said.

She shook her head. "No. Not that. It's just that Daddy was...I don't know, a man's man. He was big and strong, and everyone admired him. And he cared about what people thought. He cared too much about it, really."

"I'm not like that, Jessica. I have always hated that hero worship. You can't satisfy people when they start thinking you're perfect. I took all sorts of crap from 'Bama fans when I wrecked my knee doing something other than football. For a whole year, I was the talk of the town around Tuscaloosa. I hated every minute of it."

"Really? I didn't know that about you. I didn't realize that you hurt your knee doing something other than playing."

"I tore my ACL on the ski slopes between freshman and sophomore year. I went down to South America after my father died, just to get away and to ski at Las Leñas. It was the middle of the summer, but I took a bunch of stupid risks because I was sad and hurt and angry . . . and alone."

"Oh. I'm sorry."

"Don't be." He shoved his hands in his pockets feeling vulnerable. He'd never told anyone how little he cared about football. It had started out as something he did with Granddad, but it had morphed into something else. Something that had taken on a life of its own because it had given Dad so much pride and joy.

But after Dad died, it didn't matter so much. And he'd never liked being in the spotlight. Even when he'd been playing high school ball.

"Anyway," he continued, "the thing is, I never really cared what anyone thought of me." He stopped, realizing that was no longer true. "Well, until recently," he added.

"Oh?"

He hauled in a breath. "I care what you think. I care desperately."

* * *

The poor man. Jessica didn't really pity him in that moment—her heart was too full for that. No. She felt an overwhelming sense of remorse.

She'd kept him guessing, hadn't she? And he wasn't nearly as confident as he pretended. And that night they'd spent together, when they hadn't said a word, had been mostly because she was frightened and he was unsure.

That needed to stop right now. She closed the distance between them until she stood right before him. He was so much taller than she was, and his eye was bright with the morning sky.

"I'm so sorry for misjudging you."

He reached down and put his warm fingers against her mouth. "Hush, now. There isn't anything to forgive. You were hurt, and you lashed out. I get it. I have been guilty of doing the same."

She gently took his hand away from her mouth, interlacing her fingers with his. "Maybe. But...the thing is...I don't want to run away from you. I don't want to run away from my hometown. I want to stay. Here. And I want to love you."

"You want to love me?" He seemed utterly surprised.

"Yes. Because you've been loving me for all this time, and I was just a little slow figuring it out. So I'm really sorry about that. But can we, you know, start over?"

"You love me?"

"I do."

"I love you back. I—"

She rocked up on tiptoes and smothered whatever else he was about to say. The man wasn't great with words, but who cared? She knew now that he was a master at speaking with his heart.

# EPILOGUE

A week later, Jessica found herself having a Cinderella moment. Dressed in an off-the-shoulder ballgown of pink lace and tulle, she put her hand in Topher's and let him help her out of his BMW.

Which wasn't exactly a coach and four, but it did have leather seats. And she knew good and well that he was nothing like Prince Charming, even if he'd managed to pull the wool entirely over Granny's eyes.

Granny, who was up at the yacht club hobnobbing with the cream of Magnolia Harbor's society for this Heritage Day ball, was probably crowing about how her grand-daughter had landed a very rich man with a long and storied last name.

Which was also a lie. Jessica hadn't landed anything. She'd fallen into it. But Topher had given her a soft landing spot. Right in his arms.

"Ready?" he asked, giving her his arm. He looked dashing in his tuxedo and eye patch, like some character out of a spy novel. Although she much preferred him in Hawaiian shirts.

"Granny is going to say something about the color of my dress."

"Who the hell cares what she thinks? I think you look good enough to eat."

She blushed. "You do?"

"Yes. And after we drink some champagne and dance, I intend to consume you."

"We're going to dance?"

"Yup." He clipped the word as they headed toward the yacht club's door, but before they could enter, Harry Bauman intercepted them.

"Jessica, you look fabulous tonight."

"Thanks." Her cheeks warmed again.

"I saw you getting out of the car, and I wanted to intercept you before you heard the news from someone else. The City Hall design committee met last night, and we've narrowed down our selection to two firms. Blackwood Designs is one of them."

"What? Really? You're kidding."

"There's a lot of support for the idea of selecting a local architect. But since your company is so much smaller than the other competitors, we're going to need a few more details before we make the final selection. I hope that's not a problem?"

"No. Not at all. Thank you so much."

Harry nodded and shot Topher a glance before he turned and headed into the party.

Topher tugged her forward, but she resisted. "Wait a second. What was that look he just gave you?"

"What?" Topher sounded suspiciously guilty of something.

"Did you make a contribution to the building fund?"

He stared up at the stars for a moment. "I might have. I mean, I'm living here now. I feel as if I should, you know, contribute. And besides, I want to make sure that Rose Howland's letters and diary make it out of the vault in the library and into a display in the new museum. Especially now that everyone knows about them. I'm insanely proud of Jackie for winning a blue ribbon on his Heritage Day project."

"You don't think your contribution had anything to do with my being selected?"

He turned and faced her. "What if it did? Would you hate me? And besides, you haven't won the contract yet. Sounds like the selection committee wants you to jump through a few more hoops."

"You can't go around buying stuff for me, Topher."

"No?"

She shook her head.

"That's no fun. I like spending my money. And I want to buy you things. Expensive things."

"I don't—"

"How about this?" He pulled a small red leather case from his suit pocket. He opened it to display a necklace studded with pale-pink rubies.

"I can't."

"Of course you can. Here, let me put it on you." He took the necklace from the case and gave her an adorable look until she turned around for him. His fingers were warm against her nape as he did up the clasp. He leaned in and brushed a kiss there, which sent shivers of desire down her spine.

"If I thought you were ready," he whispered in her ear, "I would have bought you a diamond ring."

She turned and glared at him.

He smiled back. "You're not ready. But you'll come around eventually. I just have to keep telling you how much I love and admire you."

He was right about that. It wasn't his money or his name that she loved. It was him. He was kind and good. And she should let him buy her pretty things because it gave him joy.

He gave her his arm, and she walked into the yacht club, where Granny was waiting, beaming as if Jessica had finally done something right for the first time in her life.

Which was annoying in the extreme. Her inner rebel didn't want to do anything that might please the grumpy old woman.

But when Topher took her in his arms and danced her around the ballroom, letting her lead because his left side was still weak, she knew that she'd made the right choice.

Even if Granny agreed with her.

# Did You Miss the Start of This Wonderful Series?

Jenna Fossey's life is about to change. An unexpected inheritance and the chance to meet relatives she never knew existed has her heading to the charming little town of Magnolia Harbor. But as soon as she arrives, long-buried family secrets lead to even more questions, and the only person who can help her find the answers is her sexy-as-sin sailing instructor.

Please turn the page for an excerpt from *The Cottage on Rose Lane*.

*Chapter One*———————————

Was this her father's boat? The one he'd been sailing the day he died?

Jenna Fossey stood on the sidewalk, shading her eyes against the early-September sun, studying the boat. It was small, maybe fifteen feet from end to end. It sat on cinder blocks, hull up in the South Carolina sunshine, its paint blistered and cracked. Much of the color had faded or peeled away, leaving long gray planks of wood. Even the boat's name had bleached away; only the shadow of a capital *I* on the boat's stern remained. Some kind of vine—was that kudzu?—had twisted up the cinder blocks and crawled across the boat's hull, setting suckers into the wood and giving the impression that only the overgrown vegetation held the pieces together.

A thick, hard knot formed in Jenna's chest. She held her breath and closed her eyes, imagining the father she'd never known. In her thirty years on this planet, she'd imagined him so many times. In her fantasies, he'd been a fireman, a detective, a handsome prince, a superhero, a scoundrel, a bastard, and an asshole. That last role had stuck for most of her life because, before she died of breast cancer three years ago, Mom had refused to talk about him. In fact, by her omission, Mom had made it plain that Jenna's father had been a mistake, or a one-night stand, or someone Mom had met in college but hardly knew.

And then, one day out of the blue, Milo Stracham, the executor of her grandfather's will, arrived at her front door and told Jenna the truth. Her father had been the son of a wealthy man, a passionate sailor, and he'd died before she was born.

She took another breath, redolent with the tropical scents of the South Carolina Low Country. Musty and mossy and salty. This was an alien place to a girl who'd grown up in Boston. It was too lush here. Too hot for September.

She shifted her gaze to the house where Uncle Harry lived. It was a white clapboard building bristling with dormer windows and a square cupola on top. Its wraparound veranda, shaded by a grove of palmettos at the corner, epitomized the architecture of the South. She stood there listening to the buzz of cicadas as she studied the house, as if it would tell her something about the man who owned it.

At least Uncle Harry didn't live in a big, pretentious monstrosity like her grandfather's house on the Hudson. She would never live in her grandfather's house. She'd told Milo, who had become the sole trustee of her trust fund, to sell the place. But, of course, her grandfather's will restricted such a sale, just as it had restricted her ability to sell her grandfather's stock in iWear, Inc., the company he had founded and which now was the largest manufacturer and retailer of optics in the world, including sunglasses that regularly retailed for two hundred dollars or more a pair.

The *Wall Street Journal* may have dubbed Jenna the Sunglass Heiress once the details of Robert Bauman's will had become public, but that was so not who she was.

She'd been raised in Dorchester, a neighborhood in Boston, the daughter of a single mother who'd worked two jobs to keep her in shoes and school uniforms. She'd been a good student, but even with scholarships, Jenna had taken out huge loans for college and graduate school. But she'd earned her MBA from Harvard, and landed a job in business development with Aviation Engineering, a Fortune 500 company.

But her inheritance had cost her the job she loved, because iWear was a direct competitor in the advanced heads-up optics market that was so important to Aviation Engineering's bottom line.

The company she'd devoted eight years of her life to had made her sign a nondisclosure agreement and had booted her out within a day of learning of her good fortune. It was as if the universe were sending her a message that just ignoring the money or refusing to accept it was not sufficient.

So she did what she'd been thinking about doing for years—she took a year-long trip to the Near and Far East, intent on deepening her understanding of meditation and Buddhism. Her goal had been to learn how to handle the karmic consequence of the inheritance her stranger of a grandfather had given her.

She needed something meaningful to do. But what? She needed a cause. Or a reason. Or something.

After a year spent mostly in India, she'd come to the conclusion that she could never build a new life for herself without confronting the secrets of the old one.

Which was why she'd come to Magnolia Harbor, South

Carolina, with a million questions about her father, seeking the one person who might be able to answer them—her uncle Harry, Robert Bauman's younger brother.

She crossed the street and leaned on the picket fence. It would be so easy to ascend the porch steps, knock on the door, and explain herself to the uncle she had never known. But it wasn't that simple. The rift between Robert and Harry had been decades wide and deep, and she didn't understand the pitfalls. She couldn't afford to screw this up. She'd have to gain Harry's trust before she told him who she was.

She walked away from the house and continued down Harbor Drive until she reached downtown Magnolia Harbor. The business district comprised a four-block area with upscale gift shops, restaurants, and a half-mile boardwalk lined with floating docks.

On the south side of town, an open-air fish market bustled with customers lining up to buy shrimp right off the trawlers that had gone out that morning. On the north side stood a marina catering to a fleet of deep-sea fishing boats and yachts. In between was a public fishing pier and a boat launch accessed from a dry dock filled with small boat trailers.

Presiding over this central activity stood Rafferty's Raw Bar, a building with weathered siding and a shed roof clad in galvanized metal. Jenna found a seat on the restaurant's terrace, where the scent of fried shrimp hung heavy on the air. She ordered a glass of chardonnay and some spinach dip and settled in to watch the sailboats out on the bay.

"The Buccaneers are always fun to watch," the waitress said as she placed Jenna's chardonnay in front of her.

"Buccaneers? You mean like pirates?"

"Well, they're obviously not pirates, but they do pretend

sometimes. Some of them love to say *arrrgh* at appropriate moments. They also regard Talk Like a Pirate Day as a holy day of obligation."

Jenna must have let her confusion show because the waitress winked and rolled her eyes. "Oh, don't mind me. I'm a sailing nerd. Those sailboats are all Buccaneer Eighteens, a kind of racing dinghy. The Bucc fleet always goes out on Tuesday afternoons for practice races."

"So, sailing is a big thing here, huh?"

"It always has been. Jonquil Island used to be a hangout for pirates back in the day. And the yacht club is, like, a hundred and fifty years old."

Had her father belonged to the yacht club? Probably. It was the sort of thing the son of a rich man would do.

"Oh, look," the waitress said, pointing. "They're done for the day, and *Bonney Rose* is leading them in. Her skipper is a crazy man, but so cute. He's got a chest to die for." She giggled. "My friends and I sometimes refer to it as 'the Treasure Chest.'" The waitress pointed at the lead boat with a navy-blue hull and crisp white sails.

The boat was heading toward the floating dock with the others behind it. The two sailors sat with their legs extended and their bodies leaning hard over the water in an impressive display of core strength. The guy in the back of the boat was shirtless with his life vest open to expose an impressive six-pack. His skin was berry brown, and his curly dark hair riffled in the wind.

Jenna caught her breath as a deep, visceral longing clutched her core. He resembled a marauding pirate. Dark and handsome with a swath of masculine brow, high cheekbones, and a full mouth. Like someone with Spanish blood and a little Native American or Creole mixed in. Or maybe African too.

Had they met before? Perhaps in a past life?

She watched in rapt attention as the boat came toward the dock at a sharp angle. He was going to crash. But at the last moment, the boat turned away, stalling in the water, allowing the second sailor, a man with a salt-and-pepper beard, to step onto the dock in one fluid motion, carrying a mooring line. The big sail flapped noisily in the wind as the shirtless sailor began pulling it down into the boat, his biceps flexing in the late-afternoon sun.

Five more sailboats arrived in the same noisy manner, and for the next few minutes, an orderly chaos ensued as boats arrived and dropped sail and got in line for the launch. Jenna had trouble keeping her eyes off the man with the too-curly hair and the dark skin.

It was probably because she'd spent the day thinking about her father and the way he'd sailed here, and died here. Had her father been like a dashing pirate ready to buckle some swash? She pulled her gaze away and allowed a wistful smile. She was doing it again. Inventing a father for herself instead of seeking the real one.

"Can I get you anything else?" the waitress, whose name tag said Abigail, asked.

"Yes. What's his name? And why is the name of his boat misspelled?" She pointed to the man and the boat, where BONNEY ROSE was painted in gold letters along the stern.

"That's Jude St. Pierre. And the boat's name is a tribute to Anne Bonney, a female pirate from back in the day. It's also a tribute to Gentleman Bill Teal's boat, which broke up over near the inlet back in the 1700s. That boat was named the *Bonnie Rose*, after Rose Howland."

"And who is that?"

"She's the lady who planted jonquils all over the island in memory of Gentleman Bill, the pirate."

"I sense a story."

"It's basically the town myth. Explains all the pirate stores in town. You can pick up a free Historical Society pamphlet almost anywhere. I'd give you one, but we're out of them. It's the end of the summer, you know. Things are starting to wind down here."

"Do many boats go down in the inlet?" Jenna asked, a little shiver running up her spine. Is that what had happened to her father?

Abigail nodded. "The currents can be treacherous there if you don't know what you're doing or you get caught in a squall. Can I get you anything else?"

Jenna shook her head. "Just the check."

As Abigail walked away, Jenna turned to study the man named Jude St. Pierre. Her skin puckered up, and her mouth went bone dry. She pushed the attraction aside. That was not what she wanted from him.

She wanted a sailboat ride to the place where her father had died. But since she didn't know where that might be in the vastness of Moonlight Bay, maybe the best she could do was a sailing lesson so she could find it later herself.

"You've got an admirer," Tim Meyer said, nodding in the general direction of Rafferty's terrace. "Easy on the eyes, dirty blond, with big brown eyes."

Jude didn't follow Tim's glance. Instead, he concentrated on the job of securing the mast to its cradle with a couple of bungee cords. He didn't have time to flirt with tourists.

"She's a cutie. Aren't you even going to look?" Tim, newly divorced and constantly on the make, had spent the entire summer chasing female tourists who were too young for him, so this comment rolled right off Jude's back.

He'd learned the hard way that tourists always went home. Besides, he had a rule about blondes. His mother had been a white woman with blond hair, and she'd abandoned the family when Jude was fourteen. He could do better than a blonde. He wanted a Clair Huxtable who could also speak Gullah, the Creole language of his ancestors.

"I can't believe you aren't even going to check her out," Tim said. "She's got a hungry look in her big brown eyes."

Jude raised his head without meaning to.

Big mistake. The woman's gaze wasn't hungry exactly. It was steady and direct and measuring. It knocked him back, especially when her mouth quirked up on one side to reveal a hint of a dimple, or maybe a laugh line. And she wasn't blond. Not exactly. It was more cinnamon than brown with streaks of honey that dazzled in the late-afternoon sun. Her hair spilled over her shoulders, slightly messy and windblown, as if she'd spent the day sailing. She was cute and fresh, and he had this eerie feeling that he'd met her before.

Her stare burned a hole in his chest, and he turned away slightly breathless. Damn. He was too busy for a fling. And never with a woman like that.

"See what I mean? She's maybe a little skinny but . . . kind of hot," Tim said.

Jude ignored the sudden rushing of blood in his head and focused on snapping up the boat's canvas cover. "Stop objectifying. Haven't you heard? It's no longer PC."

Tim chuckled. "Objectifying is a scientific fact."

"So says the science teacher. If the parents of your students could hear you now, they'd—"

"Come on. Let's go get a drink and say hey," Tim interrupted.

"No. I have a meeting tonight."

Tim rolled his eyes. "With that group of history nuts again?"

"They aren't nuts. Dr. Rushford is a history professor." And he'd donated his time and that of his grad students to help Jude get several old homes listed on the historic register. Jude's last chance to preserve those buildings was the petition he and several of his cousins and relatives had made to the town council, asking for a rezoning of the land north of town that white folks called "Gullah Town." The area wasn't really a town at all, but a collection of small farms out in the scrub pine and live oak that had been settled by his ancestors right after the Civil War. Jude's people never used the term "Gullah Town." To them, the land north of Magnolia Harbor was just simply home.

The council was having a hearing this week. Jude had been working on this issue for more than a year with the professor's help. He wasn't about to miss a meeting to flirt with a tourist. An almost-blond tourist at that.

"Okay. It's your loss." Tim slapped him on the back. "But thanks for leaving the field of play. You're hard to compete with, dude." Tim strode off while Jude finished securing the last bungee cord. When he glanced up again, the woman with the honey hair was still staring at him, even as Tim moved in.

Tim was going to crash and burn. Again.

Jude turned away. He wanted nothing to do with another one of Tim's failed pickup attempts. Instead, he headed down the boardwalk toward the offices of Barrier Island Charters, his father's company, where Jude had parked his truck. He needed to get on home and take a shower before the meeting.

"Can I have a minute of your time, Mr. St. Pierre?" someone asked from behind him.

Jude turned. Damn. It was the woman with the honey hair. She had a low, sexy voice that vibrated inside his core in a weird, but not unpleasant, way. "Do I know you?" he asked.

"Um, no. Abigail. The waitress? At the raw bar? She told me your name."

"Can I help you with something?" he asked.

"Well," she said, rolling her eyes in a surprisingly awkward way. Almost as if she was shy or something. Which she was not, since she'd chased him down the boardwalk. "I was wondering if you might be willing to give me sailing lessons."

"What?" That had to be the oddest request he'd gotten in a long time. He was not a sailing instructor.

"I'd like to learn how to sail a small boat."

"Did Abby put you up to this?"

She shook her head. "No. Of course not. I was watching you sail, and, well, you seem to know what you're doing out there." A telltale blush crawled up her cheeks as she talked a mile a minute. She was a Yankee, all right, from Boston. He didn't need the Red Sox T-shirt to tell him that either. She had a broad Boston accent. She must be here soaking up the last of the summer sun before going back north.

She'd be gone in a week.

"I don't give sailing lessons," he said in a curt tone and then checked his watch. He really needed to go.

"Oh. Okay. I'm sorry I bothered you," the woman said in an oddly wounded tone. Her shoulders slumped a little as she started to turn away.

Damn.

He'd been rude. And stupid too. If she really wanted sailing lessons, it was an opportunity to earn a few extra bucks doing the thing he loved most. Barrier Island Charters could use all the income it could get this time of year. "No, uh, wait," he said. "How many sailing lessons do you want?"

She stopped, midturn. "I don't know. How many would it take?"

"To do what?"

"Learn how to sail? On my own, you know."

"No one sails by themselves. I mean, even in a small boat like *Bonney Rose* you need a crew."

"Oh?" She frowned.

"Unless you're learning on an Opti or a Laser. But I don't have an Opti or a Laser."

The frown deepened. "Oh."

"Optis and Lasers are one-person boats. They capsize. A lot."

"Oh."

"If you want to learn on a bigger boat, you know, with a keel, you should check out the group courses in Georgetown."

"What's a keel?" she asked, cocking her head a little like an adorable brown-eyed puppy.

He fought against the urge to roll his eyes. "A keel boat has a...Never mind. It's bigger and more comfortable. And safer."

"Okay, then I want to learn how to sail the other kind. Does *Bonney Rose* have a keel?"

"No. She has a centerboard."

"Perfect." Her mouth broadened.

"I'm not a certified teacher. In Georgetown, you can—"

"So you've already said. But I'm not interested in

group classes in Georgetown. I don't want that kind of thing. I want to learn how to take risks. Live on the edge. Sail fast."

"Look, sailing can be dangerous, and I don't do thrill rides."

She folded her arms across her chest, her eyebrows lowering a little and her hip jutting out, the picture of a ticked-off female. "I'm not looking for a thrill ride."

"No?" He gave her his best levelheaded stare.

She blushed a little. "Okay. I know nothing about sailing. But I want to learn."

"Go to the sailing school in Georgetown."

"Is that where you learned?"

Damn. She had him there. He'd learned from one of the best sailors on the island. He shook his head.

"Okay. So, can you give me the name of your teacher?"

"No. My teacher is retired now."

"Oh." She seemed crestfallen. Damn.

He checked his watch again and huffed out a breath. He was going to be late to the meeting. "Okay, look, I don't know if I'd be any good teaching you how to sail, but if you want to charter *Bonney Rose* for a couple of hours, the going rate is two hundred fifty an hour." That should shut her up. Judging by her worn-out flip-flops and threadbare camp pants, she didn't look like someone who could afford that kind of rate.

Her face brightened. "Okay."

"Okay?"

She nodded. "Tomorrow?"

Damn. "Yeah. I guess. At the public pier. Four o'clock." He turned away before she could argue.

"Hey. Wait," she called as he scooted down the boardwalk.

He didn't wait.

"Hey. Don't you even want to know my name?" she hollered at his back.

He turned around and backpedaled. "Why? I'll recognize you if you show up tomorrow. Oh, and bring cash."

# About the Author

Hope Ramsay is a *USA Today* bestselling author of heart-warming contemporary romances set below the Mason-Dixon Line. Her children are grown, but she has a couple of fur babies who keep her entertained. Pete the cat, named after the cat in the children's book, thinks he's a dog, and Daisy the dog thinks Pete is her best friend except when he decides her waggy tail is a cat toy. Hope lives in the medium-sized town of Fredericksburg, Virginia, and when she's not writing or walking the dog, she spends her time knitting and noodling around on her collection of guitars.

Learn more at:
  HopeRamsay.com
  Twitter @HopeRamsay
  Facebook.com/Hope.Ramsay

# Fall in love with these charming contemporary romances!

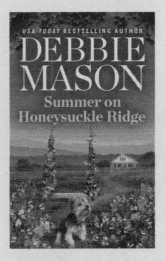

### SUMMER ON HONEYSUCKLE RIDGE
**by Debbie Mason**

Abby Everhart has gone from being a top L.A. media influencer to an unemployed divorcée living out of her car. So inheriting her great-aunt's homestead in Highland Falls, North Carolina, couldn't have come at a better time. But instead of a cabin ready to put on the market, she finds a fixer-upper, complete with an overgrown yard and a reclusive—albeit sexy—man living on the property. When sparks between them become undeniable, will she be able to sell the one place that's starting to feel like home?

### PRIMROSE LANE
**by Debbie Mason**

Olivia Davenport has finally gotten her life back together and is now Harmony Harbor's most sought-after event planner. But her past catches up with her when she learns that she's now guardian of her ex's young daughter. Dr. Finn Gallagher knows a person in over her head when he sees one, but Olivia makes it clear she doesn't want his companionship. Only with a little help from some matchmaking widows—and a precocious little girl—might he be able to convince her that life is better with someone you love at your side.

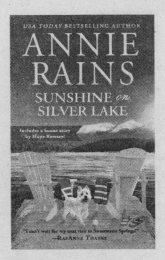

**SUNSHINE ON SILVER LAKE**
**by Annie Rains**

Café owner Emma St. James is planning a special event at Evergreen State Park to honor her mother's memory. Which means she'll need the help of the ruggedly handsome park ranger who broke her heart years ago. As their attraction grows stronger than ever, will Emma find herself at risk of falling for him again? Includes a bonus story by Hope Ramsay!

**STARTING OVER AT BLUEBERRY CREEK**
**by Annie Rains**

Firefighter Luke Marini moved to Sweetwater Springs with the highest of hopes—new town, new job, and new neighbors who know nothing of his past. And that's just how he wants to keep it. But it's nearly impossible when the gorgeous brunette next door decides to be the neighborhood's welcome wagon. She's sugar, spice, and everything nice—but getting close to someone again is playing with fire. Includes a bonus story by Melinda Curtis!

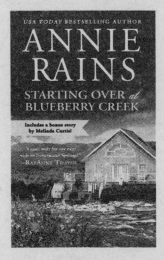

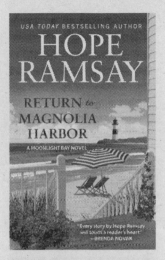

**RETURN TO MAGNOLIA HARBOR**
by Hope Ramsay

Jessica Blackwell's life needs a refresh. So while she's back home in Magnolia Harbor, she's giving her architecture career a total makeover. The only problem? Jessica's new client happens to be her old high school nemesis. Christopher Martin never meant to hurt Jessica all those years ago, and now he'd give anything to have a second chance with the one woman who always haunted his memories.

**CAN'T HURRY LOVE**
by Melinda Curtis

Widowed after one year of marriage, city girl Lola Williams finds herself stranded in Sunshine, Colorado, reeling from the revelation that her husband had secrets she never could have imagined, secrets that she's asked the ruggedly hot town sheriff to help her uncover. Lola swears she's done with love forever, but the matchmaking ladies of the Sunshine Valley Widows Club have different plans...Includes a bonus story by Annie Rains!

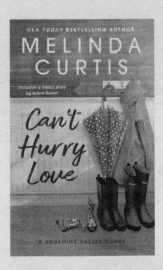

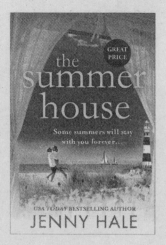
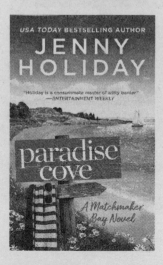